On The Dodge

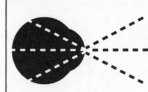

This Large Print Book carries the
Seal of Approval of N.A.V.H.

On The Dodge

William MacLeod Raine

Thorndike Press • Thorndike, Maine

1397
Pub
3-93

Library of Congress Cataloging in Publication Data:

Raine, William MacLeod, 1871-1954.
  On the dodge / William MacLeod Raine.
    p. cm.
  ISBN 1-56054-581-X (alk. paper : lg. print)
  1. Large type books. I. Title.
[PS3535.A385O5   1993]   92-36433
813'.52—dc20   CIP

Thorndike Large Print® Western Series edition published
in 1993 by arrangement with Houghton Mifflin Company.

Cover design by Ron Walotsky.

This book is printed on acid-free, high opacity paper. ∞

On The Dodge

CHAPTER 1

Blake Forrest Reads a Poster

The rider drew up at the summit and shifted his weight to ease muscles cramped from travel. A long slant of light was streaming over the hilltop through the greasewood and flooded the ugly sprawling little town with its main street running crookedly along the edge of the creek. There was a heat in the sun that set a coma of listlessness over Fair Play. A flop-eared hound wandered across the road. Otherwise there was no sign of life except the smoke drifting lazily from the chimneys.

'Safe as a Sunday school — maybe,' the man murmured aloud, a doubtful sardonic grin on his hard brown face.

Danger might be waiting in that innocent atmosphere to jump out at him if he went down. He had seen more than one morning of Sabbath peace shattered by the sudden roar of guns, just as he had known friendly smiles mask sinister intentions. But the chance of peril had to be risked. One could stay in the brush on the dodge only as long as a food

7

supply lasted. Moreover, he wanted news.

Blake Forrest was not a man to count the cost closely. Recklessness was in his blood. It had pounded through his veins from youth and driven him along many rough and crooked trails.

'We'll rock along, Maverick,' he said to his chestnut gelding. 'You never can tell till you try.'

But before he descended the steep path he made sure the .45 rode lightly in its holster fastened to the leg of the shiny leather chaps. He was not looking for trouble but if it was forced on him he wanted to be impressively present.

Maverick jogged down a stony ravine and came out of a gully to a road coated with a yellow powder made fine by a thousand trampling hoofs. Fair Play was still asleep. Even the dog had disappeared. At the hitch rack in front of a corner store three saddled horses drowsed lazily in the sun. On the false front of the building was painted a sign.

SAMPSON & DOAN
Dry Goods & Merchandise
POST OFFICE

Forrest swung from the saddle and tied at the rack. But caution was still strong in him.

There was a likelihood that he might have to leave in a hurry. He put his mount at the right of the line and fastened the bridle reins with a slip knot.

When he sauntered into the store there was a deceptive lethargy in his manner. It showed in the drag of his spurred feet, in a certain sleepiness of the half-hooded eyes. Yet the glance that seemed to sweep the room so indifferently missed nothing — took in the proprietors and the clerk, two cowboys sitting with chairs tilted against a counter, a very young man engaged in talk with them. The slow look even picked up the intent of a poster tacked to the wall of the post office division in the rear of the store. From that placard stared back at him a face remarkably like his own. The well-trained blue eyes just touched the printed sheet in passing, but long enough to get a phrase in black-faced type. 'One Thousand Dollars Reward for the Arrest of Blake Forrest.'

At the entrance of the stranger, conversation hung momentarily suspended. Those in the room observed him with the quiet Western steadiness that has nothing of offence in it. They saw a face brown and strong, all the loose uncertainty of youth hammered out of it. They saw a body compact, lean, graceful, a hint of tigerish litheness in the ease of its movements.

Forrest nodded casually to those present before he turned to Doan with his order for coffee, bacon, flour, sugar, and canned goods. Though his mind seemed to be on the purchases, he was very much aware of the three loungers in the store. One of them he labeled dangerous, the lad talking to the cowboys. Though he wore no uniform to mark his occupation, Texas Ranger was stamped all over him. Outlaw though he was now, Blake Forrest had once been in the force himself. There was no prescribed costume, yet the rangers did not dress quite like other men on the frontier. A novice could not have told the difference, but it stood out like a sore thumb. This youngster had on a flat black Stetson. The legs of his jean trousers were thrust into the tops of high-heeled dusty boots. From the sagging belt around his waist, garnished with cartridges, hung a scabbarded revolver. No doubt a pair of leathers were hitched over the horn of his saddle outside the store.

The ranger strolled to the front of the room, stood there a moment watching the newcomer covertly, then returned to his former position. His eyes studied the picture on the poster, shifted to the stranger, and back again to the photograph.

The reckless gaiety that had snatched Forrest from humdrum paths and largely dominated his life began now to drum in his blood. He thought, Mr. Ranger is loaded to the hocks with suspicions but would hate to make a mistake. The horoscope of the outlaw had marked him for perilous paths. Moreover, there was a stubborn streak in him. He meant to take his groceries with him when he left. To make a bolt for the door now did not suit him.

He lit a cigarette and moved toward the rear of the store. 'Hot for this time of the year,' he mentioned.

'That's right,' one of the cowpunchers said.

The ranger asked a question, not offensively. 'Stranger about here?'

'Yes,' Forrest answered.

'Working for some cow outfit?'

'Ridin' the chuck line right now.'

'From down Santone way, maybe?'

It was not good manners to ask casual strangers in Texas from where they came. Forrest showed surprise innocently.

'From most everywhere in my time,' he said gently, indifferently.

'Takes in some territory. Ever been in Rosedale?'

'Why Rosedale?' he wanted to know, with a smile that did not encourage curiosity.

The younger man persisted. It was his business to find out things.

11

'I'm a ranger,' he said, 'so I thought you might have met or heard of some of the wanted men on our list.'

'Might have,' admitted Forrest coolly. 'There are plenty of them.'

'Ranger Steve Porter,' one of the cowboys said by way of introduction.

'Pleased to meet you, Mr. Porter,' the newcomer said cheerfully. 'It's a good job for a young man, if he does get only thirty a month and find his own horse and weapons. Think of the service to the community, running down scalawags and putting them out of business. By and by you'll have Texas all combed up nice and respectable as Iowa. All good citizens stand back of you when you go to smoking out the bad men. Quite a way back of you, though. Healthy life too — if you live to enjoy it.'

'Don't suppose you've been down in Bexar County recently,' Porter said.

'Your don't suppose is correct.'

The ranger tried another lead. 'No reason why a top hand should be out of work these days. Plenty of outfits are shy of riders.'

'I'm a little particular who I work for,' the stranger explained, his low voice almost a drawl.

'Where was your last job?'

The suspected man laughed. 'My goodness,

you'll be asking me next where I got my horse. Maybe you think I'm in yore little "Gone to Texas" book.'[1]

Forrest had the advantage age and experience gives. He was sure of himself, a confidence born of many dangers safely passed. Young Porter's mind was like an open book to him. The ranger was strongly of the opinion that he was Blake Forrest, wanted for bank and train robbery. But he was not sure, and he could not afford to make a mistake. The officers of the force had drilled it into the men that innocent citizens were not to be arrested on long-shot chances.

'I'm no Paul Pry,' the ranger said, flushing. 'But I thought you might have picked up some information on your travels about this Forrest who robbed the T. & P. Maybe you noticed that poster.'

Since it was called to his attention the stranger noticed it more particularly now. Porter watched him while he read, and caught a look of startled surprise on the man's face erased by a swift cynical smile. If guilty, he was a cool customer.

Beneath the photograph Forrest read a very

---

[1] The Texas Rangers carried a book containing a list of three thousand outlaws, most of whom had migrated from other states hurriedly. It was a custom for the law officers of the communities where they had previously lived to mark opposite the names of the missing bad men the letters G.T.T., an abbreviation for 'Gone to Texas.'

accurate description of himself. The bandit was set down as about thirty years old, weight 165 pounds, height five-foot ten, hair black, eyes blue. His color was given as coffee brown. Body muscular and graceful. Manner pleasant and friendly unless angered. A dangerous man who would probably resist arrest. The only known mark to distinguish him was a scar on the back of the right hand from the base of the thumb to the wrist.

'Can't be more than fifty thousand guys in Texas the description fits,' commented Forrest casually.

'With that scar on the back of his right hand,' the ranger differed.

The man under observation happened just now to have thrust his right hand under the open vest he wore. Steve Porter had tried several times to get a look at it and had not yet succeeded.

'That's right,' assented Forrest genially. 'All you got to do is collect the fifty thousand I mentioned and take a look at the back of their hands. You-all won't have more than a couple of hundred suspects then.' He eyed the picture carefully. 'This Forrest guy sure looks tough. We'd ought to thank you rangers for riding on his tail so close.'

'He looks a heap like someone I've seen lately.' The ranger turned to one of the cow-

14

boys. 'Don't he remind you of someone, Bill?'

Bill would have bet his pay check against a 'dobe dollar that he could put a finger on the original of the picture without rising from his seat, but he had no intention of saying so. This was strictly none of his business.

'Cain't say he does,' was his non-committal answer.

'He looks like a dozen birds I've known,' the stranger said hardily. 'Why, he might be my own brother.'

'I don't think you mentioned your name,' the ranger suggested. 'Meet Bill Andrews and Joe Means.'

It was a neat little trap, but Forrest avoided it. He did not remove his hand from under the vest but stretched out the other.

'Glad to meet you, gents. I crushed my right hand and it's sore. My name — well, one name is as good as another. Call me Jim. My father used it except when he was waiting in the woodshed for me. Then he called me James. Jim — Brown.'

'I don't want to be annoying,' the ranger said, 'but —'

'So you can't go round treating honest men like outlaws — asking to look at their hands, and that sort of thing. You're p'intedly right. A decent citizen wouldn't like that. He would think it an insult.'

'An honest citizen would be willing to give an account of himself, Mr. Brown.'

'Sure. Why not? I'll start. The other boys can give their life histories later. Mine is short and sweet. Ran away from my stepfather when I was fourteen. Came West. Got a job. Lost it. Got another. Quit it. Moved on to another place. Finally I got to Fair Play.'

'Have you any identification papers, Mr. Brown?'

Forrest had been taking stock of the situation. The back door was nearer than the one he had entered, but his horse was at the front of the building. A showdown was coming, and he did not like it. Two first considerations were in his mind. He did not want to be arrested, nor did he want to kill this young fellow. It was bad business to wipe out a ranger. The man's companions would keep coming until at last they got him. Moreover, he was no killer by temperament. He had nothing against Steve Porter, outside of the fact that just now he was devilishly in the way. He must use strategy.

'You're putting the wagon before the horse, Mr. Ranger,' he remonstrated. 'Every man is presumed to be innocent until he is proved guilty. See the Constitution of the U.S.A. If you want to arrest me legally that's different. Get a warrant and I'll surrender like a lamb.'

'A ranger doesn't need a warrant.'

'Hmp! Personally I'd rather be arrested by due process of law than at the whim of some wise ranger who is particular where I wear my scars. But let that go in the discard. The poster mentions two holdups, one of the Rosedale bank and the other of the Texas & Pacific express. For which one are you collecting me?'

'For either one — or both.'

'Perhaps I was at Northfield too with Jesse James and the Younger boys,' the stranger suggested. 'I had as much to do with that stickup as with the Texas & Pacific one.'

'You can explain all that to the judge.'

'Decided to have me tried, have you? With or without evidence?'

'There's evidence enough. It's my duty to arrest you.'

The stranger's face broke into a swift winning smile. 'We're going at this the wrong way, Mr. Porter. What say we walk over to the sheriff's office together and put our cards on the table? If you're not satisfied with my explanation you can take me into custody until you have checked it up.'

'Suits me,' the ranger replied, greatly relieved.

'Good enough.'

Forrest walked to the counter, ran his right

17

hand swiftly into a hip pocket for money, and paid for the goods he had purchased.

'I'll put these supplies on my horse,' he said to the ranger. 'Come along out with me.'

He led the way to the door, his right hand under the parcels. As he went, he chatted cheerfully. 'I got a couple of cans of peaches. They're kinda bulky, but I have a craving for them. A fellow gets tired of sowbelly and coffee.'

Steve Porter wished he had been longer with the rangers and was more experienced. He did not doubt this man was Forrest. Why otherwise would the fellow frustrate all attempts to see the back of his hand? But he had to be sure before he arrested him. After all, it would be better to do this after the showdown at the sheriff's office.

'I'll tie this flour on behind the saddle and stow the other things in the saddlebags,' the stranger said. 'Be ready to go with you in a jiffy.'

'You-all bought quite a lot of grub,' the ranger said pointedly, 'for a man drifting from camp to camp.'

'Yes. I'm kind of a lone wolf. Like to sleep in the hills sometimes. A fellow gets thataway — feels crowded with too many neighbors.'

'Some fellows,' agreed Porter, and slanted

a long look at him.

Forrest filled the saddlebags and lifted the flour to the back of the horse.

'I'll help you tie it,' the ranger said, and stepped forward, still intent on finding out if this man had the advertised scar.

'I'm obliged to you,' the older man said easily. 'If you'll hold it a minute I'll tie the other side.'

He walked round behind the horse to the other side, reached forward and jerked loose the slip knot, and vaulted to the saddle. Swiftly he swung his mount and started it with a jump. His body low, he dashed up the road in a cloud of dust.

The ranger, left holding the sack of flour, stared after him in startled surprise. When he dropped it, to drag out a revolver, the galloping rider was forty yards away. He fired twice, aware that it was a waste of ammunition.

Forrest turned, to wave a derisive hand at him. Already the ranger was fumbling at the knotted bridle of the nearest horse. Before the fugitive was out of sight young Porter was astride the cowpony and in pursuit.

CHAPTER 2

A Meeting in the Desert

Before he had gone three hundred yards Forrest knew that the ranger had not horse enough under him to catch Maverick. The chestnut was a powerful rangy animal with plenty of endurance and a fair amount of speed. Steve Porter was already driving the little cowpony hard and was not gaining. Soon he would begin to fall farther behind.

For about a mile Forrest held to the road. He topped a sharp rise and looked back. The ranger's mount was beginning to take the slope a couple of hundred yards in the rear. As soon as the fugitive was out of sight he turned up an arroyo which twisted its way into the hills. The brush was thick, and before he had traveled a stone's throw the cactus and the mesquite had him completely hidden. He drew up for a moment to listen.

To him there came the sound of pounding hoofs on the road. The ranger did not stop at the arroyo but held a straight course ahead. He would pull up at the turn just in front of him when he discovered the man he wanted had deflected into the chaparral, but that extra two minutes of time ought to be enough for Forrest. Porter would not know at what point he had disappeared and before he had picked up the trail Maverick would be among the cowbacked hills which rose like the waves of a rolling sea. Once lost in these, he would be no easier to find than the proverbial needle in a haystack.

The arroyo ran into a hill pocket, the sides of which were sown with a thick growth of prickly pear. Forrest took the left-hand slope, and presently looked down on the tops of many folded hills. Back of these was the ridge toward which he was working. For another hour he rode steadily, then decided to tie up for dinner at the first good place that offered. What he wanted to find was water for his horse, but he knew the chances were that he would have to put up with a dry camp.

He was pushing his way up a shale bluff when he stopped abruptly. Down in the valley to the left something had crossed from one bunch of mesquite to another. The object had looked to him like a man, and if so almost certainly one in trouble. Whatever it was seemed to be dragging itself along with difficulty.

He watched for a minute and saw the object reappear in the open. A man or a boy weaved forward weakly. What was he doing here on the desert on foot? Presently the figure stopped in the shade of a mesquite and sank to the ground.

Forrest turned Maverick down the slope toward the valley. This was not a trap, since nobody could be expecting to find him here. Somebody desperately needed help. He rode across the spine-covered plain at a canter. When the figure rose and moved toward him, hands outstretched, he could see by the slender lines that this was not a grown man. But when he leaped from the horse and moved to meet the wanderer he was startled to see a woman. She was in boots and Levis, and in spite of her youth was haggard from exhaustion.

'I've been lost all day and all night,' she said hoarsely. 'Have you any water in that canteen?'

He untied the canteen from the saddle and handed it to her. She drank, as if she would never stop. The desert heat had given her an intolerable thirst.

From one of the saddlebags he got a can of peaches and from a scabbard beside the saddle a small hatchet. With the heel of the blade he slashed open the top of the can.

'The juice will be fine for your parched throat,' he said. 'And the fruit will slip down easily. Be sure you don't cut yourself on the jagged edge.'

'My throat's swollen so I can hardly swallow,' she croaked. 'It's been terrible. I thought —'

She stopped, to keep from breaking down.

He knew what she had thought, that she was going to die alone in the desert of thirst. From this terror, which had been riding her for many hours, he tried to deflect her mind.

'How did you get lost?'

'I was riding from the Granite Gap ranch to Fair Play. My horse got scared at a rattler, acted up, and threw me. When I tried to catch him he bolted.'

'A girl ought not to tackle this desert alone. . . . There are live oaks up on the bluffs where you'll get more shade. Soon as you've finished those peaches I'll put you in the saddle and we'll ride up there. I'm going to let you sleep. You're young and tough. In a few hours you will be good as new.'

She fished a peach out of the can with a forefinger. 'My throat is a lot better already. I'm hungry too. My stomach feels as flat as an empty mail sack.'

'You don't want to eat too much all at once. The peaches will do for a start.'

When she had drained the can he brought Maverick up alongside of her. The face of the girl was streaked from tears and grimy with dust. Her eyes were sunken and red. But he could see that in other circumstances she would be very pretty.

She looked at him, and he noticed she was fighting back tears. 'If it hadn't been you —'

'It would have been someone else,' he said, and did not believe it. 'We'll go now.'

The rescued girl tried to raise one foot to the stirrup and could not get it high enough. She was too near exhaustion. He put a hand round the blue overalls at the ankle, said 'Now,' and gave her a lift into the saddle. After he had fitted her feet into the leathers above the stirrups they moved across the valley and up the slope to the grove of live oaks on the bluff.

She started to dismount without help, but from behind he took her round the waist and lowered her lightly. He noticed that though she was slender and not tall her poundage was sufficient. The flesh on her body was solid and not too soft. He judged from her tanned face and hands the young woman had led an outdoor life.

'I'll light a fire and fix you up some food,' he said. 'By that time you'll be ready for some more. Go rest under that tree till I tell you to come and get it.'

'You're babying me. I ought to help.' She

was coming back to normal, but her smile was still a little wistful. When he had met her she had been very close to a complete collapse.

When dinner was ready he saw that she did not eat too much. His manner was matter of fact, almost brusque. This was no time to help her feel sorry for herself.

He spread the saddle blanket for a bed. 'Don't worry,' he said. 'It's all over. Nothing is going to harm you now.'

'You're good to me,' she told him, with a swift look of gratitude.

Though she had not expected to sleep her eyes closed almost at once. When she awakened it was from the cold. His slicker had been stretched over her. It was night, and a million stars lit the sky.

She saw the man sitting beside a fire not far away. He sat cross-legged, as riders of the range usually do. While she watched him he rose to replenish the fire. He chopped some dry branches and brought them back with him. Never had she seen anyone move more lightly and surely. The coordination of his muscles was fascinating. Something of the same rippling grace she had noticed once in a panther when she had been hunting with her father. She had drawn a perfect bead on the animal, then deliberately shot wild, unable to destroy such beauty of motion.

She was curious about this man. He too was wild and untamed, in his way a specimen flawless as the panther had been. Back of his quiet poise was a repressed and hidden fire that might become explosive if the occasion warranted. Janet guessed that he had trod through colorful years to this hour of stillness in the empty hills. She was slept out, and the desire for talk was strong. The urge was in her to discover what manner of man he was.

'What time is it?' she called.

'About four o'clock.'

She rose, shook her clothes together, and moved over to him. 'I must have slept about fifteen hours. Why didn't you wake me?'

'You needed the rest. How you feeling now?'

'Hungry.'

'That's a good symptom. I know the cure for that.' He brought food from the saddlebags and began to rake the coals of the fire together.

'Sorry I can't give you flapjacks. No flour. I left town in a hurry without any.'

As he worked, she studied him with interest. The man talked without revealing himself, yet his manner was careless and not wary. There was strength in the dark brown sardonic face. He had a hard and reckless look. That he had

26

walked in forbidden paths was possible. But he would do to trust. Her fathar's phrase came to mind, one used in speaking of the men who had settled this part of the country, that there were mighty few culls in the herd. This man was no cull.

'Funny you forgot flour,' she said. 'You're no tenderfoot.'

'I didn't exactly forget it,' he drawled. 'I gave it to a fellow to hold and he didn't hand it back to me.'

This cryptic explanation stimulated curiosity and told her nothing. But though the glance she slanted at him was a question, he did not elaborate his meaning. She was too much of the West to press for an interpretation. The code of Texas was to ask a stranger few questions and to be sure these were of a harmless kind.

'My name is Janet King,' she mentioned. 'Curtis King of the Granite Gap ranch is my father.'

He had to think a moment what name he was using. 'You may call me Brown — James Brown.'

The hoarseness had gone from her throat. The sound of her light laughter was lovely. 'You say it as if you're not quite sure,' she challenged.

Her audacity brought a smile, a little grin,

to his face. 'I mentioned it to a man this morning who didn't seem at all sure.'

'I've held you here all night,' Janet said. 'It was very good of you to look after me, but I'm sorry to have detained you.'

He was cutting open a can of tomatoes. 'No trouble at all. I'm as well off here as anywhere, except that I must get Maverick to water soon.'

'If you're looking for work, my father could probably use you as a rider,' she ventured hesitantly.

'I had some notion like that this morning, but I've changed my mind,' he told her, thinking of the poster he had seen in the post office. 'I'm expecting to move on quite some distance from here. But I'm much obliged, Miss King.'

Dimples flashed in her piquant young face. 'What are you going to do with me?'

'I've been thinking about that. I could take you back to your ranch.'

'No. There are papers at Fair Play I have to sign, not later than today. It's important that I be there.'

He thought, with comical humor, that it was important he be not there, but he did not say so. Instead, he hummed in his soft slurring voice some words of an old camp-meeting hymn.

'I want to be ready,
I want to be ready,
I want to be ready,
To walk in Jerusalem just like John.'

Janet could see he was considering what she had said. The song was an accompaniment to his reflection.

'If you're too busy to take me —,' she began.

'I'm not doing a frazzling thing. Just fiddlin' around. But I wasn't exactly heading Fair Play way.' With his hunting knife he cut some slices of bacon and dropped them in the frying pan. While he watched and turned them he contributed another stanza of the hymn.

'When Peter was preaching at Pentecost,
Walk in Jerusalem just like John,
He was endowed with the Holy Ghost,
Walk in Jerusalem just like John.'

'If you-all have an appointment to preach somewhere just take me as far as the road. I'll get to town all right.'

He laughed at the demure sarcasm in her voice. 'I'm the son of a preacher, even if I'm not one.'

'I've heard about ministers' sons,' she mentioned.

'It's a fact they're mostly scalawags,' he admitted. 'I wouldn't know why. . . . But about getting you to Fair Play, I'll fix it somehow.'

While they ate breakfast the first thin line of blue along the horizon's edge proclaimed the coming of day. He brought in Maverick and saddled. The saddlebags containing the provisions he left hanging to the limb of a live oak.

'I'll pick them up when I come back,' he said.

He gave the saddle seat to Janet and rode behind her.

CHAPTER 3

Ranger Steve Porter Gets His Man

That Fair Play was no place to show himself now Blake Forrest knew. But some devil of recklessness rose in him, as often had happened before. It was the last spot in the world where anybody would be looking for him, since he had just left on the gallop to escape capture. The cowboys he had met in Doan's store would now be back on the ranch where they worked. That left only Sampson, Doan, their clerk, and Ranger Steve Porter who would be likely to recognize him immediately. Three of these would be busy at the store, and he had no intention of dropping in there. If by bad luck he met Porter he would have to trust again to Maverick's speed. It had always been easy for Forrest to persuade himself of the wisdom or at least of the safety of any course on which he had set his mind. Just now he wanted to see Janet King to the hotel, where she was going to stay until she could get some clothes to make a presentable appearance at the home of the friends with whom she meant to stop. Her original plan had been to change

31

before she reached town, but her horse had made that impossible by running away with the bundle wrapped up in her slicker.

Young girls did not greatly interest him. They simpered and giggled and assumed coyness. But he was prepared to make an exception of this one. It was not only her good looks, of which she had more than her share. She was frank and direct, affecting no prudery because circumstances had flung them closely together overnight. He liked her spirit and her gaiety. Silver bells rang in her laughter. Moreover, on occasion she had a touch of dry wit he found amusing.

He was not under any delusion about the position in which they stood to each other. No friendship was possible between her and him. He had made that out of the question when he had left the straight path to ride crooked trails by night. Nor would he have had it otherwise. He was a man's man, and he wanted women in his life only during hours of relaxation and not as an embarrassing permanency.

Except for a pair of Mexicans squatting in the shade of a wall the street was as deserted as it had been when Forrest arrived the previous day.

'I'm glad there isn't a band to meet us,' Janet said, laughing back at him over her shoulder. 'I'm so grimy and dirty people would think I was your squaw coming in to buy a new blanket.'

'I'm being glad with you about that welcome committee,' the man behind her agreed dryly. 'You never can tell. Some of them might think I ought to stay permanently.'

'Are you as popular as that, Mr. Brown?' she asked lightly. If there was a thought of sarcasm back of her words he had to guess at it.

"Popular isn't quite the word, Miss King. Well, here you are at the hotel, right side up, delivered with care.'

He slipped from the horse, and a moment later Janet stood beside him on the two-plank sidewalk. She notice the sweep of his swift keen glance up and down the street. It disturbed her a little. If he was going to have trouble she did not want it to be at Fair Play, after he had brought her here. Of course it was possible she just had too much imagination. He might be only a range rider out of a job.

'I'll not forget your kindness — not ever,' she said.

The palm of her hand met his in a quick firm pressure.

'It's been a pleasure, Miss King. I don't reckon we'll meet again, so I'll say you've been a game little lady with heaps of sense and I'm wishing you all the luck in the world.'

He could not doubt the friendly warmth in the eyes so quick with life. It told him, what the look of many a woman had told him, of an interest that might grow keen if given an opportunity.

'Not all the luck,' she corrected. 'I hope you have your share and more.' On swift impulse, she added: 'I'm afraid you are going to need a good deal.'

'You know me?' he asked, a sardonic smile on his reckless face.

'I never saw you before yesterday, but — you don't look tame.'

'Not very well curried,' he admitted, 'and doesn't always stay put even when hitched.'

'I was sure from the moment I saw you that . . .'

'That I'm a bad *hombre*,' he finished for her.

'No, that — you are in trouble and may need a lot of luck.' In her brown throat a pulse beat fast. 'I know you are not bad, but I think you are too — too wild and reckless.'

'Those blue eyes of yours take in plenty,' he said. 'I can stand quite a bit of luck right now, all of it good.'

'I hope you haven't made a mistake bringing me here. If you have, I won't forgive myself soon.'

Carelessly, he shrugged his well-muscled shoulders. 'Don't worry about me. I'll do fine.'

'Then, good-bye, and thank you, oh, a thousand times.' Janet wanted to say more. But what could she say? He had dismissed her. The episode was ended. Yet she found it hard to tear herself away. Something new and strange fluttered in her, something a little terrifying but exciting and delightful. Abruptly she turned and disappeared into the hotel.

Forrest began to lower the stirrups, his mind full of this young woman with the eager eyes so avid of life. He was working on the second when a sharp summons startled him. A young man had walked out of the hotel and stopped in his stride. Without turning his head the outlaw knew that a revolver had flashed from a holster and was covering him.

'Stick 'em up, Mr. Blake Forrest,' a strident voice was ordering.

The outlaw had been caught napping. Even while adjusting the stirrups he had made sure nobody was approaching along the street, but he could not at the same time see behind him. He slewed his head round, grinning.

'Nice to meet you again, Mr. Porter,' he said coolly.

'Get 'em up,' the ranger commanded curtly.

'No shenanigan. Try any funny business this time and I'll pump lead into you.'

Forrest raised his arms. 'That's a fine way to talk to a man who came back to give himself up,' he said easily.

The ranger had no idea why he had come back, nor did he greatly care. It was a piece of luck for him such as probably would not happen to him again during his service. The man had made him look like a fool, and this unexpected chance was given him to rectify his mistake. He was not going to slip up a second time.

'Step back from the horse without turning,' he said. 'Keep your hands in the air. If you make a break it will be the last you ever try.'

Blake Forrest did as directed. 'Don't worry about me. I'm a lamb in wolf's clothing, Mr. Porter.'

The young man relieved him of his weapon and made sure he had no other. 'Walk down the street in front of me,' he snapped. 'Move slow — and keep your fists up.'

They turned in at the office of the sheriff, Buzz Waggoner.

'I'm turning this man over to you for safe keeping, Sheriff,' the ranger said. 'You probably recognize him from his picture. He's Blake Forrest.'

The sheriff recognized him, but not from his picture. He had known him ten years before at Tascosa. Forrest had been a hell-raising cowpuncher. Yet he had not been known as one who lived outside the law. Oddly enough, Waggoner was the one who had been under suspicion in those days.

'Jim Brown is the name,' the prisoner said mildly.

'It didn't used to be when I knew you as a kid, Blake,' the sheriff mentioned.

Forrest looked at the sheriff more closely. 'If it isn't Buzz Waggoner! You've put on sixty-seventy pounds of tallow since we have met up. Last time I saw you was just before you jumped a bronc to light out in front of Cape Willingham's posse.'

'That little matter was cleared up long ago, Blake,' the sheriff replied amiably. 'We're dealing with your troubles now.'

'Put cuffs on him, Buzz,' the ranger said.

Waggoner found a pair of handcuffs in a drawer and fastened them on the prisoner.

'Ranger Porter is just a kid, Buzz,' explained Forrest. 'Still a little wet behind the ears. Thinks it is his duty to go around arresting everybody he doesn't know.'

Steve Porter pointed triumphantly to the scar on the back of one of the hands in the cuffs. 'Knew it was you all the time,' he said.

'You were too smart about keeping it under cover.'

'Say I'm Blake Forrest. Does that prove I'm the man you want?'

'Sure it does. Your mask fell off and the express messenger recognized you. That's how come we knew it was a Blake Forrest job.'

'What is the name of that express messenger?'

'You'll find out in plenty of time.' The ranger turned to Waggoner. 'Be sure you lock this man up safely, Sheriff. He's a desperate character. Don't take any chances with him.'

'We'll get along all right,' Waggoner said. He was a big good-natured man beginning to run to fat. He laughed a good deal, and when he did his little pig eyes almost disappeared beneath the wrinkles in his face.

'Think I'll see him in a cell before I go,' the ranger said tartly.

'Seems to me I was elected sheriff, young fellow,' Buzz reminded Porter without rancor. 'You don't have to leave him with me, you know, but if you do I'll be the one taking charge of him.'

"All right. I just want to make sure. He's slippery as a barrel of snakes. You know how he gave me the horse laugh yesterday."

'Seems to me I did hear something about

that, Steve,' Waggoner said. 'Left you holding a sack, didn't he?'

Porter reddened. 'That was yesterday. Today's different. If you don't want me to see him put safe in a cell you better give me a receipt for him.'

The sheriff scrawled one. It read:

'Received from Ranger Steve Porter one prisoner named Blake Forrest.' He signed it with his name.

Reluctantly the ranger departed. He would have preferred to see his captured bandit behind bars. After he had gone Waggoner smoked a cigarette with his prisoner in the office, though he was careful to see the desk was between them and a Colt's .44 in the open drawer within reach of his hand.

'Sorry to see you here, Blake,' he said. 'You're too smart a fellow to be in a jam like this. There are plenty of fools in this world you can't ever teach a thing, but you've got brains in yore head and ought to know that crime never pays.'

'Why Buzz, I've only got to look at your career to know different,' Forrest answered. 'At Tascosa I see you lighting out like the heel flies were after you, a few jumps ahead of a posse which claimed you had been using a running iron too freely. Next time my eyes are refreshed by a sight of you, they are looking at an honest-to-God sheriff probably all lined up to be governor one of these days. If crime doesn't pay, you got no business where you are, Buzz.'

The sheriff grinned sheepishly. 'I don't say I'm any model for schoolmarms to point at, Blake. All I say is that I seen the error of my ways and pulled up in time. After what you did for me I hate like Billy-be-damn to see you go to the penitentiary.'

With much more confidence than he felt, Forrest smiled at him cheerfully. 'Then you'll be glad to know I'm not going there, Buzz.'

'Well, I hope you're right. Maybe you got an ace up yore sleeve. By the way I heard it Gildea says you robbed his bank at Rosedale without even wearing a mask. Then on top of that the express messenger of the train you robbed recognized you when you held up the Texas & Pacific. I don't see any jury in this state letting you loose against such evidence.'

'Who is that express manager who claims to have recognized me?'

'Fellow by the name of Terrell.'

'Ray Terrell?'

'That's right. One of the Terrells from Deer Trail.'

The man wearing the handcuffs relapsed into silence. The manner of pleasant friendliness was wiped from his face as a wet sponge

40

erases the writing from a slate. His blue eyes had grown hard as agates, cold as ice in a wintry pond. At present he had nothing more to say.

'Reckon I'd better be fixing you up with a room,' the sheriff said.

He drew a bunch of keys from the drawer and took his prisoner into a corridor that led from the office to the jail in the rear of the courthouse.

'I aim to make you comfortable, Blake,' the fat man said. 'If there's anything you need holler and I'll fix you up best I can.'

'I'll be all right,' the captured man answered absently.

His mind was still busy considering information the sheriff had given him.

CHAPTER 4

Janet Sees a Lawyer

After Janet King had bathed and made what first-aid repairs to her appearance were possible with soap and water, she went out in her boots and Levis to buy at Sampson & Doan's such clothes as she needed. As soon as he saw her Doan came forward to wait on her himself. The Granite Gap ranch trade was valuable, and as the only woman in a house full of men Janet had a good deal to say about where much of the spending was done.

He was surprised to see her casual costume, but did not let his astonishment reach the surface.

'It's nice to see you in Fair Play again, Miss King,' he told her. 'Let me see, it has been a month since you were here last, hasn't it?'

He was a baldheaded little man with an unctuous smile and a habit of giving his hands a dry wash when he was cajoling a customer.

Janet explained that her horse had run away with the clothes she had expected to wear in town, and that she wanted to buy what was necessary until she reached the ranch. Since she was rather particular about what she wore when she was not riding the range, it took her some time to select a print dress, underclothes, stockings, shoes, and accessories. The last thing on her list was a comb and brush. Doan led her to a showcase at the lower end of the store to let her see what he had in stock.

Her glance fell on a poster tacked to the wall of the post office compartment. From it the face of her rescuer, James Brown, smiled cynically at her. She read what was written beneath it, her heart beating a wild alarm.

One Thousand Dollars Reward for the Arrest of BLAKE FORREST, Wanted for the Robbery of the Valley Bank at Rosedale and for Holding up the Texas & Pacific Express at Crawford's Crossing. Forrest is about 30 years old, weighs 165 pounds, and is Five Foot Ten in height. Eyes blue, hair black, complexion tanned to a coffee brown. Body muscular and graceful. Manner pleasant and friendly unless angered. This outlaw is a dangerous man who will probably resist arrest. Officers are warned to take no chances.

N.B. The only distinguishing mark on

this man is a scar on the back of the right hand from the base of the thumb to the wrist.

She had known it, she had known all the time, Janet told herself, that this man was somehow living outside the law. It was written on his reckless sardonic face, was imprinted in the feral grace of his rippling motions. Nonetheless a chill went through her as at the first touch of a northern blizzard. He had not only been a friend in need. Anybody in the district would have done as much for her as he had. In the frontier country a man had to help one in distress, especially a woman. It was the unwritten law of the land. But his personality had filled her with a quick excitement. A spark in him had lit fires in her that were new and a little alarming.

'Are they sure this man is guilty?' she asked. 'I mean — is the evidence against him complete?'

'He's the fellow, all right,' Doan replied eagerly. Like most people he was glad to tell his part, though entirely a passive one, in a story as dramatic as this. 'He came in here yesterday, bold as cuffey, to buy supplies and was recognized by a ranger, young Steve Porter. Steve tried to arrest him, and he jumped his horse and lit out, leaving the boy holding

44

the sack. He actually was holding a sack of flour this Forrest had handed him. Never saw the beat of the scalawag's nerve. He planned it, cool as a cucumber, to make his getaway, and by gum, pulled it off.'

'I know, but what I mean is, maybe this Forrest didn't do these holdups. Maybe it was someone who looked like him.'

Doan shook his head. 'No chance of that, Miss King. He walked into the private office of Jake Gildea, the president of the Valley Bank at Rosedale, and forced him to hand over sixty-five hundred dollars. Gildea knows him well as I do you. Seems they weren't good friends. And when he was robbing the train his mask fell off and he was recognized.'

Janet was distressed. It was one thing to feel that he was capable of any bold and reckless adventure, another to learn that he was definitely an outlaw.

A stringy boy of about fourteen ran into the store, his eyes shining with excitement. 'Steve Porter has got that outlaw Blake Forrest,' he screamed.

Doan turned on him severely. 'What do you mean telling lies, Bud Newsome? I saw Steve in town not more than an hour ago.'

'Sure. That's where he arrested him. Right here in town. Honest to goodness. Cross my heart.'

The clerk ran out of the store to verify the news.

'Someone has been joshing you, Bud,' explained Doan. 'Why would Forrest be at Fair Play when Steve ran him out of town yesterday? It doesn't make sense.'

'I dunno why he came back. But it's so. Everybody says so. A fellow was telling it at the blacksmith shop, and I heard it again coming up the street.'

'Well, you heard a lot of foolishness, son. Stands to reason it can't be true.'

Janet walked out of the store in a turmoil. If he had not brought her back to town he would not have been captured. Why had he done such a foolhardy thing? By now he might have been well on his way to Arizona or Colorado. It was because he had befriended her that he had been taken.

'Miss King — Miss King,' a voice behind her called.

She turned. Doan had come running out of the store. 'Did you decide you want the white comb and brush?'

'Yes.'

'Shall I send all the things to the hotel?'

'Yes — yes. At once, please. I'm in a hurry.'

He promised to have the goods at the hotel inside of five minutes.

While Janet was dressing in her new clothes

her mind was busy with the problem of this captured outlaw. She was going to ask Henry Vallery, her father's lawyer and an old family friend, to see Forrest and look after his interests. There was nothing else she could do to help him. She was unhappy that he had been caught in town after bringing her here, she told herself, yet she was not responsible because his sins had found him out.

Henry Vallery took the same view. 'If a man puts himself outside the law he'll have to take whatever punishment is coming to him. You're not in this, Janet. It won't do you any good to get mixed up in it. Your father wouldn't want folks to associate your name with a bad man like Forrest.'

He was a benign-looking old gentleman, white-haired and kindly, a little fussy and nervous. But she knew he was a very good trial lawyer. After he had protested sufficiently and shot his cuffs a few times he would capitulate and do as she wanted.

'Would my father want me to desert a man who had got into trouble because he brought me in from the desert and didn't leave me to die?' she asked, forsaking the logical position into which she had earlier argued herself.

He sputtered around a good deal, then threw up his hands.

'All right. I'll go talk with him. I can't see what good it will do, since he's headed for the penitentiary. But I'll go.'

'I'd like to wipe out my debt to him. If he hasn't any money I'll take care of your fee. You know I have money Mother left me.'

'You'll do nothing of the kind,' he stormed. 'First thing you know this fool town would be gossiping about you and him. You've done enough for him. Now you can go back to the ranch and forget about it.'

She brushed some dandruff from his black Prince Albert coat and smiled up at him. 'I'll not forget how nice you've been about this, Uncle Henry. And you do see, don't you, why I've got to help him if I can?'

As a retainer in advance she kissed him swiftly and fled.

CHAPTER 5

'Standing in the Need of Prayer'

To Buzz Waggoner and Henry Vallery, walking along the corridor to the jail cells, came the sound of a fairly good untrained tenor raised in a camp-meeting song.

'It's me, it's me, O Lawd, standing in the need of prayer,
It's me, it's me, O Lawd, standing in the need of prayer,
Not my brother, but me O Lawd, standing in the need of prayer.'

'By Judas Priest, have you got a preacher locked up in your calaboose?' Vallery inquired.

'No, sir. That's my bandit, the one you come to see.' The sheriff shouted greeting as they drew near the cell from which the singing had come. 'You need prayer all right, Blake, but you need a good lawyer too. So I've brought him along with me. This is Judge Vallery, than whom there ain't no better before a jury. Judge, meet yore client.'

'Am I his client?' Forrest drawled.

'Hell! You two fix that up together.' The sheriff unlocked the cell door and Vallery entered after which Waggoner fastened the door again. 'I got business in the office, but I'll be back in about fifteen minutes, say.'

When the echo of the officer's footsteps had died away the lawyer explained his presence. 'I'm not trying to thrust my services on you. Fact is, a young lady to whom you did a kindness is — er — distressed about your plight.'

'Sit down on that chair, Judge. Sorry I can't offer you refreshments.' Forrest rolled a cigarette leisurely and lit it. 'A young lady. Interesting. What's the name?'

Vallery stretched his arms and shot his cuffs in a characteristic gesture. 'Suppose we leave her name out of this. You understand that, feeling under an obligation to you, she naturally — er — is unhappy because you were arrested on account of bringing her here.'

'I see,' the prisoner said dryly. 'But she would not like her name to get out. A good Samaritan by proxy. I'm sure obliged. Tell her with my compliments, Mr. Vallery, that when I want a lawyer I'll choose my own.'

There was a cool scorn in the outlaw's voice that embarrassed the lawyer a little. He had not expected to meet a man of this type. His natural assumption had been that the fellow would jump at a chance to get help out of the predicament in which he was. That the prisoner was one with sensitive feelings was a complete surprise.

Vallery cleared his throat and shot his cuffs. 'I have not stated the situation clearly, young man. The young lady doesn't give a tinker's damn, by Judas Priest, whether her name is known or not. But I care. I'm not going to have her name mixed up in a business like this. You ought to know how the tabbycats in a little town talk. Just give them something to start with and the finest woman's reputation can be talked away in a week.'

'You're quite right, Judge,' Forrest answered gently. 'I didn't get it correct. Now this young lady doesn't owe me a thing. I told her so. It just happens I was lucky enough to be near when she was lost and petered out. I'm a bad *hombre*, Judge. Don't let her touch pitch and nobody will even know she has ever met me. She's a right fine young woman, and we don't want gossips fooling with her name. That's important. Tell her I'm much obliged, and for her to keep out of it. Tell her I'll take her advice about a lawyer. I've just met the one I want.' He stopped, with a shame-faced grin. 'At least I would take her advice if I had any money handy.'

The old lawyer went through his usual nervous stretchings. 'I expect that could be arranged, young man.'

The keen blue eyes of Forrest rested on the attorney. 'Did the nameless young lady say she would arrange it?'

Vallery floundered. 'Well — er — in point of fact — what I meant was — er —'

'I asked a question, Judge.'

'Yes, sir, she did,' blurted out Vallery. 'She has money coming to her from her mother. That is why she is in town today to see me. But it wouldn't do. I told her so. If it got out that she had paid for your defence —'

'Of course it wouldn't do. You don't need to argue it with me. I wouldn't have it for a moment. But I want her to know I'm certainly grateful. I won't be seeing the young lady again, Judge. Will you tell her for me that I think she's a gentleman? About your fee, I'll fix that myself. I know where to get money, if I can get out of jail for a day or two — and I can.'

'How? Bail won't be allowed.'

'A fellow can always find a way,' the lawyer's client said with a bland smile.

'I don't know what you mean.' Then, bluntly: 'I judge from what I have read that you are guilty. Or are you?'

'Now you've met me, what would you think?' Forrest asked.

'I'll do my thinking after you have told me your story,' Vallery said, a little stiffly. He felt that this outlaw was too impudently sure of himself.

'I haven't had time to fix it up smooth yet, Judge.'

His nonchalance exasperated the lawyer. 'I take my work seriously, Mr. Brown — if that's what you still call yourself.'

'That name is played out. Buzz recollected me from old Tascosa days on account of me finding him a bronc to fork when he was in some hurry one time. Call me Blake Forrest.'

'I don't want to force your confidence, Mr. Forrest. Perhaps you can find a lawyer who will suit you better. But if he has your interest at heart he will not go into court with you making a jest of your crime.'

'I'm accused of *two* crimes, Judge, according to the reward poster I saw.'

'Yes. If you have an alibi for either —'

'Maybe Jake Gildea will give me one,' the prisoner answered with a hardy grin. 'I was with him at the time his bank was robbed.'

'You mean that you are guilty of these crimes?'

'Guilty and not guilty.'

'I'm not good at riddles, sir.' Vallery rose from the chair. 'I don't think we are going to suit each other as client and attorney. I will say good day.'

Forrest differed. 'We're going to get along fine, Judge. I want an honest man for my lawyer, and I have found one.' There was a flicker of reckless mirth in the blue eyes. 'A criminal makes a mistake when he gets a crook to defend him. I want our firm to be fifty percent respectable. Sit down, and I'll tell you the sad story of how a poor young cowboy who was a preacher's son and brought up proper went wrong through associating with a bank president when he'd ought to have known from his copy book that evil communications corrupt good manners.'

'Very good,' assented Vallery dubiously. 'Let us be serious about this.'

'Not if I can help it, Judge. I'm going to have twenty years to be serious after I'm locked up in the penitentiary. Got to keep my grin working while I can. Well, here's the yarn.'

Forrest told his story and the lawyer listened, now and again interrupting with a question. When the outlaw had finished, the older man commented:

'There are one or two points to hang a defence on, but I must say you have managed to get yourself into a pretty bad jam."

'I don't need a high-priced lawyer to tell me that,' Forrest said. 'Point is, can you get me out of it?'

'I don't see how. Even your own story will convict you, and your reputation is unfortunately bad. But I'll do the best I can.'

'That's straight talk. The kind I like. No palaver. All right. I'll round up for you what evidence I can get.'

'By letter?'

'Personally. Didn't I tell you I expected to be out of here in a day or two?'

'Yes.' Vallery looked at him keenly from beneath shaggy gray eyebrows. 'Don't do anything foolish. Your case is desperate enough now without your making it any worse.'

Buzz Waggoner sauntered back and unlocked the door. 'You fellows chewed the rag enough yet?' he asked.

'For the present,' the lawyer said. 'I'll be back tomorrow morning.'

The sheriff saw him out of the jail and returned.

'Everything in my hotel first class?' he inquired of his prisoner. 'Grub all it should be?'

'Fine and dandy, Buzz. But I'm thinking of moving.'

'Soon?' the sheriff wanted to know, with a lift of quizzical eyebrows.

'Yes. I need to get some money that I have cached in the hills. That's one thing, and the least important. I'm going to put my cards on the table with you, Buzz. I didn't rob that Texas & Pacific train, and I can prove it if I have a chance to round up evidence. But I'll have to be busier than a candidate before election, or I'll be railroaded through on false testimony and on my record.'

'I don't reckon you can get bail, Blake.'

'I know I can't.' The cool hard eyes of Forrest fastened on his jailer. 'I'm depending on you for a little help, Buzz.'

'Now looky here, fellow,' Waggoner protested, instantly alarmed. 'I'm sheriff of this here county. If you think I'm going to turn you loose —'

'I wouldn't expect that, Buzz. It had better be a jail break, don't you reckon?'

'No sir, I don't. Like I said, the people of this county elected me sheriff. I stand for the law. I'd look fine turning loose any old friend who happens to be in here. You-all got no right to expect any such thing.'

Waggoner began to sputter excitedly. He knew his prisoner would not mention the time when he had supplied a horse for Buzz to get out of Tascosa and had turned aside at some risk Cape Willingham's posse from the pursuit. But he was thinking of it, just as the sheriff himself was.

'Do you think I would lie to you, Buzz?'

'What's that got to do with it? I'll loan you

56

money. I'll do anything personal I can, but I don't aim to renege on my oath of office.'

'When I tell you I didn't rob that train, do you believe me?'

'I reckon so. Sure. Anything you say.'

'Haven't forgotten, have you, that some years ago I had to kill Buck Terrell, brother of this express messenger who swears he recognized me as one of the train robbers?'

'That's so.' The sheriff stared at him. 'Meaning that this is a frame-up against you?'

'Meaning just that. I can prove where I was at the time of the train hold-up, if I can get out to find my witnesses.'

'You'll have to send some other fellow to dig 'em up for you, Blake,' Waggoner protested, little beads of sweat on his forehead.

'No other fellow could do it. There are reasons.' The blue eyes held fast to the light gray ones of the officer. 'If I promised to give myself up to you in two weeks you know I would do it, don't you?'

'Maybe you would, and maybe you wouldn't,' Waggoner answered angrily. 'No use you talking, Blake. I ain't a-going to turn you loose. Might just as well save yore breath.'

'Keep cool, Buzz,' the outlaw advised. 'You're too fat to get all het up thataway. When you boil up and turn red as a gobbler I get scared of apoplexy. Take it easy and you'll live longer. I asked you a question. Don't you know that if I promise to show up here at a certain date, hell and high water can't keep me from coming?'

'I expect you'd be here. What of it? Am I to tell the folks who elected me that I let out the most wanted man in Texas and that he has promised to show up again in a couple of weeks? I'd look like a blamed fool.'

'Just slip me a file and forget all about it. By the way, where is my horse Maverick?'

'At Daggett's wagon yard.' Waggoner exploded violently. 'No, damn my buttons, I won't do it. What's more, I won't talk about it. That's what a fellow gets for trying to be nice to a guy in trouble.'

The sheriff turned and clumped noisily down the corridor.

Forrest smiled. He had sown seed in fertile soil. Waggoner was not going to enjoy the next twenty-four hours. He was going to remember how his prisoner had been Johnny-on-the-spot in *his* hour of need. Old memories were going to churn up in him. Buzz was of the old school. An obligation to a friend was more important to him than an abstract sense of official duty, especially when he knew that he was permitting only a temporary escape. If the sheriff did not weaken, Blake Forrest would be greatly surprised.

CHAPTER 6

Forrest Rides

Blake Forrest descended to the ground by means of a blanket from his bed. He had found it no trouble to file the flimsy bars of the window. Once outside, he crept around the back of the building into a grove of live oaks. Buzz Waggoner had pointed out to him the house where Doan lived, to the right and just back of the trees. Three minutes after he had gained his freedom he was knocking on the door of the merchant's house. The sheriff had flatly refused to give him back his revolver, and he was going to need a weapon.

In his stocking feet Doan came to the door.

'What you want?' he asked of the man standing in the shodow of the porch vines.

'Want to buy a few things at the store.'

'You'll have to wait till morning,' Doan said irritably. 'We've been closed an hour.'

'Sorry, but I've got to get out of town tonight,' Forrest said mildly. 'I'd be obliged if you would step over and sell me what I need.'

'I suppose you've been sitting around a livery stable or a saloon gabbing all day,' Doan

59

snapped. 'Well, I'm not going over to the store this time of night. That's flat. We'll be open at eight in the morning.'

He started to close the door, but Forrest's foot was in the way. A strong brown hand reached out, caught him by the coat lapel, and dragged him forward with a jerk.

'You're going with me to the store, Mr. Doan,' a quiet voice said, almost in a murmur.

'Who are you?' Doan asked, startled at such cavalier treatment.

'The name is Blake Forrest. I'm sure if you think about it again you'll be willing to accommodate me.'

The storekeeper gasped. In the darkness he had not recognized the outlaw. 'C-c-certainly,' he stammered. 'Anything you want, Mr. Forrest. I'll just get my shoes and be with you right away.'

'Is the store key in your pocket?'

'Yes.'

'Then we won't bother about your shoes. It's not far through the grove.'

'May I t-tell my wife where I'm going?'

'Just call to her that you'll be over at the store a few minutes. Make it sound natural.'

Though Doan did his best, there was a quaver in his voice. The customer comforted him as they walked through the live oaks. 'I'm not going to hurt you, Mr. Doan. In ten minutes

you'll be back with your family fit as a fiddle
— if you behave reasonably and don't get pan-
icky. All I'm asking of you is a little service,
for which I'll say "Thank you kindly." Don't
be afraid.'

'I'm not af-f-raid,' Doan replied, his teeth
still chattering a little. 'I haven't done you
any harm.'

'Not a bit, and I won't do you any,' his
captor said cheerfully. 'Just remember that we
have to be careful about being seen, since I've
moved from Buzz Waggoner's calaboose un-
beknown to him. Does that key fit the back
door of the store as well as the front one?'

'Yes.'

'Then we'll go in that way.'

They turned up an alley, to avoid the people
on the street. Inside the store Doan struck
a match and lit a lamp with trembling fingers.

'I'll look at your guns,' Forrest said. 'I want
a .45 and some ammunition.'

He selected a weapon and a belt. The latter
he filled with cartridges after he had loaded
the revolver.

'I'm a little short of money just now, Mr.
Doan,' he explained. 'Have you any objection
to letting the payment ride a couple of weeks?'

Doan assured him eagerly he had not.

'Good enough. I'll be back then and settle
for the goods. I want you to walk down with

me to Daggett's wagon yard, where Buzz left my horse. Better pick a pair of boots out of stock and put them on. Get a pair that is comfortable.'

They walked down the alley and across the live oak grove. The escaped prisoner wanted to meet as few people as possible. Through the greasewood of a vacant lot they cut across to the wagon yard. Inside the little office near the entrance two men sat in tilted chairs, one of them with his boots on the table. He was in his early fifties, a big rawboned fellow with a goatee and a gray mustache. He wore an open vest, but no coat. His companion might have been twenty-five, and he had fiery red hair and a snub nose.

The older man glanced at the newcomers and continued with the story he was telling.

'So after this inspector had asked a mess of questions and had given plenty of instructions about how this and that report would have to be filed or there would be trouble sure enough, why old Snell was sore as a boil. He reached under the counter and handed a cigar box with a letter and a circular in it to the inspector. "Take yore damn post office back to Washington," he says, "and get the hell out of here." So that's how the old man quit being postmaster.'

Forrest waited until the narrator had got

his laugh before he mentioned his business.

'Like to get a horse of mine that has been left with you, Mr. Daggett.'

The big man stroked his goatee and looked at the outlaw out of keen light blue eyes. 'I don't recollect your leaving a horse here, sir,' he said.

'Buzz Waggoner brought it in for me,' Forrest drawled. 'A chestnut gelding with white stockings.'

The gaze of Daggett remained fixed on this lithe lean stranger standing in the doorway. The owner of the corral had been brought to instant alert attention. The voice of his visitor was gentle, the half-hooded eyes almost sleepy. The outlaw leaned lazily against the upright, a thumb hitched carelessly in the sagging belt. But Daggett knew that between two heart beats this man could be wakened to violent and explosive action.

'You are Blake Forrest?' the proprietor of the place asked.

'Correct, sir.'

Daggett played for time while he considered the situation. He stroked his goatee thoughtfully. 'Fixed up yore little difficulty with Buzz, I take it?' he suggested.

'Or else I wouldn't be here, would I?' countered Forrest, his smile suavely cynical.

The keeper of the wagon yard did not discuss the point. He suspected that something was wrong, but he knew who was master of this exigency. The bank robber had the drop on him just as surely as if he had him covered with the gun which rested so close to the indolent brown hand.

From the face of Daggett the harshness was wiped out as completely as a sponge obliterates writing on a slate. Its rigidity relaxed to a smile. This was a case that called for non-resistance.

'Yore horse has been well taken care of, Mr. Forrest,' he said, and lowered his boots from the table. 'We'll find him in the fourth stall.'

He led the way out of the office. Forrest motioned the red-headed man and the storekeeper to follow. He brought up the rear.

'There's a bill for two dollars,' Daggett mentioned. 'Does the sheriff pay that?'

'No, I'll settle it now,' Forrest said, and did. 'Mind saddling for me, Mr. Daggett? I mashed one of my hands the other day.'

A faint satiric smile rested for a moment on Daggett's bronzed face. It might be true that one of the outlaw's hands was disabled, but he was quite sure the other was fit for swift business. He brought the horse from the stall and saddled it.

'The cinch not quite so tight, please,' requested Maverick's owner courteously. 'I'm a light rider and easy on my mount.'

'Can I go now?' asked Doan, still uneasy in his mind.

'In just a minute, Mr. Doan,' his customer said cheerfully. 'You came down to see me off, and you wouldn't want to leave before I go.'

The red-headed man gave a nervous giggle. Since he did not know this outlaw's intentions he too would feel easier a little farther away from him.

Forrest swung to the saddle. 'I've had a very pleasant time in your little town, gentlemen,' he said with a grin. 'It's sure a nice hospitable place, but I mustn't outwear my welcome. . . . Now if you'll kindly all step to the other end of the corral. . . . That's fine. *Hasta la vista, señores.*'

He swung his horse out of the gate and trotted down the street. To the men in the corral there drifted back the words of a Mexican lullaby.

> 'Arriba del cielo,
> Esta un ventanito,
> Por donde se asoma
> El nono chiquito.'[1]

[1] High up in the sky
Is a little window;
From where it peeps,
The baby small.

The red-headed man flung his old Stetson into the dust at his feet. An oath ripped out of him. 'The son-of-a-gun!' he said vehemently. 'If I'd only had a six-shooter with me.'

Out of opaque eyes Daggett took the measure of the man. 'Sorry you didn't mention it earlier,' he answered, contempt edging his voice. 'I would have been glad to let you have mine, seeing I wasn't using it.'

'He made me go to the store with him, in my stocking feet, and let him have that gun he's wearing — on tick,' Doan said bitterly.

Daggett laughed. 'I'd call him about the coolest customer I've seen since Heck was a pup. Well, gents, shall we call on Buzz and condole?'

They walked uptown to spread the news.

CHAPTER 7

Forrest Takes a Nap

As soon as Forrest had crossed the bridge at the end of the street he quickened his pace. The lullaby died on his lips, and he smiled at himself. Sometimes, when in a tight spot, with danger lurking in the background, a queer exultation would bubble up in him and express itself in melodramatic fashion. He had seen would-be bad men, *poseurs,* pull this sort of stuff and it had always seemed to him ridiculous, a part of the stage properties they pulled to inspire fear and admiration in the audience. Blake was no amateur showing off. He had been a ranger for years and had many times given proof of his cool daring. When he 'put on a show,' as he called it, the act was born of some inner amusement rather than a desire to impress others.

Leaving Fair Play, he rode over a land drenched in moonlight. More than once he stopped to listen for sounds of possible pursuit. None came to him. Buzz Waggoner would make a bluff, of course, to save face, but it would be entirely a perfunctory one.

The town below him, with its lights strung out in a crescent like the jewels of a necklace, looked as peaceful as old age. No doubt weapons and mounts were being gathered for a posse, but he knew this would be wasted energy.

He departed from the road at the same point where he had left it a few days before. Maverick plodded through the brush and came at last to the bluff where Forrest had left his supplies before going to town with Janet King. The saddlebags were still hanging from the tree branch to which he had attached them.

Clouds had come up, and moon and stars were under wraps. He sniffed rain in the air. After he had unsaddled and picketed the horse he chopped some branches and built a fire. He had to find a certain cache he had left near here, and light was necessary to check the landmarks by which he could identify it. There was not a chance in ten thousand that a posse would stumble on him after he had picked his sinuous way through such a tangle of arroyos. His head had hardly found the softest spot in the saddle before he was asleep.

With the morning light at his back he wound deeper into the ribbed desert. He came at last to a sort of pass, wooded with mesquite on both sides of the trough, and here he swung to the left and pulled up at a thicket of wild plums. A fault ran across the terrain, a low rock ridge. Between two quartz outcroppings his gaze picked up the remains of a campfire. With his hatchet he slashed into the ashes and tossed aside the loose dirt. He dug out a sack. From it he took gold and bills to the amount of five hundred dollars. The rest he put back in the hole and heaped the loose dirt on it. Over the place he built a fire and cooked a late breakfast. When he had eaten he emptied the coffee grounds on a bare rock, evidence that somebody really had camped here. He even left part of an old newspaper pegged down by a stone.

He saddled, humming gaily a Negro song:

'What you gwine to do when the meat runs
    out, my baby?
What you gwine to do when the meat gives
    out, my honey?
What you gwine to do when the meat gives
    out?
    Gwine to set 'roun' my do' with my mouf
    in a pout, for sometime.'

Playfully Maverick pretended to bite at his arm. He dodged the lunge, tightening the cinch as he went on with the song.

'What kind o' pants does the gambler wear,
  this mo'nin'?
What kind o' pants does the gambler wear,
  this mo'nin'?
What kind o' pants does the gambler wear?
  Big-legged stripes cost nine a pair
    this mo'nin'.'

Mounting, he rode back to the pass through
the mesquite and swung to the left. He traveled down a lane to the end of an alley from
which he could look down on the shining
plains stretching to the far horizon.

Maverick jogged down, into a tangle of cactus clutching at him as he picked a careful
way. A river of silver snaked through the valley, and along it ranches were dotted. From
some of their checkerboard fields, on both
sides of the river, the sun's rays were helio-
graphed to him when the blades of the wind-
mills caught the light. Descending through the
lomas, he reached the first of the ranches as
he followed the road to the town of Deer Trail.

He let Maverick choose his own pace. There
was no hurry, since he did not want to get
in until after dark. There were one or two
men he wanted to see, but he did not care
to have his presence advertised. It occurred
to him, a wry grin on his brown face, that
in these late years he had done a good deal

more business at night than in the daytime. The text of a sermon preached by his father when he had been a small boy flashed to mind: 'And men loved darkness rather than light, because their deeds were evil.'

Forrest did not think his deeds had been evil, not in the sense that they had sprung from a bad heart. A certain wildness, born of his hot-blooded zest for living, had made of him a rebel, and since he had never cared to build himself up in the opinion of others he had ridden far and thrown a wide loop. This had brought him into contact with hard, lawless men, often not to his profit. Sometimes the resulting explosions had been violent. He had a reputation as a dangerous man, but he could truthfully say he had never killed except in self-defence, even in the ranger days when he had combed the brush country after criminals. Now he was on the dodge himself. The men with whom he had camped a hundred nights, the comrades of earlier days, were on the lookout to round him up.

He came into Deer Trail through Wingate's pasture. Since Maverick might be recognized he picketed the horse in the field and walked to the lane which ran along its west side. He could hear a fiddle going in the Longhorn saloon, the stamp of shuffling feet at a dance hall. Deer Trail woke up a little at night.

By an alley he reached the rear of 'Mother' Holloway's boarding-house. Through a window he could see her in the kitchen giving the cook instructions for the next day's meals. A maid was at the sink washing dishes. Stepping back to the shadow of a cottonwood in the yard, he gave the hoot of an owl. He saw Mrs. Holloway glance out of the window, then continue with her directions to the cook. It was perhaps five minutes later that she opened the back door, stepped out, and closed it behind her.

Forrest whistled softly, and she moved forward to the cottonwood.

'The bad penny back again,' said the outlaw with a flash of ivory teeth in a wide smile.

'Don't you know better than to come here, Blake Forrest?' answered the boarding-house keeper severely.

'I came back for one of yore custard pies,' he drawled.

'I know why you came back — to get into more trouble, you crazy galoot,' she snapped.

'To get out of the trouble I'm already in,' he corrected. 'And honest, Mother, my mouth is watering for yore good home cooking.'

He put an arm round her shoulders and gave them a hug. She was Irish on her father's side, a plump short little woman with a plain homely face, but many a cowboy within a radius of fifty miles would have fought to a finish in her behalf. She had never refused a hungry man a meal, regardless of whether he could or could not pay for it. The sick she nursed, the wounded she gave food and shelter. A hundred rough young fellows called her Mother, and if they owed her money would have sold their saddles to see she was paid.

'Don't blarney me, you scamp,' she told him, but with a smile that transformed her face. Gray-headed and fifty she might be, but few women were too old to respond to the charm of Blake Forrest when he took the trouble to warm up to them. 'Now what is it you're wanting?'

'Food — shelter — information.'

'You ought to be in Mexico — or somewhere — instead of projecting around here. Don't you know every sheriff in West Texas is looking for you, let alone the rangers? You're not safe here, and well you know it.'

'I want to make myself safer. That's why I came to see you. Have you a room you can let me have, Mother?'

She frowned, considering. 'Wait out here half an hour. By that time Mattie and Juanita will be gone home. I'll come out and get you then.'

Forrest would have liked to smoke, but he

knew it would not be wise. A man in the yard with a lighted cigarette might cause investigation. He sat behind the trunk of the cottonwood with his back propped against it and let his body relax.

The kitchen light went out and two women came from the house. They disappeared around the corner of it toward the street, chatting as they went. He waited, with the patience life in the brush had taught him.

Mrs. Holloway appeared on the porch. He rose and joined her. In the dark kitchen she gave him instructions.

'Go up the back stairway to the little room above the dining-room. The third door on the right. I'll fix some food for you and be up in a jiffy.'

'All I want is a sandwich,' he explained. 'Don't bother about cooking.'

'Just let me be minding my own business,' she ordered. 'I'll slap a steak in the fry-pan soon as I can light up.'

He tiptoed up the narrow stairway and felt his way along the hall. The narrow room in which he found himself had a faint light from the window. It was enough. He took off his boots and lay down on the bed. In two minutes he had dropped into a light nap.

The sound of the door opening awoke him. Somebody, light-footed and swift, walked into the room. A match scratched just as Forrest spoke.

'Am I to come down for my steak?' he asked, swinging his stockinged feet to the floor.

The match went out. He knew something was wrong. This was not Mother Holloway.

'Who is it?' swiftly demanded a startled voice, the rich husky timbre of it young and feminine.

Forrest grinned wryly. This was a pretty how-do-you-do.

CHAPTER 8

Mrs. Holloway Tells a Story

'Your servant, madam,' Forrest said, and bowed from his hips to the slender form facing him in the darkness. 'I have to apologize for being in the wrong room. Of course I'll leave at once.'

The woman was about to tell him to be quick about it, but a thought stopped her. She was a school-teacher, and before supper had put her month's salary for safekeeping in a rolled-up pair of stockings tucked away in the lower drawer of the bureau.

'No, you don't,' she warned. 'You'll stay here till I've had a look at you, or I'll scream for help.'

'Pleased to stay,' he assured her. 'If you'll allow me, I'll light the lamp.'

He struck a match and put it to the wick of the little coal oil lamp set in a wall bracket. While he did this and put the globe back in place the eyes of the young woman swept over and appraised him. At the first sound of his voice she had been startled but not really frightened. There was a quality in it, gently

76

modulated but clear, which gave complete reassurance as to her personal safety. Now she thought — why, he's handsome — not a ruffian at all but quite genteel. It was exciting to meet him in this strange way. She felt a queer exhilaration at the adventure, and because of it decided to be severe with him.

'Well, sir?' she asked crisply, and left him to make explanation.

He took his time, making up his mind what manner of young woman this was. She was tall and slenderly full, erect and graceful as a fawn of the forest. Her abundant red hair was electric with life, and the tawny eyes that met his fearlessly were direct as those of a man.

'I'm a plumb idjit, miss,' he said with a smile. 'Mrs. Holloway told me how to get to my room, and I got mixed up somehow. Don't know my right hand from my left, I reckon, and drifted into the wrong room.'

She did not like his manner of assurance, but it was not possible to look into his cool, amused eyes and treat him as a sneak thief. Indignation simmered in her. Even if it was only a mistake — and she supposed now that it was — she chose to consider his attitude insolent. He ought to be humble and apologetic.

'It's very funny, isn't it, for me to come

into my room and find a strange man waiting there in the dark?' she said haughtily.

The heavy brows of the young woman met in a frown. He noticed tiny gold flecks in the pupils of the irate eyes.

'I can only regret my stupidity.'

'I suppose you didn't notice it is a lady's room.'

'I don't see right good in the dark,' he mentioned sedately.

'Didn't you light the lamp?'

'No, ma'am, I didn't.'

'That's queer,' she said, and there was still accusation in her voice, challenge in the firm mouth and chin. 'You come into a strange room in a boarding-house, one you have never been in before and don't know anything about, and you go to bed without even lighting a lamp to see where things are.'

'I didn't exactly go to bed,' he corrected. 'I lay down because I have been riding all day and was fagged.'

'What's your name?'

There was the usual instant of searching hesitation before he found the one he wanted. 'James Brown.'

'You don't live at Deer Trail.'

'Not here, but Mrs. Holloway will vouch for me. I haven't even a pair of yore earrings in my pocket.' He dragged the last sentence, drolly, as if the thought of being a sneak thief gave him amusement.

He could hear Mrs. Holloway puffing up the winding stairway with a tray in her hands. She stopped outside the door and looked in, surprised at what she saw.

'What you doing in Miss Decker's room, Blake?' she asked.

'I got in the wrong room by mistake,' he said. 'Miss Decker thinks maybe I came to burgle the house.'

'Blake what?' the girl asked her landlady. 'I mean, what's his other name?'

'His name is —'

Mother Holloway stuck. She had just remembered that his name was not to be used and she did not know under what one he was passing.

'Brown,' volunteered the fugitive blandly. 'James Blake Brown.'

A light flashed on the mind of Helen Decker. She had been puzzled by some familiarity in the face of the man that evaded recognition. But now she had it definitely fixed. A picture of him on a poster was tacked on a wall at the post office. He was Blake Forrest, the outlaw for whom a reward of one thousand dollars was offered, the bad man who had killed her cousin Buck Terrell two years ago.

'If you can vouch for him, Mother Holloway, of course it's all right,' she said, her eyes fixed on the stranger. 'Naturally when I came up and found him here I was frightened.'

Watching her, Forrest was of opinion that she was stalling for time while she decided what to do. Though she was trying to veil it, he read hostility in her hot eyes. He had seen that flare of astonished discovery. She meant to turn him over to the authorities and was trying to think out the best way to do it.

'A thousand dollars is a lot of money,' he drawled, almost in a murmur. 'More than a school-teacher earns in a whole year.'

'So you *are* Blake Forrest,' she cried. 'You admit it.'

'With a girl like you, Miss Decker, smart as a whip, there wouldn't be any use denying it, would there?' he said with ironic gentleness.

'Whether I'm smart or not,' she retorted swiftly, 'I don't intend to let a criminal and murderer escape if I can help it.'

'That's fine. A schoolmarm should be an example to the community, and as I said, a thousand dollars —'

'Jeer all you please. It doesn't make any difference to me what you say. As soon as I get a chance I'll do my best to get you captured. You killed my cousin Buck Terrell.'

'Was *he* your cousin?'

'Yes, he was.' The color flamed in Helen's cheeks. Buck had been a bad lot, no credit to the family, but he was dead now and oblivion softened his sins. Once when he was a big boy and she a seven-year-old child, he had stopped a runaway horse and perhaps saved her from a bad fall.

Forrest made no explanation. He did not tell her that he had been forced to drop Buck to save his own life, nor that the man had been a scoundrel and a traitor. Since Terrell was kin to her he would not blacken his name.

But Mother Holloway was held back by no such inhibition. 'Blake wasn't to blame for that. You know that, Miss Helen, or you would if you'd study the facts fair. Buck hounded him till he had no choice.'

'So *he* says. Naturally he had to make out a case for himself with you. I suppose he has talked you into believing he isn't a bank and train robber, one of the worst outlaws in Texas.'

'He doesn't have to talk me into believing that,' Mrs. Holloway said simply. 'I know him. He has been wild and foolish, but he isn't bad. If we can all sit down a minute and be reasonable, Miss Decker, I'll tell you a little story.'

'I'm not going to sit down in the same room

81

as that man,' Helen answered, the color high in her cheeks. 'I'll listen to you because I like you, as everybody does, but I'll hear it standing, and nothing you can say will change my mind about him.'

'So why waste yore breath, Mother, since what the young lady thinks about me isn't important?' Forrest asked with light indifference.

'Be still, both of you,' the stout little woman ordered. She pointed to the tray which she had put on the bed. 'Better begin on that steak while it's still hot, young man. Keep busy eating, and don't interrupt me.'

'Good advice,' Blake said, and fell to work with knife and fork.

The landlady sat down on a home-made chair with a rawhide leather seat. She was so short that her feet hardly reached the floor. 'It's a kinda long story, but I'll cut the corners,' she began. 'When Mr. Holloway died I was in a money jam. We had borrowed from Jake Gildea to keep the store going, and right soon after the funeral he began talking about foreclosing. My husband had paid him back seven hundred of the thousand borrowed, so I scraped the bottom of the barrel and finally got together the other three hundred and interest. But I couldn't find the receipt for the money paid back. Jake swore to me Sam never had paid him back a cent. I'd seen the receipt and knew better, but I couldn't prove it. The upshot was I gave him a mortgage on the house here for five hundred and turned that over to him on account. I've done right well with the boarding-house, but you know little Billy's lame leg has been a terrible expense. I had to take him two-three times to Kansas City to a hospital before it was finally fixed right. First Jake took over the store, and about six months ago he began pressing for the money on the house. I could see he meant to take it too. With times the way they are I wasn't able to borrow anywhere else.'

She stopped, her faded blue eyes pleading with the younger woman for a kindly consideration of the case.

'Jake Gildea always was a penny-pinching scoundrel,' Helen said, with angry contempt.

'Yes,' Mrs. Holloway agreed. 'And one day a man came to me and dropped an envelope in my lap. It contained my note to Jake, and across the face of it was written "Paid in full," with Jake's signature beneath it.'

'You mean that Gildea sent it to you?' Helen asked, puzzled, but certain that this was not the explanation.

'I'm not asking any questions about that, but I've seen Jake since then, and he acknowledges the note as paid.'

The tawny eyes traveled from Mrs. Holloway to Forrest. A light broke on her. 'You're saying that the man who robbed the bank made Jake Gildea sign your note as paid.'

'I'm not saying anything more than I have told you,' the little woman replied doggedly. 'I didn't owe Jake the money and he has decided to let it go at that.'

'I see,' Helen replied, her gaze on Forrest. 'I'm very glad for you. Did this Robin Hood leave with you as a gift too the seven or eight thousand in cash he took from the Valley Bank?'

Blake Forrest smiled, unabashed. 'I've heard the sum was six thousand four hundred and twenty-two dollars, Miss Decker.'

She said, standing very straight, 'I don't find crime amusing, sir.' There was the crack of a pistol shot in her resonant voice.

'I'll laugh about it while I can,' he answered hardily, his voice bitter. 'You see, I happen to know the circumstances. Gildea robbed the mother of this fellow who visited him at the bank of just six thousand four hundred and twenty-two dollars, regardless of the fact that she was a widow with a son who was only fifteen years old. She died soon after that.'

Looking at him, his fearless eyes fastened on her, it was impossible to doubt that he was telling the truth. She did not like him, but he did not look like a liar.

'Did the Texas & Pacific Railroad owe him a lot of money too?' she asked scornfully.

'No. That job is being handed to him free gratis. He didn't do it.'

'My cousin is an express messenger on the train. He recognized the leader.'

'Your cousin named the wrong man.'

'That's what you say.'

'In the excitement he might easily make a mistake,' the landlady suggested.

'He might even want to make one,' Forrest said.

'I suppose you hate Ray because you killed his brother,' Helen countered swiftly.

The outlaw pushed away his tray and rose. 'I'll be going, Mother. I'm obliged to you for a good supper. Tell Billy I'll be seeing him one of these days, and for him to be a good boy to his mother.'

Mrs. Holloway fluttered in front of him. 'Wait a minute, Blake. I don't want you to go before we know what Miss Decker means to do.'

The girl flushed. She was annoyed, at herself and at them, for the position in which she found herself.

'If you're so innocent why don't you give yourself up and let them try you?' she demanded of the man.

'I'm not so innocent as that,' he told her, and his smile was wise and crafty. 'There are a lot of people in this part of the state would like to see penitentiary walls close on Blake Forrest. But it's not going to be that way if I can help it. When I stand trial my witnesses will be ready as well as theirs.'

'When will that be?' she asked.

'I'll send you an invite, Miss Decker,' he said pleasantly. 'I wouldn't know the exact date right now.'

The girl picked up a school reader, riffled the pages, and laid it down again. 'All right,' she said impatiently, turning to Mrs. Holloway. 'Get your friend out of my sight, please. I ought to let the sheriff know he is here. But I won't. On your account. I'm doing wrong, and I know it. But presently he'll be caught and put away safely, so it doesn't matter much.'

Forrest bowed, a gleam of mirth in his eyes. 'Glad to have met you, Miss Decker. I can see you must be a right good teacher. I'll bet you make the little rascals jump plenty when you whack them with that hickory stick. No sparing the rod in your school. I was born twenty years too soon to be the nice respectable citizen I would have been if I'd learned my reading and writing under you.'

The tawny eyes blazed anger at him. 'If

you'll kindly leave my room, sir.'

He left, smiling amiably. To the women in the room there drifted back a drawling snatch of a camp-meeting song:

> 'See that sister dressed so fine,
> She ain't got Jesus on her min'.'

Helen Decker stamped her foot. 'He's the most insolent man I ever met.'

Mother Holloway wiped out an embryonic smile. She had to admit that Blake certainly could be aggravating.

CHAPTER 9

Blake Meets a Friend and an Enemy

Deer Trail was an anaemic town, gaunt as the country in which it was situated. A dispirited creek, yellow and shallow, wound through the village sluggishly, on its banks a number of Mexican *jacals*. In the doorway of one a lean native, wearing his shirt outside the trousers, strummed indolently on a guitar. Under a cottonwood two burros laden with wood waited for their master to come out of a *tendejon*. Not a town bursting with gay night life.

Forrest crossed a frail bridge floored with rotting planks that spanned the stream at the lower end of the village. He moved leisurely toward the one lighted street. There was no sense of hurry in him. Close to the shadowed wall of a blacksmith shop he waited, watching the figures that drifted up and down the wooden sidewalk of the dusty street. There was a man he wanted to see. There were others he did not want to see him.

The saloon was the club of the old West. Here the life and light of the drab frontier towns gathered to refresh spirits oppressed by drought, blizzards, low cattle prices, and the encroaches of sheep. So Forrest kept an eye on the Longhorn, satisfied that sooner or later somebody would come out of the front door who would be a safe source of information. He saw a dozen come and go before he selected his man.

A big rawboned fellow came down the street headed for the Longhorn. By his garb he was a cattleman. He wore a shabby wide hat tilted on one side of his head, a wrinkled coat dusty with travel, a flannel shirt, salmon-colored striped trousers, and a pair of run-down-at-the-heel boots.

The outlaw moved out of the shadow of the blacksmith shop and called to the big man. ' 'Lo, Craig!'

The cattleman stopped, looked round. 'Someone call me?' he asked, a little warily.

Even a peaceable man had enemies in West Texas. In a country so infested with bad men, rustlers, and horse thieves a man who ran cattle had to fight for his own. Foes were a matter of course.

'Come over here, you doggoned old sand-lapper,' invited Forrest, 'and shake the hand that shook the hand of John L. Sullivan.'

'Have you done bust a leg that you can't come over here?' the cowman wanted to know.

Forrest moved a little farther forward into the light.

'By jinks,' the big man yelped, and strode across the dusty road. 'Thought you were in Chihuahua by this time, you old vinegaroon.'

He shook hands with the fugitive and grinned at him. Forrest drew him back into the shadows.

'I'm a little mite particular who I meet these days, Craig,' he said.

Craig Shannon viewed him with reluctant admiration. He approved of this young man without endorsing all his follies. Even when he did not approve, he found a difference between him and ruffians known generically as 'bad men.' When Blake Forrest stepped outside the law he did it with a frankness that redeemed his action from meanness.

'What in heck you doing here, Blake?' the cattleman wanted to know. 'Don't you know there's a whole passel of sheriffs looking for you in West Texas and a couple of companies of yore own old pals the rangers?'

'Someone mentioned it to me. I'm to be arrested for robbing a train when I was 'most a hundred miles from the spot.'

'So I've heard tell. Bill Crabb gives you an alibi, if that's worth anything.'

'I was with Bill and Stone Heath at the time.'

'Yeah. Point is, *where* were you with them?'

'At a cow camp of the Circle Three B. We spent the night with two line-riders of that outfit.'

'Well, you better dig 'em up, young fellow, if you don't like to be surrounded by stone walls with guards on them.'

'Do you know where either Bill or Stone are?'

'Saw Bill at a roundup Saturday a week ago. He was riding for Old Man Blevins. Likely he's still with him, though you never can tell about a wild coot like Bill. He may be in Arizona or New Mexico now.'

'Like to meet up with Bill *muy pronto*. I'm aiming to build that alibi till it listens respectable to a jury. Could you get word to him I'll be hanging around the line shack at the southwest corner of the Nine R ranch — say Thursday or Friday?'

'Might. Is Jake Gildea going to be one of the alibi witnesses in the Valley Bank case when it comes to trial?'

"I certainly didn't run my boot-heels over side-steppin' trouble that time,' Forrest drawled. 'Fact is, Craig, I hadn't the slightest notion of pulling off that darned holdup when I saw Jake's weasel face at the window of the bank. He looked so dad-gummed satisfied I couldn't stand it, since I'd just been hearing from Mother Holloway how he was foreclosing on her house after he had beat her out of seven hundred dollars and made her pay usurer's interest for ten years. So I walked into his private office in the bank, figuring on asking him to lay off Mother Holloway. Still innocent as a pink-faced cherub, you understand. Well, sir, he had a pile of gold and greenbacks in front of him that he was counting.'

'Must have been expecting you,' grinned Shannon.

'First off, he barked at me, "What you mean coming in here without permission?" I asked him if he was the angel Gabriel or Jay Gould that a man couldn't see him without a "Please" and his hat in his hand. That didn't go so well, and he wouldn't listen to a word I had to say about the five-hundred-dollar mortgage. Sat there hunched up over his money like a big spider and told me to get out and mind my own business. I got to thinking about that damned scoundrel robbing Mother Holloway, the salt of the earth, and how hard she works for every dollar she gets, and all of a sudden I saw red. What started the fireworks was his saying he would surely bear down harder on her on account of my butting in.'

'Jake would be like that,' the cattleman agreed.

'I made him get the note and write "paid" on it. He did it and mentioned that he aimed to send me to the penitentiary. Figuring I might as well be hanged for a sheep as a lamb, I collected from him the money he had stolen from my mother.'

'You crazy, high-handed galoot, don't you know better than that? Right then you bought yoreself a one-way ticket to the pen.'

'Looks like.'

'Unpopular as Jake is, you can't get away with holding up a bank.'

Forrest smiled ruefully. 'I explained to him I wasn't taking it from the bank but from him.'

'Hmp! A lot of good that will do you. It was bank money, and you knew it.'

'It's a private bank owned by Jake. I never claimed to be a lawyer. Seems to me it wouldn't matter whether it came out of his right- or left-hand pocket.'

'If I was you I'd light out for parts unknown.'

'Can't do it. I'm under a sort of promise to go through to a finish.'

Shannon shook his head. 'Maybe a slick lawyer may do something for you, but I'd say you've done hogtied yoreself so you can't wriggle loose.'

Out of the Longhorn came four men and stood for a minute talking on the sidewalk.

The light from the saloon windows flooded the spot and Forrest recognized three of them. One was Webb Lake, a small neat man whose hard, flat, pallid face did not belie his reputation as a tough citizen too handy with a gun. The bulky heavy-shouldered fellow standing next to him was Wes Terrell, brother of Ray and Buck. The third one known to the fugitive called himself Pres Walsh. He had once just missed serving a term in the state prison for shooting two Mexicans who had tried to recover stolen stock from him.

The party separated. Terrell crossed the road and the rest started up the street. Shannon saw that recognition was unavoidable and moved in front of Forrest to cover his identity.

' 'Lo, Wes,' he said. 'How are tricks?'

'Betwixt and between. Stock some gaunted. Need rain out our way.'

'We been having mighty heavy rains up Dry Valley and vicinity. Enough is plenty, I say. We don't need any more now for the grass.'

'Expect the water is sure enough boiling down Funnel Creek then.'

'Wouldn't surprise me if it swept out the railroad bridge at Cranmer.' He added, by way of comment, 'It certainly has been a gully washer. Funnel bank-full when I crossed it an hour ago and there's a lot more water to come down from tributaries higher up.'

Terrell craned his neck to peer past the cattleman at the figure behind him. 'Who's yore friend?' he asked.

The man in the shadows said quietly, eyes hard and glittering like agates, 'The name is Forrest.'

A shout of astonishment broke from the throat of Terrell. 'Come a-running, fellows. I've got Blake Forrest here. We'll settle his hash right now.' He dragged a revolver from the scabbard under his arm.

Forrest had been backing to the corner of the building. He dodged back of it, turned, and ran. He heard the roar of Terrell's .45 as he vaulted a gate leading into a vacant lot. Shouts, oaths, the slap of running feet came to him. He raced through the knee-high fennel to the opposite fence and went over that lightly. More guns barked at him. Two or three men squirted out of the back door of a dance hall like seeds from a pressed lemon, intent on finding out what all the shooting was about.

'Hell has broke loose in Georgia,' he panted, not slackening his pace.

Straight through the dance hall he went and out of the front door, leaving disorganized behind him a quadrille through which he had plunged. By this maneuver he had gained a dozen yards, since his pursuers had been forced to ask whether he had stopped in the hall. But as he scudded up the street he knew they had followed him out of the front door. A bullet whined past him. In front of him three men had just come out of a building.

Someone in the rear called, 'Head him off, boys.'

Forrest ducked through a gate that opened into a wagon yard.

CHAPTER 10

Guns Blaze in the Wagon Yard

The wagons in the yard were lined up on both sides and in rows down the center. Some were loaded, some empty. Within the inclosure were two buckboards, an old buggy, a few ranch wagons, and eight or nine large ore-carriers. Deer Trail had two reasons for existence. One was to serve as a supply depot for the ranches of the neighborhood, the other because it was a halfway point between the mines at Oroville and the nearest railroad connection. The mule-skinners driving the company wagons could make it in a day to the shipping junction if they started early enough, but a good many of them stopped at Deer Trail either coming or going.

When Blake Forrest dodged into the yard he turned sharply to the left where the shadows were deeper. Never in his gusty lifetime had he been in peril more imminent. Four men at least were racing at his heels. There might be two or three more, adherents of the Terrell crowd, lured by the lust of a man-hunt and by hope of sharing in the reward. They

97

would not try to capture him. It was easier and safer to kill, besides being more satisfactory to his enemies. The story given out would be that he had been shot down while resisting arrest, and in due time the reward would be paid.

Crouching low, Forrest ran along the fence back of the ore wagons.

A raucous voice came to him. 'He ducked in here, boys. We've got him trapped. Hold the gate, Phil, while we comb the corral. No monkeying with this bird. Fill him full of lead first and order him to surrender afterward.'

Wes Terrell talking, the cornered man thought grimly as he drew his revolver. As yet he had not fired a shot, though a dozen bullets had been flung at him, some of them wildly into the darkness where he had disappeared. To give himself up to these ruffians would be suicide. They would shoot him down as he approached. He had to fight.

To him there came the rumor of men moving, faint whispers of sound hardly to be distinguished from the murmur of the night. He knew his foes were spreading to search the yard. They would not all come at him in a body probably, though they would keep fairly close to one another. The reputation he had won as a fighting man would suggest caution. Since they had closed the way of escape, he would have to go out with his gun blazing. Hardy ruffians they were, but none of them would want to be the victim of their own victory.

The stockade fence was more than ten feet high, made of whipsawed planks with the ends packed solidly in a trench and bound stoutly together. There was no chance to climb it, unless he could leap for the top from the rear of an ore wagon backed close. Unfortunately none of the wagons were near enough for him to use one as an aid.

Yet he had to make an attempt to scale the fence. He picked one wagon not so far from the stockade as the others and clambered into it. A gun roared, halfway across the yard. Instinctively he ducked, though he knew it had not been aimed at him. No doubt one of his hunters, a bit goosey with the strain, had turned loose at a shadow.

Forrest leaped for the top of the fence. His fingers caught the edge of a thick plank but could not hold the grip above the drag of his weight. A second time he climbed over the wheel into the wagon.

Soft footsteps sounded . . . drew closer. Very likely the noise of the impact of his body against the stockade had been heard. He crouched low, behind the high sloping sides of the carrier's bed.

A head was thrust forward cautiously around the tail of the wagon. Pres Walsh, taking as few chances as he could. The man crept forward, keenly alive to danger. Forrest waited until Walsh was just below him, then sailed out of his hiding-place and landed like a hod of brick on top of his foe. The hinges of the man's knees gave way and he went to the ground, his body jammed against the wheel. Swiftly, before Walsh could let out a cry, Forrest smashed his head hard against the iron tire. The revolver slipped from the lax fingers of the man. His torso slumped down.

The outlaw tossed the weapon over the stockade. He had lost his hat while vaulting the fence during his escape from Terrell. Now he borrowed the dusty old sombrero of his unconscious enemy. The rim flopped down over his face and partially concealed it. There was a chance that in the darkness he might be mistaken for Walsh and get near enough to the gate before discovery to make his escape.

Abruptly he stopped. A shout lifted, not twenty feet from him. Two guns sounded, almost simultaneously. Someone groaned. Forrest edged noiselessly around another wagon and saw two men facing each other. One of them had caught hold of a spoke to keep himself from falling. It was Wes Terrell. He stood there, knees bent, head sunk forward, glaring at Webb Lake. From the barrels of both their guns flowed thin trickles of smoke.

'God, Wes!' Lake said thickly, horror in his bulging eyes. 'I thought it was Forrest. You came at me shooting.'

Terrell's body began to slide along the tire. Lake moved forward to support him, but stopped abruptly. His gaze had fastened to the face of the man they were hunting. His right arm swept up, but too late. Forrest was waiting, ready for the play.

The crash of the two revolvers sounded almost as one. But the split second of time difference spoiled Lake's aim. A puzzled surprise showed in the flat pallid face of the man. He caught at his shattered elbow as the weapon dropped from his paralyzed fingers. The bullet from his gun had passed through the rim of the hat Forrest was wearing.

'I ought to finish the job while I'm doing it,' the outlaw said, his eyes drilling into those of the man he had just wounded.

'No, don't do that,' Lake begged. 'You've done enough to me.'

Forrest turned away, without answer. A possible way out of his trap had flashed into his mind. He had been lucky so far. Lake was too busy being sorry for himself to have any fight left in him, and too glad at being left alive to interfere with his enemy's flight. Walsh and Terrell were out of the battle. Now was the time to be gone. He pulled the rim of the hat farther down over his face and swaggered into the open, revolver in hand.

A name stuck in his mind. Terrell had called the man he had left at the gate Phil.

'It's all over, Phil,' the hunted man called. 'I got him. He's dead as a stuck shote. Webb plugged him one too. But he had done wounded both Webb and Wes before I finished him.'

He walked fast, almost at a run, as if excitement were surging up in him. The man at the gate was puzzled but not suspicious. Pres Walsh looked somehow different even in the darkness. That was probably because he was agitated.

Not until the man with the floppy hat was actually at his side did Phil Decker know that he had been fooled. He let out a startled cry and started to raise his gun. Again Forrest had the advantage of understanding the situation while his enemy did not. He pistol-whipped Decker above the temple with the long barrel of his .45 and the young man staggered back against the gate.

Half a dozen men were gathered in the street. Apparently they had come to watch the finish of Blake Forrest rather than to take an active part in it. The barrel of the fugitive's six-shooter made a sweeping half circle in front of them.

'Don't try to stop me or I'll fire,' he ordered.

A moment later he had crossed the street and was diving into the shadowy darkness between two adobe buildings. Behind him he left a Babel of shouts, excited explanations, curses, and shuffling feet. As he rounded the rear of the adobe building to the right he saw over his shoulder that nobody had as yet started in pursuit. He reckoned on plenty of time. With four of his foes wounded there would not be many to take up the chase, even if the casualty list had not been enough to daunt enthusiasm.

Through a barb-wire fence he went into Wingate's pasture. He found the saddle and blanket under the mesquite bush where he had left them. His picketed horse he saddled swiftly. Maverick cantered across the field. There was a gate at the east end, and through this Forrest led his mount.

From the main street came on the breeze a murmur of excitement. There would be plenty of it. The town would buzz for hours about what had taken place. Talk of it would last a long time, not because of its intrinsic importance but because a small town keeps alive its dramatic memories. Thirty years from now some oldtimer sitting in the sun would say to a neighboring loafer, 'Remember that night Blake Forrest made his getaway from the Terrell crowd?' and the other old gaffer, who very likely had been home in bed during the shooting, would boast he had been an eyewitness of the battle.

Forrest struck the street outside of the business section. In some of the scattered houses there were lights, but he did not meet a soul on the deserted road. Unmolested and unnoticed he drew out from Deer Trail at a jog trot. He knew that his luck had been amazingly good. Against all probability he had come out alive and unhurt without having been forced to kill any of his assailants. He had pistol-whipped one and hammered the head of another against a wagon-wheel, but a broken head meant only an unpleasant surface wound and a headache. Webb Lake he had left with a shattered arm which might be stiff for life, but Webb was too poison mean to die of a bullet not in a vital spot.

None the less Forrest knew he had not improved his position by this shooting scrape. Though his enemies were worthless scamps, they were in their home terrain. He would be blamed for starting this trouble, and it would add to his reputation as a notorious criminal. He was a dog with a bad name. Nothing he could do would be right. Probably the story would be given out that he had come to town looking for Wes Terrell. Some of the rest of the crowd would swear they had heard him make threats. Craig Shannon knew he had not been the aggressor, but the cattleman could not be expected to make trouble for himself by talking too much.

He traveled through a low country, thick with brush. A cold rain began to fall and he put on his slicker. As he rode he brushed against the plumed huisache and scattered showers of moisture. In places the ground was soggy from the heavy pounding rains that must have beaten down.

A small branch running high cut across the road. The water in it was pouring turbulently down to Funnel Creek. Forrest knew he must be close to the main stream. When he reached it a few minutes later he saw that the bridge across Funnel had been swept away. This was a nuisance. He would have to ride miles out of his way to cross the railroad bridge five miles lower. Moreover, he would have to leave the road and pick a way through the thorny chaparral.

The foliage was so laden with raindrops that when he pushed into the shrubbery it was like being sprayed by a shower bath. If it had not been for his slicker he would have been wet to the skin. As it was, branches heavy with water whipped back against his face and washed it or shook their contents down his neck.

Whenever he came in sight of Funnel he saw that it was a raging torrent. White-crested waves tumbled over one another in a rush to get down to the Rio Grande. He decided that there must have been a cloudburst in the country back of him.

The rain had thinned, but it was still chill. Pecan trees and wild plums were abundant along the banks of the stream. . . . A spike buck, startled out of sleep, went crashing wildly into the chaparral. . . . Travel was slow, and the cruel thorns clutched fiercely at the flanks of the horse and the legs of the rider.

Forrest made the best of it. He had not lived for years in the brush country without having become inured to discomfort. It was a harsh land, one in which both vegetation and animal life had to fight for existence. A rattlesnake sounded its warning, and the rider clutched at the saddle horn when Maverick leaped sideways.

After a long detour he came back to the Funnel. The stream had widened, and the force of the deep rushing current was terrific. Here the scrub was less thick, but the ground was still boggy. Though horse and man were both tired, Forrest decided to keep going. This was a spot too miserably inhospitable for a night camp. On the theory that the sound of his own voice might make for cheerfulness he sang another camp-meeting ditty.

'Keep a-inching along, keep a-inching along,
 Jesus will come by and by;
Keep a-inching along like a poor inch worm,
 Jesus will come by and by.'

He rode out into the clearing made for the railroad track and came upon a startling discovery. The bridge across Funnel Creek was gone. A moment later he heard the shriek of an engine's whistle. A train was rushing to destruction. He was on the wrong side of the creek to give warning.

CHAPTER 11

Through Troubled Waters

Blake Forrest has never forgotten the sight and sound of the train crashing into Funnel Creek. He had faced death earlier in the night coolly enough, but that had been a personal adventure with all his being attuned to the swift excitement of peril close and immediate. Here he was an insignificant atom watching helplessly an appalling catastrophe. As the engine smashed down, dragging cars after it, the stomach muscles below his heart collapsed weakly. He sat laxly in the saddle, sick to the very core of his entity.

The cries of the injured and the drowning beat through his weakness and brought him back to urgent life. From his waist he unbuckled the heavy belt and from his feet dragged the high-heeled cowboy boots. The loop of the lariat he fastened under his armpits, then tied the other end securely to the saddle horn. Swiftly his eyes swept the scene. Two cars had gone down, a third hung precariously on the edge of the broken bridge. Passengers were trapped in the coaches. Others struggled in the rushing water. Borne by the current, wreckage tossed like chips on a windswept lake.

His gaze picked up a girl clinging to a handrail. The pounding waves submerged her. In a moment her head reappeared. She was still holding fast. Even as Forrest leaped into the stream he saw that she had been swept away.

With powerful reaching strokes he drove through the flood that flung itself at him like a moving wall. He went under — came up again. In the tossing billows the girl had disappeared. Blake thought her gone, but something soft plowed into him beneath the surface. His fingers caught an arm. The pressure rolled him over. Still clutching the arm, he was hurled downstream as far as the taut rope would permit.

Caught in a comparative eddy back of a projection in the bank, he fought his way to a plum tree partially uprooted by the inundation. By gripping branches he pulled first himself and then the girl ashore.

Her eyes were shut. Whether she was alive or dead he did not know. Nor had he time to find out. For the head of a man showed in the turbid waters. Forrest saw him — lost him — caught sight again of a hand lifting feebly. The swimmer was trying to bring a child ashore with him.

Once more Forrest dived. Though the stream was narrow, the drag of the pounding swell was tremendous. Driftwood hammered against Blake and hurled him around. He shook away the weakness and steadied himself. His overhand stroke was still powerful. Somehow he reached the man, who was clinging to a spar.

Above the noise of the roaring river, words could not make themselves heard. Forrest reached for the boy, just before the leaping scud tore them apart. The clutch of the undertow carried him to the end of the rope as before and into the less furious waters behind the promontory.

He saw, without giving it present weight, that good old Maverick was standing on the bank, front feet braced, having done his job as he had learned to do it from a hundred experiences at the end of a tight rope fastened to an angry longhorn. Clinging to the plum tree, he rested in the chill current while he gathered strength.

The girl he had rescued was sitting up. She crawled toward him on hands and knees, reached down, and took the little boy from his arms. Forrest turned, kicked his foot against the bank, and headed out into the river for the third time.

When Forrest reached the man in the creek,

the swimmer was sinking. To get him to land was a long hard struggle. More than once the outlaw thought he would have to give up. Cold had sapped his force, and he was nearly exhausted. He set his teeth and slowly fought to the bank.

By gestures he told the man to hang on to the plum tree while he dragged himself out inch by inch. Kneeling on the slippery bank, he managed to help the rescued passenger from the water.

Both of them collapsed. Presently, the man said, weakly, 'My little boy?'

The girl spoke, a sob in her voice. 'He's sick from swallowing water, but he'll soon be all right."

Still breathing deeply, Forrest looked across at her. He judged she was fifteen or perhaps sixteen, a slim immature adolescent, still in the gawky years. In her wet clothes she had the slinky look of a drowned rat. She was, unless he missed his guess, fighting against hysteria. It was perhaps fortunate that she had the small boy to look after.

The rescued man moved with leaden feet across the few yards that separated him from his son. He had the look of one mortally stricken. Forrest did not then know that there had been three members of the family in the coach that had crashed.

The roar of the Funnel was still as heavy as thunder. No longer could one hear cries and screams. Those inside and outside the cars in the creek had been drowned. The coach poised on the edge of the bank still hung suspended there, but people were being helped out of the tilted upper end of it. They could be seen plainly, but their voices were lost in the sound of the flood.

Forrest rose. 'I'll light a fire and we'll dry off,' he said.

A cry from the girl stopped him as he was walking toward Maverick to get the hatchet.

'Look!' She was on her feet, pointing across the Funnel, fear vibrant in her voice. 'It's Myra — little Myra Hunt. She was on the train.'

A child not more than two or three years old was clinging to the branch of a tree on the opposite bank. Her perch was far out over the rushing water, the waves of which lapped up to her feet and at times covered them. It was plain that she had been washed there and flung into momentary safety.

The outlaw stared at her, and a cold wind of despair chilled his heart. So far he had come through alive, but his job was not done. If it was possible he had to save that baby. If not, he had to go under trying.

Since the rope was not long enough to reach

across the creek, he unfastened it from his waist.

'I won't have time to light the fire,' he told the girl.

'You're not going into the water again!' she cried, staring at him out of big dark eyes.

'Got to get the kid if I can,' he said harshly.

'Let the men on the other side get her.'

'They don't see her.'

'Call to them. Point her out.'

Blake shook his head. 'Wouldn't be any use. They couldn't hear us for the noise of the water,' he said. 'And if someone gets her it will have to be soon. She won't hang on much longer.'

He did not like the job. Heavy floating timbers from the bridge and the wrecked cars were pounding a way down the creek. Twice he had just missed being hit. Moreover, he would have to reach the other side without the rope as a safety belt. Tired as he was, he doubted if he could make it.

'I wouldn't go,' the girl begged. 'Someone may see her.'

'And they may not,' he replied grimly. From an inside pocket of his shirt he drew a small oilskin package. 'Matches,' he explained. 'Get a fire going if you can and dry your clothes. Wear my slicker in the meantime.'

He pointed for a bluff on the opposite shore that jutted out about thirty or forty yards below them. As his body shot out into the river he realized that the flood had passed its highwater mark and was decreasing in volume and in the violence of its pressure. In another hour all of its fury would be spent.

A wave rolled over him. When his head emerged he caught sight of one of the bridge piles leaping straight at him. He tried to dive and succeeded in missing the direct impact. Wrenched sideways by the current, the log struck his shoulder and sent him under again.

More than halfway across, he fought with all the strength in him to span the raging twenty-five or thirty feet between him and the bank. There were times when he felt it could not be done, that the torrent was too powerful to be breasted. But his weary arms still reached forward, and at last he was swept against the bluff completely exhausted. He clung to the root of a plum tree for a few moments while he gathered force to drag himself ashore.

A minute later he was calling to the little girl in the tree. 'Hold on, Sugar. I'll have you out of there before a cow can shake its tail.'

The child stopped sobbing to watch him climb the tree. He crawled out on a limb below the one on which she rested. The branch gave with his weight so much that he was not sure it would not break. He leaned out as far as he could, and his fingers just touched her dress.

He smiled at her. 'Inch this way just a mite, honey, and give me your hand,' he said cheerfully. 'Then we'll shin down the tree together and go back to the folks.'

The child did as he directed. his grip closed on her arm just below the shoulder. Carefully he edged back toward the trunk of the tree, his legs dragging in the swirling water. Presently they were safe at the stem of the tree, dry land beneath them. He slid down, the child in his arm, and carried her to the group of people standing beside a car that had not been torn from the track.

A brakeman stared at this battered specimen who was coming out of the darkness from nowhere. His face was grimy from the muddy waters. He wore no boots. The shirt had been torn from his back and a bloodstained bruise covered the left shoulder. His feet dragged, as do those of a man who has come to the end of his strength.

'Goddlemighty!' the trainman cried. 'Where in Mexico did you come from, brother?'

'Someone take this little girl and get her into dry clothes,' Forrest said.

A woman stepped forward and took the

child. 'Your baby?' she asked.

'No. I was on the other bank and saw her in a tree.'

'You swam the river?' the conductor asked incredulously.

'Yes. Had to get to her.' The woman was disappearing into the car with the infant. 'I reckon she was in one of the front cars and her parents were drowned.'

The conductor's memory functioned. 'No. She was traveling with a colored nurse to her folks. They own a cattle ranch somewheres near Fair Play.' He let his gaze linger on this stranger wonderingly. 'Pardner, how did you ever make it across that damned Niagara?'

'I don't know. It nearly beat me.'

'This has been a terrible business,' the conductor said. 'Luckily the first two cars weren't very full. I had about eight or nine passengers in them. Not sure which. Counting the engineer and fireman, we've lost either ten or eleven.'

'Not quite that bad,' Forrest corrected wearily. 'I fished three out alive. They are on the other bank.'

'That's fine,' a passenger said fulsomely. 'I'd like to know the name of our hero. My name is Jonathan Stevens, and I'll see personally that you are rewarded for this. I'm a banker — from Kansas City.'

The outlaw looked at him. For a moment there was a flame of contempt in the tired blue eyes. It died down. Forrest turned away without answering. It was not worth while holding anger, not on a night like this.

The creek was going down very rapidly. During the past ten minutes it had fallen more than a foot. Moreover, the sky had cleared. The rain had ceased and a few stars were out.

A man thrust a flask into Forrest's hand. 'Drink, stranger,' he said. 'You need it.'

Blake Forrest was no drinking man. In his youth he had done his share of it, but of late years he had known that his nerves and general condition had to be fit if he wanted to survive. Somehow he had managed to acquire a good many enemies, and dissipation was one thing he could not afford. Now he drank. Tonight was an exception. Any whiskey he drank would be a medicine.

Presently he noticed that a fire was burning on the other side of the creek. The rescued passengers must have found his matches dry and been able to ignite the brush they had gathered.

'I'm going to sleep for an hour,' Forrest said to the conductor. 'Wake me at the end of that time, prompt, if you please.'

He went into the smoker, made himself

comfortable in a seat, and fell asleep. It seemed to him he had hardly closed his eyes when the conductor shook him awake.

CHAPTER 12

The Hero Disappears

'Hate to wake you, but your hour is up, young fellow,' the conductor said.

Forrest stretched himself. His muscles were stiff and his shoulder ached. He rose and followed the railroad man out of the car.

As he had known it would be, the creek was now running at almost normal flow.

'Have you sent for help?' he asked.

'A brakeman hoofed it back to Lang's Crossing. A wrecking crew will be here before morning. I'll have to make a report on this. Like to have your name as a witness, if you don't mind.'

The outlaw drawled, a faint sardonic smile touching his eyes, 'Call me Anon. I've seen that name considerable in my McGuffey's Reader.'

Judging by the puzzled look in the conductor's eyes, he was struggling to get this clear. 'He's the fellow that wrote all those poems, ain't he? Like "The Boy Stood on the Burning Deck" and "Young Lochinvar" and "The Assyrian Came Down Like a Wolf on the Fold." But you're not exactly claiming —'

'I wouldn't want to claim a thing that belongs to Sir Walter Scott and Mrs. Hemans and Byron,' Forrest assured him.

'You don't get the idea, Ed,' explained the brakeman, out of his fund of erudition acquired at a crossroads country school in Missouri. 'When McGuffey didn't know who wrote a poem he just put the word "anon." under it, short for author unknown, as you might say. This gent here means, I reckon, that for reasons of his own he ain't mentioning his real name.'

'Oh, I savvy now,' the conductor said with a grin.

Forrest leaned toward him and whispered, 'I'm really the Prince of Wales, but I'm keeping it quiet because my mother doesn't know I'm out. You can call me Eddie if you like.'

The eyes of the brakeman grew big with excitement. It came to him that there was another name by which he could call this stranger that would be worth cash in the box to anybody who spoke it at the right time and place.

The conductor was too busy for persiflage.

'There are some folks on this train won't ever forget you, Mr. Anon.,' he said seriously.

'Hard to forget a night like this,' Forrest answered. 'I'll remember it myself for quite a while. . . . How's the kid I got out of the tree?'

'She's all right. Sound asleep in the last coach. The ladies are looking after her.'

'Good. Got to get back to my boots and my horse. See you later.'

The crushed cars and the engine were piled up in the bed of the stream. Forrest waded out and used the debris as a bridge on which to cross. At the farther side he splashed through waist-high water to the shore.

The girl he had rescued rose from her place beside the fire and came to meet him. He noticed that the little boy was sleeping on the man's lap.

'We saw you got across and saved the baby,' the girl cried eagerly. 'It was the bravest thing I ever saw. You almost didn't make it. When that log hit you . . .'

She did not complete the sentence. Her meaning was clear.

'I've heard it claimed I can't drown because I'm all set to be hanged some day,' he answered carelessly.

'How can I ever thank you for saving me?' she said, her voice breaking. 'My folks will want to —'

He interrupted, his voice gruff with embarrassment. 'Don't try to thank me. I've been going into creeks all my life after cow critters, so I figured I might as well yank out a human or two for a change. You pretty well played out?'

She caught sight of his shoulder. 'You've been hurt!' she exclaimed.

'Nothing but a bruise. If I were you I'd lie down and get some sleep. I tucked away an hour of it myself. Exactly what you need.'

'I can't sleep.' Her long-lashed eyes rested on his. 'I keep thinking about those poor people who . . . lost their lives . . . and that if it hadn't been for you . . . I would have been one of them.' She dropped her head on her arm and began to cry, softly.

He patted her arm. 'Now — now, don't you cry. It's all over. You didn't lose any folks in the wreck, did you?'

'No. I've been away at school, and I'm on my way back home.'

'Good. Well, I'm the doctor, and my orders are for you to lie down and sleep while I dry my clothes at the fire. Thing to do is to relax and forget a while.'

His cheerful matter-of-fact voice brought existence back to normal. The girl smiled at him, wanly, and said, 'All right, doctor, but can't I be nurse and tie up your shoulder?'

He saw that would please her and distract her attention from the horrors through which she had passed. 'What with?' he asked.

She flushed scarlet and said, 'Look the other way.'

He did so, and heard cloth ripping.

'You can look now,' he was told.

In her hand was a wide ribbon of cotton torn from one of her petticoats.

Since he had lived most of his life on the open range he had dressed a good many wounds and even set a few bones. Now he gave her instructions for tying the bandage. It was a waste of energy, he thought, but it might do her more good than it did him.

He replenished the fire while she tried to find a soft spot on the ground. With his hatchet he chopped branches from trees and dragged them to the fire. The girl was already sound asleep.

The man with the boy on his lap asked a low-voiced question. 'Were any saved except us and the baby?'

'Not any of those in the two cars that went down after the engine. The conductor thinks about seven must have been lost.'

Bleakly, the man said, 'My wife was with us when we went down.'

Forrest had no words of comfort for that. He said, gently, 'I'll hold the boy while you try to get a little sleep.'

'I can't sleep,' the man replied hoarsely. 'I keep thinking. Only yesterday I got annoyed and spoke rough to her.'

Looking at this kind-faced man, Forrest knew he had been a good husband. 'Don't you reckon,' he said in a low voice, 'that where she has gone she knows how much you cared for her?'

The man stared at the fire, agonized thoughts crowding his brain.

The outlaw stepped back from the light of the flames and stripped. He wrapped his naked body in the slicker. His clothes he spread in front of the fire to dry.

'I'll watch them,' the other man said. 'You go to sleep.'

'I could use a few hours sleep, but I have to be on my way before daybreak. Will you waken me?'

The man said he would. Forrest waited till the clothes were dry before he slept. He dressed, then lay down as he had a thousand times before in camp.

Before daybreak he was in the saddle.

The sun was up when the girl awoke. She sat up, startled, then remembered what had happened. She looked around and shuddered.

'Where is the man who saved us?' she asked.

'He left an hour and a half ago,' the other man made answer.

'But we don't know who he is,' the girl

cried, dismayed. 'We don't even know his name. Where has he gone?'

'He didn't say. Just mentioned he had important business.'

'Didn't you ask him his name? Or where he lived?'

'Yes. He said his name didn't matter and that he lived under his hat. Once he did mention that he was riding the grub line.'

'I meant to thank him properly. Now I can't find him.'

'He didn't intend for us to know who he is. As for thanks, he's the sort of man who doesn't want to be reminded of any good deed he does.'

'Why not?' she asked with spirit. 'He can't expect to save my life and not have me say even "Thank you." I don't think he ought to have gone like that.'

The man did not say what he suspected, that their rescuer was living outside the law. He did not want to wound the feelings of the girl.

His little boy began to cry. 'I'm hungry,' he wailed. 'I want my mamma.'

Hastily the man moved over to his son to comfort him.

A brakeman picked his way across the creek over the debris, wading through the water when it was necessary. He carried a pail and a pot of coffee.

'I've brought you some food,' he called. 'The wrecking crew just got here.'

Again the unhappy husband asked a faltering question. 'Were any others in the wrecked cars rescued except us and the baby in the tree?'

The man in uniform shook his head. 'No, sir. That's all.'

'Not a black-haired woman about thirty — in a brown dress?'

'No. I'm sorry.'

The bereaved man turned away despondently.

'One man rescued all of us,' the girl said. 'The same man who swam across and got the baby out of the tree. Do you know who he is?'

'Said his name was Anon. Isn't he here with you?'

'No. He left before I wakened. I don't see why he didn't stay.'

'Finished his job here, hadn't he?'

The girl flushed. 'I want to thank the hero who saved my life.'

'He's some hero all right, but he is a hard citizen too.'

'How dare you say that?' she cried, and turned away indignantly.

From a poster he had seen, the brakeman was doing some guessing.

CHAPTER 13

Blake Forrest Has a Hunch

Blake Forrest leaned against the door jamb of the line rider's cabin and looked out into a night lit by a sky of stars. He rolled and lit a cigarette, then immediately dropped it to the ground and pressed the fire out in the sand with his boot. The faint rhythmic beat of a horse's hoofs had come to him. Swiftly he walked across the open to the nearest brush, some clumps of prickly pear. Behind one of these he crouched. He was expecting a visitor, but he wanted to make sure this one was not self-invited.

The clump of the galloping horse came closer. Some distance from the house — it might have been fifty yards — the rider pulled up abruptly. The call of a coyote sounded.

Forrest stepped out from the shelter of the cactus.

' 'Lo, Bill,' he called. 'Come on up and rest yore saddle.'

Crabb rode forward. He crossed his hands on the saddle horn and looked down with a derisive grin that masked friendliness. 'You doggoned old horn-toad, I come to collect you and a thousand pesos. I hear you done held up a train and robbed it.'

'Want to talk with you about that.' The outlaw put a hand on the mane of the cowpony. 'But first off, did you bring me any grub?'

'Grub. Why, no! Was someone telling you I'd started a feed store for jackasses?' asked the cowboy, a dry chuckle in his throat.

His friend caught him by the arm and hauled him from the horse. Before Crabb could set himself to resist, he found himself on the ground with Forrest astride him.

'I was mentioning grub,' the outlaw suggested.

'So you was, you ornery old vinegaroon.' The man underneath flashed white teeth in a smile. 'You win. It's in that gunny sack back of the saddle. Best I could rustle unnoticed from Old Man Blevins's chuck wagon. If you don't like it —'

'I'll like it. I ran out of food last night. My belly button and my backbone are saying "How d'ye do?" to each other.'

Crabb picked up his hat and brushed the dust out of his red hair. He was a homely freckled man with big protruding ears, a large mouth, and faded blue eyes. For years Blake Forrest had been his hero. He had been captivated by the man's reckless courage, his generosity, and the surprising largesse of his friendship. Bill was a humble soul, and there welled out of him a great loyalty toward this paragon who had brought to him a warm and happy pride in their comradeship. Always he covered his feeling with badinage.

'I'd ought to know better than to play good Samaritan to a locoed criminal who holds up banks, robs trains, and assaults innocent cowpokes,' he said. 'Beans and bacon and a jag of flour I borrow from old Blevins, unbeknownst and feloniously, and the skunk I'm bringing the chuck to bites the hand that feeds it. When you're in the pen, fellow, and I'm outside looking in —'

'Where do you get that idea about you being outside?' Forrest asked. 'When that Texas & Pacific train was being robbed, you were right by my side. But you're right about me and the pen being likely to get acquainted. Every place where I poke my nose I jump up a bunch of guys looking for that thousand pesos you mentioned. . . . Sit in the doorway, Bill, and admire the scenery while I fix me up a couple of stacks of flapjacks and a fry-pan of bacon. I'm kind of particular who drops in on me tonight.'

'Think you would be, with all West Texas reading reward posters,' Crabb jeered. 'If I was in yore jam I'd be making myself an absentee fast as my bronc could drag it.'

Forrest lit a lantern and set about making supper. The cowboy stared at him. Usually his friend took pride in his appearance. He not only had a good horse and saddle, but also wore expensive clothes. His boots were custom-made, his wide hat the best that money could buy. Now he looked as if his clothes had been salvaged from a dump. The shirt had been half torn from his back, and on the left shoulder there was a great livid bruise. A dusty, torn, and floppy old hat drooped over his head. He would have looked like a disreputable tramp, if it had been possible for one who carried himself as Blake Forrest did to convey that impression.

'Say, have you been bucking a cyclone?' Crabb asked.

'Well, a cloudburst,' Forrest substituted, putting a match to the kindling he had already set in the stove.

'Craig Shannon was telling me, Blake, you had a rookus with some of the Terrell crowd at Deer Trail. Did they do this to you?'

'No. But I had a little mixup with them. Nothing serious. They kind of crowded me.'

His friend grinned at him admiringly. 'You're the doggondest cuss I ever did see.'

'But after our little party I thought it best

to go over the hill and hunt the turkeys for a while.'

'Hmp! The way Craig told it, you had the damndest bear fight with a whole mess of them.'

'There were some fireworks,' Blake admitted, and lifted a lid of the stove to make way for a frying pan.

'Nothing serious. Hmp! What d'you call serious, fellow? Wes Terrell and Webb Lake have took to their beds account of having some lead pills slapped into them. Pres Walsh was 'most scalped, and young Phil Decker had stitches plenty sewed in his head.'

'Phil Decker. What kin is he to Miss Helen Decker, the schoolmarm at Deer Trail?'

'Brother. You know the lady? She's pretty as a new-painted wagon.'

'I've met her. She wouldn't tell you I was one of her best friends. What is the story going round about our fracas in the wagon yard?'

Bill opened his wide mouth in a grin. 'Depends on who tells it. Seems by the Deer Trail *Journal* you attackted these peaceable citizens when they was tee-totally unprepared. I reckon they was just going home from prayer-meeting. The sooner the state is rid of such miscreants as you the better it will be. And what the hell are the rangers doing anyhow that they don't collect you?'

131

'So that's the way the *Journal* sees it? And what's the other side of the story?'

'All I know is what Craig Shannon says. According to him, these nice gents went for you all spraddled out, and you kinda showed them up. I will say Craig says his piece real loud and often. What did you ever do for that guy, Blake?'

'Not a thing. He just happens to be a white man. Bill, I'm out of jail hunting evidence. In about a week I've got to give myself up to Buzz Waggoner, so I'm in a tight to round up my witnesses. I've got to gather them and prove an alibi on the Texas & Pacific robbery. First off, where is Stone Heath?'

Bill scratched his head. 'I dunno, exactly, he sashays around so dadgummed much, but I reckon we can dig him up somewheres in the brush. Likely those two line riders we spent the night with are still at the Circle Three T. But you never can tell.'

'My trial will be set for some time during the next term of court, unless we can convince the district attorney that I was nearly a hundred miles away at the time the express was held up.'

'I'll get my time from Old Man Blevins and help you run down these lads. When we all come through with our testimony they can't do a thing to you. But what about that

Valley Bank business?'

'I'm in a tough spot there,' Forrest grinned, ruefully. 'I must have been plumb crazy that day when I saw that old scalawag Gildea counting the money he owed me and Mother Holloway and persuaded him to let me keep it for him.'

'Why don't you light out, Blake?' Crabb asked. 'No use you hanging round here. You can't stay on the dodge all yore life, and if you give yourself up you'll land in the pen sure.'

His friend poured some pancake batter into the frying pan. 'Keep your trap shut, Bill, and don't ever mention this, but Buzz Waggoner gave me a chance to break jail on my promise to show up in two weeks. So I've got to go back.'

Bill rasped his stubbly chin with the palm of a hand. 'Doggone it, that's sure too bad,' he lamented. 'Now you can't light out.'

'No, sir, I have to go through.'

'You haven't told me yet about that bruise on yore back, Blake.'

'Oh, that. I tried to swim a creek and a floating log hit me.'

'When? What creek?'

'Funnel Creek. When it was bank-full.'

'What did you do that for, you crazy galoot? Why'n't you ride round to a bridge?'

'The bridge was washed out.'

'So it was. The railroad bridge too. That was a terrible accident.'

'Yes. I was there next morning and saw the wreck.'

'I hear two-three were saved from the flood.'

'Yes. They managed to get out.'

Forrest sat down at the table to a meal consisting mostly of flapjacks and bacon and black coffee. He ate with the appetite of a healthy outdoor man who has fasted for twenty-four hours.

For a few minutes Crabb watched him, then drew his chair up to the table. 'Seeing as I rounded up this grub, I'll sit in and sample yore cooking. It has been 'most two hours since I had a whack at any food.'

When Forrest drew back from the table it was with a sigh of contentment. 'To enjoy eating, a man ought to fast for a couple of days every once in a while,' he said.

'Not me,' Bill differed. 'I enjoy my beans and bacon any time I hear that holler, "Come and get it." The best thing I do is eat.'

Blake tilted back his chair and laced sinewy fingers back of his head. He looked at the coffee-pot, eyes narrowed in thought. 'A notion has been roaming around in my nut quite some time,' he told his companion. 'Maybe there's nothing to it, but on the contrary other hand, as old Jig Fisher says when he is making oration, I call it to your attention for your consideration, gentlemen, as a possible solution of this vexing problem.'

The outlaw brought the front legs of his chair to the floor sharply and looked across the table at the cowpuncher. 'Ray Terrell claims he recognized me as the leader of the gang that held up the Texas & Pacific express at Crawford's Crossing. Why did he do that?'

'I go up to the head of the class on that one, Blake,' his companion said, and stopped to lick the paper of the cigarette he was rolling. 'Because you bumped off Brother Buck once upon a time.'

'That's one reason, but it may not be the only one. I'll ask another question. Why did Wes Terrell and the rest of his gang try to put me out of business Monday night?'

'Same answer — Brother Buck. Though that's only part of it. The whole outfit have hated yore guts ever since you made them crawfish in public when they were all set to wipe out Stone Heath because he had whaled the stuffing outa Pres Walsh.'

'True enough, but half a dozen times since then I have met up with the bunch and not one of them lifted a hand to his gun. They bristled up like strange dogs all set for a fight

135

— and didn't make the jump.'

Crabb considered that. 'Maybe this time they had been chewing the rag together and were all set for trouble. Maybe they were drunk. Maybe they thought that in the dark they could get away with it.'

'Or just possibly, having shifted the blame for robbing the express from themselves to me, they figured it would be hunky-dory to have me dead so I couldn't prove myself innocent.'

Bill stared into the cold hard eyes of his friend while his mind wrestled with the suggestion just made. 'Meaning that the Terrell gang pulled off the holdup themselves. By granny, they might have done it. They're poison bad, the whole kaboodlum. The devil and Tom Walker! Till right now I never suspicioned them, but I'll bet my time check against a 'dobe dollar you've shot a bull's-eye.'

'Let's say they did it. How did they know there was a big money shipment that night — unless someone gave them the tip?'

'Ray Terrell,' guessed Crabb, almost in a whisper.

'Why not? He could have wired his brother from up the line — sent a blind telegram, perhaps addressed to somebody else, after he had made sure the money was on board.'

The faded eyes of the cowboy gleamed.

There was a chance this might turn into an exciting adventure. He had his own personal grudge at the Terrell outfit, and if they could get something on them he would be no end pleased.

'You mean — send the telegram after he had seen the loot loaded in the express car?' he asked.

'He'd wait till then, I would guess, even if he had a confederate in the office to tip him off.'

'Wouldn't do any good to wire to Deer Trail. The gang couldn't reach Crawford's Crossing before the train got there.'

Forrest nodded. 'Might have been sent to some station on the line of the Texas & Pacific within twenty miles of where the train was to be robbed, or twenty-five at most, say. If we could run down such a message and could show that Wes Terrell, Webb Lake, and Pres Walsh were away from Deer Trail on the twenty-second and twenty-third of last month, why we would have picked up sign on a cold trail worth following.'

'We'll start right here from the chunk,' Crabb said, with a little whoop of enthusiasm.

'Don't expect too much, Bill. This is only a hunch. May not amount to a thing. But we'll get busy and see where it takes us. Dig up Stone Heath if you can. I want you and him to cover the Deer Trail end of this, since I can't show up there. Find out all you can about the movements of these birds around the time of the holdups. If they were out of town check up the horses they rode and get a description of the mounts. But do it all absolutely on the q.t.'

'Y'betcha! Not a peep outa me. I'll get my time from Old Man Blevins tomorrow morning and hop to it right away.'

'Wes Terrell is one of these flannel-mouthed braggarts who have to talk. If he has a woman he may have spilled the whole story to her. Stone has always been the fair-haired lad with the girls. Maybe she'll open up to him.'

'I'm on my way, fellow,' Crabb said, and reached for his hat.

CHAPTER 14

One of Blake's Witnesses

The new rider at the Granite Gap ranch watched Janet King as she walked across the dusty square from the house to the stables. He was shoeing a horse, efficiently, but with a manner of easy indolence that was deceptive. From a distance he had observed Miss King before. She was worth a second look, and that called for several more, to make sure her young good looks were as dazzlingly vivid as earlier impressions had recorded. In her movements was the grace that comes from perfect muscular coordination. The sun and the wind that had browned her hands and face had given her strength and vigor expressing themselves in rhythmic beauty.

Janet pulled up in her stride. The young man in chaps hammering a horseshoe on the anvil was singing softly to himself. The words of his song had drifted to her.

> 'I want to be ready,
> I want to be ready,
> I want to be ready,

To walk in Jerusalem just like John,'

he sang.

She remembered, with startled certainty, the only time she had ever heard the words before now. A man whom she could not get out of her mind had sung them. Was this just a coincidence? Or was it possible Blake Forrest had chosen this means to get into touch with her?

Her footsteps turned in the direction of the man at the forge. He was a blond, tall, lean, and muscular. When he raised his head she saw he had an attractive face, with a flashing smile that showed fine white teeth.

'You haven't been with us long, have you?' she said.

'Not long, Miss King. Came this week. My name is Stone Heath.'

'I hope you'll like it at the Granite Gap. . . . Funny about that song you were singing. I never heard it but once before, and that was the other day. A man sang it who found me lost in the desert and took me to Fair Play.'

The blacksmith plunged the horseshoe into a tub of water. 'I picked it up from a side-kick of mine who is loaded up with camp-meeting songs,' he explained.

'Of course he wouldn't be the man who helped me.'

'Not likely.' The cowboy rested a muscular brown forearm on the rump of the bronco he was about to shoe. He was willing to prolong this conversation indefinitely. At the present moment he did not remember ever having met a young woman who had more to offer than this one. She was like a boy, and yet not at all like one. It was the vogue for girls to be shy and demure. Miss King was direct and simple. Her fine eyes met and held his without fluttering down to the cheeks. She was in high-heeled cowboy boots, custom made. None the less, her slender person was vibrant with femininity. 'No, I don't reckon you would be meeting my friend. He's not a lady's man.'

'Neither was this one who saved me. He thought I was a nuisance, but he was too polite to say so.'

'Might have been Blake, at that,' he admitted.

The blue eyes of Janet sparkled to quicker life. 'If you mean Blake Forrest, that's exactly who it was,' she cried. 'When he brought me to town he was arrested.'

'They didn't hold him long,' Heath said, smiling at her.

'No. I wish I could do something for him, after what he did for me. You don't know where he is, do you?'

'No, ma'am, I don't. On the dodge somewhere. I'd like to meet up with him, too. I've been aiming to ride in and see Buzz Waggoner. You see, I'm one of Blake's witnesses. He was with me when the Texas & Pacific was robbed. We were 'most a hundred miles from Crawford's Crossing at the time, so he couldn't have been in that job.'

'I'm so glad to hear it,' Janet told him, and her heart was lifted with joy. 'I don't mean to hear he wasn't in the train holdup. I knew that. He told my friend, Mr. Vallery, that he wasn't. But to know he has reputable witnesses to prove what he says.'

'I ain't so blamed reputable, Miss King,' Heath admitted. 'I've been in plenty of scrapes with Blake. We raised trouble in couples, he and I. So I won't make such an all-fired good witness. Fact is, I reckon Buzz will want to arrest me as one of the bandits soon as I come through for Blake.'

'But you'll come through,' she said quickly. 'You won't let that interfere.'

The gray eyes looking at her grew hard. 'Do I look like some kind of a yellow dog that runs away when it is kicked?' he asked.

'No, you don't. I'm sorry I said that. You'll forgive me, won't you?'

From his tanned face the chill vanished. 'When you say pretty please that way I reckon

I will. After all, you can't tell how good a watermelon is by looking at it. Maybe I might be a coyote. No way for you to know.'

'There is, too,' she contradicted. 'I can tell by looking at you, and I know that Blake Forrest wouldn't have a friend who wasn't true.'

'You like that old scalawag,' he said.

A slow flush crept beneath the tan of her cheeks. 'Yes. Wouldn't you like somebody who had saved your life and then risked going to prison by bringing you back to safety?'

'I'd like Blake Forrest if he'd never brought me anything but trouble. And come to think of it that's about all we ever did bring each other except some of the best times two guys ever had.'

'So would I,' she said, and her steady eyes defied him to think evil of her confession. 'It isn't what he does for you. It's what he is.'

'You're shouting, Miss King. Both Blake and I have stepped outside the law a few times, I wouldn't wonder. Laws aren't made to fit conditions. A bunch of soft politicians sit at Austin and put a lot of statutes on the books that won't stand up when you're on the range fighting drought, blizzards, rustlers, and general hell. At times Solomon himself couldn't guess which cow was the mother of some pot-bellied little dogie gone astray. It belongs to the first cowman who finds it, either in person

143

or through one of his riders. You know that. It's common sense. But the law doesn't say so.'

'If that was the only crime your friend has committed they ought not to be hunting him down like a wolf,' Janet told him, a flash of resentment in her eyes.

'Maybe there are others,' he conceded cautiously. 'When a young fellow is helling around he rips a lot of ordinances to pieces. But what I claim is that Blake is a white man and will do to take along. He has the rep of being a killer. To hear some folks talk you'd think he had massa-creed about forty instead of having wiped out three sneaking ruffians in self-defence.'

Janet recalled that her father had once shot down a rustler who fought back when he was caught red-handed. Curtis King had never mentioned this to her, but she had heard it from others. She knew he had not been to blame but had been driven to fire to protect himself. Perhaps it had been that way with Blake Forrest, too.

'He seems to have a knack of getting into trouble,' Janet answered, harking back to the absent friend of the horseshoer. 'Take this fight he has just had at Deer Trail. The paper says he attacked several peaceable citizens and left them all wounded behind him when he lit out in the dark.'

'Don't you believe it. Don't believe a word of it.' The friendly gray eyes of the cowboy had grown hard as agates. 'You have brains, Miss King. Use 'em. Would a hunted man, who is trying to hole up till he can get out of the country, go to shooting up a lot of citizens who weren't bothering him? A cool customer like Blake, who never was known to be goosey? It's not reasonable. Now, is it? I ask you.'

'But he did shoot them.'

'All I know about this is what I've read in the paper, and what I know about Blake and the riffraff he had the fracas with in the wagon yard. But that's enough for me to be sure this story has been twisted into a lie. They jumped him — figured they would get the reward — figured after he was dead nobody would raise a rumpus about it, account of his bad rep. The mistake they made was in thinking four-five of the Terrell bunch was enough to tackle a thorough guy like Blake.'

'You're certainly a good friend of his,' the young woman said, and there was warm approval in her starry eyes.

'I'd ought to be,' Stone Heath replied. 'He yanked me out of the Canadian when it was bank-full and a drifting log had knocked my horse from under me. That was two years ago.

We were taking a herd up the trail for Shanghai Pierce. . . . Maybe I'd better give you an idea how-come this Terrell outfit to be such enemies of Blake — and of me, too, for that matter.'

'If you will, please,' she assented eagerly.

'First off, I got to admit Blake and I were wild young coots. We weren't no-ways trained to travel in harness and stay hitched. When we'd go to town we would get roostered and raise merry cain. Mostly, what we did was harmless and we would pay later for anything we busted. But we got a bad name, and a lot of cowmen figured it would be a good thing to pass us up when they were hiring riders. So gradually we drifted into a crowd of rapscallions who were tough hombres. We weren't in the inner circle but kinda outsiders fooling around with them. They flattered us, and we were young enough to like it. Of course we were a pair of suckers, and they were drawing us in so that we'd go so far we couldn't back out.'

Janet drank in the story, not lifting her gaze from his. 'Go on,' she said.

'There was another young fellow ran with us, a lunger with lots of money out here for the ozone. He came from Connecticut, seems to me. Name of Brooks Phelps. A nice young cuss but weak, all filled up with romantic notions about the West. Pretty soon Blake and I saw the Terrell crowd were aiming to take Phelps for his wad. From remarks they made we gathered they thought him a tenderfoot and fair picking. They sure made him think he was the fair-haired lad. We kept our eyes open and learned they were going to take him out on the range and sell him the Sawbuck brand, a sizable herd they didn't own any more than I did.'

'And you protected him?'

'We picked up our information late, after they had all been out to look the herd over and had come back to the hotel to sign up. Blake and I walked into the room just as Phelps was starting to sign the check. There had been a lot of drinking and back-slapping. We could see that. Well, ma'am, we could see we had arrived at a mighty awkward moment for the gang. Buck Terrell was the leader. He looked at us plenty black and asked what we meant by butting into a private room without knocking. Blake played innocent and was awful sorry he had interrupted if he wasn't welcome. I forgot to tell you that we had been breaking away from the bunch for four or five months and had been trying to get Phelps wised up about them. So they were already hos-tile, you might say.

'Phelps spilled the beans, not knowing he

was doing it. "I'm buying the Sawbuck brand," he says. "Writing a check for it now." Blake looks around, cool and easy. "I don't see Old Man Flandrau," he comes back. "I should think he'd be here when he was selling you his herd." That started the trouble. Buck had been cock of the walk in a kind of way. He was a bully-puss fellow always lookin' for trouble. So he told Blake he was a liar and for him to get outa the room. Blake didn't turn a hair. In that gentle even voice of his he suggested to Phelps he go to the courthouse, look up the Sawbuck brand, and find out who was a liar. You could see the tenderfoot was taken plumb in the wind. He says to Buck, apologetic-like, that it would be a business way to do that.

'Buck knew his crooked deal had gone sour and he saw red. He dragged out a gun and turned loose on my friend. Blake dropped him in his tracks. By that time my .45 was out and I had the others covered. We beat it, young Phelps along with us. Two days later one of their crowd, fellow named Pres Walsh, met me in the post office. One thing led to another and I had to lick him. His friends heard about it and came running, all set to wipe me off the map. Blake drifted in, simultaneous. In front of the post office, with twenty people looking on, he bluffed them out and made them back down. Ever since then they have wanted to get even.'

'You think they tried to murder him at Deer Trail the other night?'

'That's the word for it, Miss King. If it had been anybody but Blake they would have got him, too, but that lad is a sure-enough hell-a-miler. He is in a class by himself.'

'It's an outrage,' Janet cried indignantly, 'that he should be blamed for these things when it isn't his fault at all.'

'Nice if you could get the law to thinking that way, too,' he drawled. 'Trouble with Blake is he never stops to explain. Like it or lump it, he rides his own high-headed way. Once we were rangers for about a year. We liked it fine, but we got in a jam with our lieutenant about some doggoned fool business and were thrown out on our ears. I'll bet Blake was the best-liked man in the company, but somehow he couldn't stand discipline. Now our old friends are combing the brush for him. It's a crazy world. With Texas full of bad men and criminals everybody suddenly decides Blake is the worst of the bunch. I'm not saying he hasn't ridden high, wide, and handsome. But he can look in the glass and see the face of a square shooter. Don't ever let anyone tell you anything different.'

'I never shall,' Janet answered.

There was such a warm and glowing color in her ardent face that Heath looked at her in surprise. She read his thoughts and reproved them.

'He took me to Fair Play knowing he might be captured.' She spoke quietly, but her hot eyes betrayed the emotion in her. 'You told me that you are not a yellow dog. Wouldn't I be one if I deserted him now?'

He said, smiling at her with approval, 'You'll do to ride the river with, lady.'

He had given her Cattleland's last word of praise. In the long trail drives to a market, the herds had to be taken across rivers sometimes filled to the banks with roaring muddy water. To guide the longhorns from shore to shore was a dangerous business, one that tested a man's courage and loyalty to the limit. Janet knew more than one gay gallant lad who had gone down in the rushing current and later had been buried in a shallow grave beside the stream.

She shook her head, brushing that aside. 'Father has hired a lawyer to defend him, you know, if he is ever tried. Mr. Vallery thinks perhaps he can beat the train-robbery charge. It's the other one that is hopeless. At least it looks so. There's no alibi there, is there?'

CHAPTER 15

Buzz Waggoner Invites a Guest

A film of wariness passed over the face of the cowboy. He trusted Janet King, but he did not intend to make any admissions not hedged with explanations.

'If you mean the Valley Bank robbery I wouldn't know about that. Jake Gildea is a skunk. No argument there. He would steal from his own mother if she was alive. How do we know there was any holdup? He claims it took place in his private office. When the clerk answered his ring Blake was sitting across the desk from Gildea smoking a cigarette. He didn't have any gun out. Gildea didn't mention any holdup. He just gave orders for Homer Packard — that was the clerk's name — to bring Mother Holloway's note.'

'Who is Mother Holloway?'

'Finest woman God ever made. A friend to everyone who is sick or in trouble. Any cowboy who is out of a job can go and stay there till he is riding again and settle with her when he gets his pay check. She is a widow. Jake robbed her of about a thousand dollars after her husband died because the receipt for what he had paid on a mortgage note had somehow got lost in the shuffle. He was aiming to foreclose on her home. Instead Blake talked him into turning over the note to her indorsed as paid in full.'

Janet's eyebrows met in a frown of perplexity. 'How could he talk him into it, unless —'

'Search me,' Heath answered dryly. 'Blake is right persuasive when he is going good. Maybe he appealed to Jake's better nature.'

'You know better than that.'

'I know Blake took the note to Mother Holloway and she had the mortgage released without a word from Jake.'

'Maybe he was afraid she had some evidence the note had been paid and didn't want to go to trial to test it. And what about the rest of the money? According to the papers, Mr. Packard says he saw it on the table when he went into the room. It wasn't there afterward, and Blake Forrest went out of the bank carrying a sack.'

'Maybe Jake's better nature had got stirred up again. When Blake was a boy Jake took advantage of Mrs. Forrest and robbed her of everything she had. He did it nice and legal, so there wasn't any comeback. Let's say remorse had been eating at his heart until he just couldn't stand it any longer. So —'

Janet interrupted impatiently. 'No jury will believe that sort of nonsense. Jake Gildea loves money and nothing else. And your friend can't walk into a bank and rob it just because he claims Gildea cheated his mother. You know that. We have laws here in Texas, and people have to respect them.'

'Well, I'm no lawyer, but I have heard of what they call extenuating circumstances. I was sorta mentioning some.'

A man in a buckboard drove into the yard, caught sight of them, and drew up a few feet distant. The driver was Buzz Waggoner. He lowered his fat body gingerly from the rig.

'Mornin', Miss Janet,' he said. 'Nice to see the sun again after all these rains. After that Funnel Creek business a fellow feels he could stand a lot of sunshine without kickin'.'

'Yes,' she agreed. 'No news yet, is there, of who the man is that saved Bess Decker and little Myra Hunt?'

'Not a murmur. He musta gone into a hole, looks like, and pulled it in after him.'

'It's the queerest thing I ever knew. Of course he must have been a stranger.'

'Yep.' The sheriff turned his attention to the man at the outdoor blacksmith shop. 'Heard you were here, Stone, so I moseyed out to pick you up.'

'Might have saved yoreself the trouble,' the cowboy said indifferently, fitting an iron shoe to the hoof of the horse. 'I was aimin' to ride down and see you in a day or two.'

The shrewd little eyes of the officer watched him. 'So? What for?'

'For the same reason you came to get me,' Heath said nonchalantly, driving a nail into the horn of the hoof.

'You know why I'm here?'

Stone Heath glanced at him, a little amused. 'I'm not a plumb fool, Buzz. You've heard talk about me being a witness that Blake couldn't have been in the Texas & Pacific robbery, so you came out to check up.'

Evenly, his eyes on the blacksmith, Waggoner said, 'I've heard you were with him at the time the robbery occurred.'

'You've heard correctly.'

'And if you're innocent he is.'

'You're loaded to the hooks with tact, Buzz,' the cowboy grinned. 'You might have put it that if he's guilty I am.'

'Probably you have witnesses as to where you were at the time. I'll be tickled if you can clear him — and yourself.'

'Three of them witnesses. But I haven't got them handy in my vest pocket.'

'Good idea to dig up those witnesses, Stone.

You can't do it even with the help of horse-shoes, sitting here at the ranch. I reckon you better come along with me.'

'To your calaboose?'

'I aim to get this business cleared up if I can.'

Janet could not keep out of it any longer. 'He really was going down to see you, Sheriff Waggoner. We were talking about it just before you drove up.'

'That's fine. If he was fixing to come any-how I won't be discommoding him by giving him a lift to town.'

'I'd like you to speak with Father before you go. He's in the house now. Let's walk back to the porch and you can sit down.'

'Suits me,' Waggoner said. 'You come too, Stone.'

'Looks like somebody else will have to finish shoeing this horse,' Heath said with a grin. 'Well, I never was crazy about blacksmith work anyhow. Soon as I've got this one shoe on I'll be with you.'

'I'll wait,' the sheriff said pointedly. To mit-igate the bluntness he added: 'I got lots of time. No need to hurry.'

A gangling youth in high-heeled boots and shiny leather chaps crossed the yard. Janet called to him.

'Bud, will you run in and tell Father that

Sheriff Waggoner is here and wants to see him?'

The boy loped to the house and disappeared through the door. Presently his father came out to the porch. Curtis King was a broad-shouldered man in his late forties. He had the strong, rugged face of a man who has fought his way through adversity to success. His shirt was gray flannel and his corduroy trousers climbed half way up the legs of dusty boots.

'Hello, Buzz,' he called. 'Glad to see you. Aren't you off your range a bit up in this neck of the woods?'

'He came to arrest our new rider Stone Heath,' Janet said quickly.

'So? What's the boy been up to, Buzz?'

'He's a friend of Blake Forrest, so Mr. Waggoner thinks he ought to be in jail.'

Curtis King looked at his daughter. 'Suppose you let Buzz do the talking, Janet. He's not dumb.'

'Stone here is an important witness in the T. & P. train robbery,' the sheriff explained. 'Claims he was with Blake Forrest at the time of the holdup. If so, I reckon he better come down and tell the district attorney and the rangers what he knows. Wouldn't you say so, Curt?'

King turned to his employee. 'Is that a fact, Heath? Were you with this man Forrest when the express was robbed?'

The eyes of the cowboy narrowed slightly. He had a perfectly straight story to tell, but he did not intend to say anything that later could be twisted by lawyers into something he had not meant.

'That's right, Mr. King. Bill Crabb and I spent the night with Blake at a cow camp of the Circle Three B. Two line riders of that outfit were with us. One of 'em was called Shorty. I disremember the name of the other, if I ever heard it.'

'At what time was the express robbed?' the cattleman asked Waggoner.

'Quarter after eight in the evening.'

'And you were at the Circle Three B, a long day's ride from Crawford's Crossing, at that time, Heath?'

'Yes, sir. Lying in front of the campfire, my head against a saddle, listening to the boys tell windies.'

'And you can prove you were there?' King asked sharply. 'No use building up a fairy tale to try to help your friend. The lawyers will tear it down in court quicker than a cat can wink and send you to the penitentiary for perjury.'

'My story is correct, sir,' Heath answered curtly.

'When did you see Blake last, Stone?' the

sheriff inquired amiably. 'I don't reckon you know where he is now.'

'No, I don't.' Heath spoke with a touch of drawling sarcasm. 'You've seen him since I have. Wasn't he a guest at yore hotel for a couple of days and then decided to check out?'

Waggoner drew the ranchman to one side for private conference.

'Stone tells the same story that Blake Forrest does about being at the Circle Three B,' he whispered wheezily. 'O' course they might have fixed it up together. Forrest and Heath and this Bill Crabb are thick as three in a bed, I've heard. Maybe all three were in the holdup.'

'And the two line riders?'

'May have been invented to help out the story. Mind, I don't say it's that way, Curt. I've a notion they are telling the truth. Blake is an old acquaintance of mine. Generally speaking I'd take his word a hundred per cent, and he tells me this is a frame-up against him. He did me a good turn once and I like him. But I'm sheriff of this county, and I reckon I'll tote Heath down to Fair Play. If his story is straight he will be able to prove it at the proper time.'

King agreed. 'Won't do any harm, though if you want to leave Heath here I'll agree to produce him at any time he is wanted.'

'If he doesn't pull his freight,' the sheriff amended.

'I don't think he will. I size him up as a man who will go through. Far as we've gone, it looks to me as if Forrest may be innocent of the train robbery. He has the name of a hardy, reckless fellow, but I am under a personal obligation to him, and if his case ever comes to trial I aim to help him any way I can.'

'Glad to hear it. But even if he makes the riffle on the train robbery he'll be convicted of the Valley Bank holdup. It's an open-and-shut case against him. I reckon I'd better take Heath with me.'

The sheriff did not think it necessary to explain his own private and personal reason for putting Heath under lock and key. He was a politician, and it was necessary for him to put up a good front before his constituents. There had been a good deal of criticism of him for having let Forrest escape. Nobody appeared to suspect him of complicity, but the town newspaper had pointed out that he must have been very lax to have permitted someone to smuggle a file into the prisoner's cell. It was Waggoner's opinion that if he bustled around and showed activity by arresting another possible suspect he might draw the sting out of the bad impression he had made.

Waggoner told the cowboy he had better pack his war bag.

'Am I under arrest?' Heath asked.

'Let's not get technical, Stone,' the sheriff evaded. 'We'll put it that you are going down as my guest.'

'At yore home or the jail?'

'I'll have to think about that.'

Heath grinned, hardily. 'Looks like I'm going to be such a welcome guest that you wouldn't hear of me turning down yore invitation,' he said.

Before they left, the cowboy found occasion for a private word with Janet. 'Don't worry,' he comforted. 'It will work out all right.'

She wished she was sure about that.

CHAPTER 16

A Brush-Popper Makes Inquiries

Maverick jogged through the chaparral in a leisurely way, expertly avoiding the thorns of the mesquite and prickly pear which reached out to clutch at him. His master wore heavy leather leggings above the boots thrust into stirrups protected by *tapaderos*. His jacket was of the same material. Gloves with gauntlets saved hands and wrists from a hundred scratches.

For an oldtimer it was comparatively easy to get through the thicket in this meandering fashion, though a tenderfoot would have thought it an impassable tangle. Blake Forrest had been a brush-popper in earlier days. Many a time he had pounded wildly through the jungle hightailing a mossy-horn racing for dear life while cat-claw, rat-tail cactus, Spanish dagger, wild currant, and a dozen other savage growths tore at him fiercely.

Blake was not hunting cattle today. He was running down information that would help him prove, he hoped, that the T. & P. express robbery was none of his doing. He was not heading for Crawford's Crossing. Any story he might have read from an inspection of that swampy terrain had long since been obliterated by the heavy rains. The outlaw was playing the hunch he had mentioned to Bill Crabb, that since the bandits had chosen for the holdup a day when the train was carrying a large shipment of money they were probably acting on direct information of treasure aboard, in which case the news must have been wired them from San Antonio or some point west of there.

This was a sheer guess, but one based on a logical premise, if as he suspected the robbers were being tipped off by inside information. Fifteen miles west of Crawford's Crossing was the station Summit Gap. Eastward about the same distance from the scene of the holdup was the small village of Horse Creek. The telegram might have been sent to either place. The hopes of Blake strongly ran to Horse Creek, for the reason that this small village was a much more likely contact point than Summit Gap for the Terrell gang. In riding from Deer Creek to Crawford's Crossing one would have to detour only a few miles to take in Horse Creek, but would have an extra thirty miles to touch at Summit Gap.

About noon Blake rode along the single dusty business street of Horse Creek. There were half a dozen adobe houses facing the railroad tracks, including a blacksmith shop, a general store, a saloon, and a tumble down shack set in a corral. The station stood by itself on the other side of the rails. He trailed the reins and sauntered into the red-painted frame building.

A girl sat at a telegrapher's desk reading a book. She was about fifteen, fresh-colored, and plump. At sight of Forrest she put her finger on the page to keep her place and waited for him to speak.

He smiled at her. 'Are you the president of the T. & P., miss?' he asked.

The girl flashed a white-toothed grin. 'No, sir. I'm just keeping the depot open while Father eats his dinner,' she answered. 'There might come a message while he is away.'

'So you're a telegrapher too.'

'He taught me. I'm not so awf'ly good.'

'I don't reckon you get a great many private messages either coming or going,' he suggested. 'You don't have to be a top hand, do you?'

'Not one a month. What would anybody want to send a wire for from here? Once in a while we swap messages with operators up and down the line, just to pass the time.'

'The world sure moves,' Blake contributed. 'To think you can send a message twenty miles

163

in a split second. Then there's this newfangled do-funny the telephone. They say you can hear a fellow's voice a half a mile.'

'We got messages a lot farther than twenty miles,' the girl said. 'Sometimes Father hears from San Antonio.'

'Think of that.' Forrest was full of rustic wondering admiration. 'On company business, I reckon.'

'Mostly. Like I said, onct in a great while somebody sends a telegram.'

His eyes were the puzzled inquiring ones of a country boy come to town. 'What in the Sam Hill about? Why won't a letter do just as well?'

'Mostly about folks sick or dead. We got one three-four weeks ago from a mother about her baby. Said there was scarlet fever in the family and she was sending the baby to a ranch on the Express that day. Kinda funny about that too. Her brother is a nester and lives back in the brush somewheres. He came in for supplies that day and was hanging around here before the message came.'

'Expecting it, eh?'

'Yes. Seems she had written him she might have to send the baby, but it was lucky he happened into town that day.'

'Wasn't it?' Blake agreed, all enthusiasm. 'Say, miss, I never did see one of these-here telegrams. You wouldn't have, I reckon, a copy of that baby one sticking around yet.'

'Sure we have. Father is very particular about that. He hangs all the private ones on that hook over there.' She smiled cheerfully. 'Course I'm not supposed to show them, but there's nothing private about that baby one. I'll get it for you — or some other one that's not important.'

From the hook she took the few copies of wires hanging there. Clearly she was proud to show her superior knowledge to this good-looking cowboy just out of the brush. One of the sheets of paper she passed to Blake. 'There it is. From San Antone. Dated April 23.'

Outwardly not a flicker of excitement showed on Forrest's tanned face as he read, but the blood was pounding in his veins. The Express had been robbed on the twenty-third. 'Scarlet fever here. Sending baby on Express today. Meet train.' It was addressed to Sam Jones and was signed Mamie.

'An' I reckon the baby arrived right side up and Uncle Sam was here on the job with a nursing milk bottle all ready,' the outlaw said with a grin.

'No, that's another funny thing. The baby didn't come, and the uncle didn't show up to meet it.'

'Well, I'll be doggoned! An April Fool joke maybe, about three weeks too late.' Blake handed back to the girl the sheet of paper and she replaced it on the hook. 'Much obliged for letting me have a look-see. You know, I'm one of these-here brush-poppers who don't get a chance to know about these up to date doodads the way you do. Maybe I don't look it, but I'm most scared to death to meet a young lady, account of not seeing one in a month of Sundays. You sure have been nice to me. Expect I'd better drift along.'

Blake stood in the doorway awkwardly clinging to his wide-rimmed hat with both hands as if it were a safety belt. He did not seem to know how to get out of the room.

The girl's moon-face dimpled to a smile. This bashful young man made her feel sophisticated. It was quite safe to tease him.

'Give my love to the longhorns, and if you ever come back this way again —'

'I'll sure drap in, miss,' he promised. 'I won't be like that forgetful guy Uncle Sam Jones. Say, like as not the bird was locoed.'

'He didn't look crazy, though I didn't like him.'

'Why didn't you?'

'I dunno. He was kinda mean and sulky, with no color in his face and dead slaty eyes. A little fellow.' The girl slanted a glance at her new acquaintance. 'And old.'

The outlaw tried to achieve a blush. 'How old is old?' he asked. 'Would you call me old, miss?'

'Not yet,' she gave information. 'Forty is old.'

'Mr. Forty-Year-Old Sam Jones didn't get fresh, did he?'

She shook her head violently. 'No, sir. He thought I was just a piece of the furniture. And when I told him there wasn't a telegram for him — that was before it had come, you understand — he snapped at me like I was an Indian squaw. Spoke to me through his teeth without opening his lips. He was certainly no gentleman.'

Forrest guessed that the name Mr. Jones usually went by was Webb Lake, but he did not say so. 'Someone ought to work that scalawag over and teach him manners. If I meet him perhaps I will. He hadn't any right to treat a little lady like you that-a-way. Did you say his hair was sort of brindle?'

'No, black.' There was a spark of excitement in the brown eyes of the girl. It began to look as if she had made a conquest. 'But don't you go getting into trouble over me, Mr. —'

'Wood — Jim Wood,' supplied Forrest on the spur of the moment.

'Glad to meetcha, Mr. Wood. My name is Willie Fulwiler.'

The young man expressed his pleasure at having met her, but he seemed to have a fixed idea that he ought to teach Mr. Jones manners.

'Was this cuss alone, did you notice? Or did he come to town with friends?'

'He was alone. I saw him when he came riding down the road.'

'Notice the horse?'

'It was gray — just like any other gray horse. Now look here, Mr. Wood. If you should happen to meet this Jones, I won't have you picking a difficulty with him just because he was grumpy to me and doesn't know how to behave the way a gentleman should.'

Her visitor appeared to drop the idea, with reluctance. He bowed himself out of the station and led Maverick across the street to the corral.

A couple of oldtimers sat there on a bench whittling. A young man in overalls seemed to have charge of the place. Forrest turned over his horse to be fed and leaned against the corner of the shack indolently.

'Come far, stranger?' one of the antiques inquired.

'Quite some distance,' drawled Forrest.

The other old man squinted up at him from faded eyes set in a face wrinkled as a last year's winter pippin. 'Ridin' for some cow outfit, I take it,' he offered by way of an opening conversational lead.

'Have been,' the young man admitted. 'Not right now. Kinda drifting, you might say.'

They discussed the rains, grass, price of cows, and came at last to the recent holdup of the T. & P. Express.

'I don't reckon they passed through this town on their way to Crawford's Crossing,' Blake said, referring to the bandits.

Instantly the two old men moved shrilly into an argument that apparently had been threshed out more than once before.

'You reckon wrong, stranger,' one of them said hurriedly, plunging in to get the first word. 'They sure done just that. Not right spang through the town, though one came in to buy grub for them whilst the others waited in the scrub for him to come back.'

The old fellow shut his toothless mouth firmly and glared at his crony, challenging the expected denial.

His companion, even more ancient and wrinkled, promptly took up the cudgels. 'Nothin' to that, Giles. Nothin' a-tall. This Blake Forrest wouldn't be such a fool as that. Just because some danged brush-popper drapped in and bought a couple of plugs of chewing tobacco and some grub don't prove any such a thing. I been tellin' you that for weeks, but you always was an opinionated old vinegaroon.'

'Me, opinionated!' shrieked Giles bitterly. 'Why, anybody in this county will tell you that the most sot jackass in our midst is Hans Reincke. Nothing less than a stick of dynamite will get a notion outa yore head once it gets lodged there. Now listen to me, stranger. Billy Boss saw these birds in the brush right outside of town and they waved him round. Now why would they do that if they didn't want not to be seen?'

Hans shook a fist in the face of the other. 'You couldn't believe Billy Boss on a stack of Bibles. Why, that lunkhead came in to the store here once and told how —'

They were off. The quarrel raged violently for five minutes, then died down swiftly to friendly accord. There was no real heat in the epithets they had flung at each other. In a quarter of an hour both would have forgotten them. The recriminations were a routine expression of camaraderie devised to pep up life and make it more interesting.

Forrest learned that Billy Boss lived in the village and looked him up. He found him leaning against a sun-baked adobe wall strumming a guitar, his long lean legs stretched in front of him along the ground. He had a lank cadaverous face and lopsided brows that twitched above humorous eyes when he was amused. It was a fair guess that he took life easily. Three or four flaxen-haired children playing about the place appeared to be his offspring.

He waited until this stranger had explained what he wanted.

'You a sheriff or a ranger, Mr. Wood?' inquired Boss, picking a note or two on his guitar as he talked. 'Because if you are, anybody in this town will tell you not to believe a word I say. I'm the doggondest liar in Texas, I reckon.'

Once more Forrest trailed the bridle reins. He sat down beside Boss and rolled a cigarette. 'I like a good liar,' he said, smiling.

Billy Boss looked at him reproachfully. 'Jumping jackrabbits, fellow, don't you know a liar ain't got any character?'

'Depends on how, why, and when he lies,' the man in chaps told him as he lit up.

A barefoot little girl came out of the house. 'Paw, maw says for you to cut her some firewood if you want any supper tonight,' she said severely.

'Sure, Melissy. Tell yore maw I'll do that right soon.' The father of the family turned a tilted and erratic eyebrow toward his guest.

171

'Sounds mighty immoral to me, mister. Tell me more. A lie is born of the devil. Or else it ain't. Now which?'

Blake shook a warning finger at the man. 'You're not foolin' me a little bit, Billy Boss. I know all about your lying.'

'I'm plumb surprised,' Billy said. 'An' you never even met me till two minutes ago.'

'Sir Walter Scott was a good liar, if you want to call him that. I've read a heap of his romances. This fellow Mark Twain is another — and this Artemus Ward. You've got what book scholars call imagination. When you sit around the store swapping yarns you tell sure enough tall stories. You top the best the other fellow pulls. But when I ask you, straight out, whether you saw three-four men in the brush who waved you around the day of the train robbery I know I'll get the truth.'

The voice of Boss was lugubrious, but his eyes twinkled. 'That's no way to go around knocking a rep a fellow has spent a lifetime in building,' he complained. 'Well, dad gum it, I did see some men in the chaparral, and they waved me round. I was looking for one of my sows that had just had a litter of pigs.'

'Sure they waved you round?'

'Plumb sure. I didn't stop to ask them why. I vamoosed.'

'Would you know them again?'

'Might know one of them, the big fellow who was nearest to me. He rode a sorrel horse. And I'd know the one on the gray gelding that rode into town and brought grub for them.'

'He was with them when you jumped up the bunch?'

'Just leaving — heading for town.'

'Notice the other horses?'

'Not particularly. Hadn't time. Solid colors, I would guess. Roan or sorrel, say. Now, brother. Turn about is fair play. Where the heck do you come in on this?'

'I'm working on the case,' Blake said. 'You'll see me in court when they are trying that fellow Forrest.'

'Railroad detective, eh?'

A slim young woman, sun-bronzed, in a faded print dress came to the door and looked down at them. A satiric smile twitched at her mouth.

'If you're rested enough you might get that wood, Billy, if it's not interfering with more important business,' she said, amiably.

Blake came to his feet with one rhythmic motion and bowed. 'Afraid I've been detaining him, madam. He's been very impatient to get to work. I'll let him go now.'

The smile of Mrs. Boss became a broad grin.

'I don't see how you kept him from it so long, energetic as he is.'

The visitor swung to the saddle and took the road.

CHAPTER 17

Bill Crabb Saddles

Crabb limited his conversation to 'Pass the potatoes, please' and 'Another cup of coffee, ma'am.' He liked to talk, but he had been educated in the 'come-and-get-it' school of eating where a fellow had to stow away the grub *muy pronto* or run the risk of losing out to a bunch of hungry wolves ready to take advantage of any tenderfoot who opened his mouth for any other purpose except to put food in it. Moreover, he did not often get a chance to try such cooking as Mother Holloway served.

He was very much aware of the good-looking red-headed schoolmarm opposite him. She was certainly as good for the eyes as Mother Holloway's food was for the stomach. Miss Decker was flanked on the right by her younger sister Bess and on the left by her brother Phil. Both of them were in from the ranch for the day, Bill gathered. Just now the slim half-grown sister of Helen Decker was much in the public eye, since she had been snatched from death at the Funnel Creek train disaster a few days earlier. In another way Phil too was attracting some attention. He was wearing a bandage around his head. Compliments of Blake Forrest, thought Bill with an internal chuckle. He wanted to ask Phil innocently if a bronco had piled him, but it did not seem a good time to devil that short-tempered youth. Bill was in Deer Trail to dig up information and not to start trouble.

Most of the boarders were single men who lived at Deer Trail. One owned the wagon yard, two worked in the store, another freighted. Most of the conversation was manufactured for Helen Decker's ears, though not always addressed directly to her. Bill did not wonder at that. Life flowed richly in her supple body. Her face was quick with vitality. The cowboy would have been willing to bet his saddle against a dollar Mex that during the school term just ending several of those present had offered their names and worldly goods to the school-teacher.

Glancing round the table, he guessed that none of them would make the riffle. They were showing off, as small boys do, mostly by 'joshing' one another, but their repartee was a little feeble. It would not be fair to call them culls. They stacked up about the way other town lads did, but they were not quite in a class with the school-teacher, who was as full of fire as a thoroughbred colt.

From the talk Bill gathered that her school would be out next week and that after the final exercises she and her sister Bess were going to visit their friends the Kings at the Granite Gap ranch. From this another piece of news developed.

Someone lower down the table mentioned a name that stopped Bill's jaws abruptly.

'Buzz Waggoner found Stone Heath working for Curtis King and took him down to Fair Play with him,' a man mentioned. 'Stone admits he was with Blake Forrest when the T. & P. was robbed.'

'That ties it,' Phil Decker spoke up jubilantly, breaking a sulky silence that had endured most of the meal, due to the fact that he was still sensitive at the defeat Forrest had handed him and his allies. 'It's the penitentiary sure for Forrest now one of his gang has confessed.'

'What has he confessed, Phil?' asked Crabb, his good resolutions giving way to a more urgent impulse.

Young Decker stared at him hardily. He knew Crabb was a friend of Forrest. 'That he helped his no-'count friend rob the Express. Didn't you hear Jake?'

'I heard him,' Bill Crabb replied. 'But you got Stone wrong. He claims he was with Blake when the train was robbed, sixty odd miles away from Crawford's Crossing, along with three other witnesses.'

'How d'you know he claims that?' Decker demanded tartly.

'I expect that's what he says, because I am one of the other three,' Bill mentioned mildly.

Decker said, angrily, 'Looks like you're talking yourself into the pen too.'

'Be still, Phil,' his sister ordered.

'I don't have to be still,' her brother replied, voice and manner truculent. 'Everybody knows Crabb is thick as thieves with Forrest. Somebody had to help him do the stickup. If Heath and Crabb say they were with him that suits me fine.'

Mrs. Holloway interfered. 'I'm not going to have any trouble started at my table. If you want to quarrel please go outside and don't come back.'

'I'm a clam from right now,' Bill promised, 'except to say I'd like a piece of that apple pie circulating around, ma'am.'

'Coming up,' the owner of the wagon yard said, helping himself to a wedge of the pie.

'And to say,' added Crabb, 'that I'm not lookin' for any fuss and won't have a thing to do with one unless it's brought right to me and laid on my lap.'

'You didn't come to town then to finish the

job your friend started,' young Decker said sullenly.

The faded blue eyes of the freckled, redheaded cowboy held for an instant a flash of derision but the voice was almost apologetic in its amiability.

'Why, I haven't heard of Blake starting any job he couldn't finish, Phil. If you was to ask me I'd say his middle name is thorough.'

Somebody farther down the table snorted. Decker glared at the man, then pushed back his chair and got up. His sister Helen rose swiftly and followed him out of the room. There was a moment of awkward silence before Crabb suggested that if it didn't rain he reckoned they would have fair weather for awhile.

After dinner Helen Decker was waiting for Crabb at the door of the parlor. She asked him if he would come in for a minute. When he did so, she shut the door behind him.

Her tawny eyes fastened on his. 'Why did you come to Deer Trail?' she demanded, and he saw that anger was smoldering in her.

'Why, miss, to buy this and that. I been out in the brush quite a spell.'

'Well, get out of here — at once. There will be trouble if you don't. No friend of that crazy killer Forrest is welcome here. You ought to know that.'

'Blake isn't a crazy killer,' he denied. 'They attacked him, and he defended himself. About me being at Deer Trail, Miss Decker. I'm peaceable as a preacher — and it's a free country.'

'You won't find it so free. They'll put you in jail.'

Watching her, he knew that was the least of her worries. Back of her anger was fear. She was afraid her brother would stir up his friends to destroy him.

He lifted his shoulders in a shrug of acceptance. 'All right, miss. I'll go. I've done finished my business anyhow. Much obliged.'

'You needn't thank me.' The resentment in her low, husky voice was clear. 'I don't want Phil to get into trouble, that's all.'

He knew she was a fine high-spirited girl and that she was unhappy because her young brother had fallen among evil companions. She could not help being aware the Terrells were a bad lot, even though they were her relatives.

'I'll saddle and get right out,' he promised.

He walked down to the corral where he had left his horse. As he rode out of the gate he saw several men coming down the street. One of them called to him. He did not answer, but turned in the other direction and put his horse to a canter. Though not sure, the impression was strong in him that they were the Terrell crowd. He was getting away just in time.

CHAPTER 18

Blake Keeps a Promise

Bill Crabb could tell that Forrest had reached the rendezvous ahead of him. A thin drift of smoke from the brush informed him that preparations for supper were under way. Since Bill had not eaten for twelve hours this was good news.

But he did not give the yelp of a coyote, wait for an answer, and then ride forward to the camp. That would have been altogether too tame. He swung from the saddle, trailed the reins, took cover behind a clump of cholla. From this he slipped back of a mesquite and crept across the open on his stomach to some prickly pear. He was making a half circle of the camp, all the time drawing closer to it. His last shift was to a spot back of some twisted bushes.

Blake was seated by the fire, his back to Crabb, who was just about to rise and order the camper to throw up his hands when Forrest took the play away from him.

'There's a lunkhead cowpoke skulking back of a mesquite with a crazy idea that he can play at being a Comanche on the warpath,' the man beside the fire drawled without turning his head. 'If he doesn't come out reaching for the sky I'll sure begin pumping lead.'

Bill came out, hands up, wearing a shamefaced grin. 'How did you know I was there?' he wanted to know.

'I've been listening to you and watching you for ten minutes. Coarse work, Bill.'

'You couldn't be sure who it was.'

'I know how that thing you call your mind works, Bill.' Forrest did not think it necessary to explain that he had seen the approaching rider from a little hill before he started his Indian tactics.

Bill picketed his horse while his friend finished making supper. They exchanged news while they ate. Crabb told his story first.

'So nobody in Deer Trail saw anything of Webb Lake, Wes Terrell, or Pres Walsh on the twenty-second, twenty-third, or twenty-fourth,' Blake said.

'No, sir. Because they weren't there. The kid at the corral told me they left early Tuesday morning and didn't show up again till Friday.'

'But young Decker was at Deer Trail during all that time?'

'No doubt about it. If there were four of them they probably picked up someone else. Afraid to trust the kid, I reckon.'

'I'm glad he wasn't one of them. The little I know of him he ought not to be in their crowd, any more than we ought to have been in it three-four years ago. But if he sticks around with them long enough he'll sure go bad . . . What about the horses they rode?'

'Webb Lake was on a gray gelding.'

'That checks. He was still on it when he rode into Horse Creek.'

'Wes Terrell had a big bay with four white stockings and Pres Walsh rode a flea-bitten sorrel.'

'Did they leave word where they were going?'

'Yep. They were going after spike buck. Funny thing is they didn't get any. They had the doggondest luck. So they claimed to the kid at the corral. All they got was one wild boar, and they didn't bother to bring that back.'

'Fishy, with the chaparral full of game. I'd guess their minds were on higher things.'

'Even the kid thought it queer,' Bill said. 'Though of course he hadn't a ghost of an idea where they had been.'

'They did the T. & P. job, all right. We haven't enough proof to convict yet, but we have plenty to give the rangers a start on the trail that ought to finish with these birds collected at the end of it.'

'Fine,' agreed Bill ironically. 'Then when

you're all rounded up in the pen, after you've been convicted of the Valley Bank holdup, you can talk over old times together while you're breaking rocks.'

Blake smiled, with no enthusiasm. 'I certainly must have been crazy with the heat that day. My luck will sure have to stand up if I get out of that.'

Bill swallowed a mouthful of flapjack and glared at his friend. His disturbance expressed itself in annoyed protest. 'Jumpin' Jehosophat! What's the sense in talkin' about luck? You've got yourself sewed up in a sack so you can't move. A guy can bluff in a poker game, but not after he has shown his hand and flung it into the discard like you have done. Luck? Hmp! Think you can persuade the jury that old Jake Gildea has become a Christian and just naturally shoved back at you the mazuma he stole from your mother a dozen years ago? That old buzzard! Why, the jury would split its sides laughing. No, sir. You go to trial and you go to jail.'

Mournfully, to plague his companion, Blake intoned a snatch of one of his camp-meeting songs.

'See that brother dressed so gay,
The devil's going to come for to carry
    him away.'

'He sure is,' agreed Crabb vindictively. 'For twelve or fifteen years, Mr. Blake Forrest, and maybe one off for good behavior.'

'And your suggestion, my cheerful and comforting friend?'

'Lemme go in and make talk with Buzz while you stick around in the brush. If things don't look good — and we know blamed well they won't — I'll report and you can light out for Wyoming or somewheres north and west of there.'

'Thought I'd mentioned to you that I had promised Buzz to come back,' Blake said carelessly.

'Sure, but no use being pernickety. Buzz is a good guy. Once you were Johnny-on-the-spot when he needed help. Now it's his turn. He'll understand. I'll fix it up with him.'

'I've already fixed it with him — promised to be back inside of two weeks.'

'Yeah, but — nobody knows he gave you the file. It won't hurt him any if you don't show up.'

Forrest shook his head. 'Nothing doing, Bill. Call it stubbornness if you like, but I'm going back.'

'Hell's bells! You don't *want* to go to jail, do you? Who ever heard of a fellow walking back and asking them to put the cuffs on him?

Of all the cussed jackasses I ever met up with —'

'I take the cake,' Blake finished for him. 'Let her ride at that, Bill. Just darned fool.'

Crabb desisted from his objections. He not only knew when he was beaten but was at heart not sorry for it. He would have been disappointed if his friend had followed his advice and run away. One of the things you liked about Blake Forrest was that you could tie to him. He would go through.

None the less the cowboy was unhappy. His gloom was still with him in the morning when they set out for Fair Play. Blake was in good spirits. He laughed and chatted, told stories, even sang, as they rode through the pleasant sunshine. Bill had noticed before that when things were not turning out well for Blake a queer reckless gaiety cropped out. He had a natural zest for danger.

Bill did not share his cheerfulness. In a few hours Blake would be behind the bars and he would never be free another moment for a great many years. At times Forrest was an enigma to the red-headed rider. The outlaw was a cool customer, a seasoned man, close-mouthed, sure of himself, entirely dependable. Then something would blaze up in him, and all his poised steadiness would be tossed aside in an instant of wild impulse. That was how he had come to hold up Gildea, but you could not explain to a jury, and get away with it, that Blake had not taken the money because he wanted to steal it or cared anything about it for itself, but only because at the moment it had seemed to him right to make that old scalawag give up the funds he had taken crookedly from two defenceless women.

'Buck up, Bill,' Forrest told him as they looked down on the smoke rising from Fair Play's huddled houses. 'One of these poet guys once said that stone walls don't make a prison nor iron bars a cage.'

'Hmp! How long did he ever break rocks in a pen?'

'I'm not breaking any yet. We'll cross our bridges one at a time. First, this train robbery. It will be a pleasure for me to hand that over to the Terrells to explain. As for the Valley Bank business, I've been in worse jams and came out all right.'

They rode along the main street to the courthouse and tied at the hitch rack in front of it. Half a minute later they opened a door and walked into the office of the sheriff.

CHAPTER 19

Blake Makes Oration About Luck

Buzz Waggoner took a black cigar from his mouth and stared at his returned prisoner.

'You're a couple of days ahead of time,' he said at last.

'Don't tell me I'm not welcome,' Forrest begged. 'Don't tell me to leave and never darken your door again.'

The little eyes of the sheriff almost disappeared in his smile. 'No, sir. I aim to make you feel right at home. I wouldn't refuse you the shelter of my roof.'

'Me too?' inquired Crabb. 'I'm one of these here prodigals too.'

'Maybe you too. I'll have to look into that.' Waggoner got up from his chair and shuffled forward to shake hands with Forrest. 'I hope things worked out for you, Blake. They been kinda ridin' my tail because I was so careless as to let you escape. I couldn't explain you were coming back.'

'Were you right sure I would?' asked Forrest.

The sheriff ran a fat hand through his hair

to help him explain more clearly. 'Well, I'll tell you about that,' he confessed. 'Most of the time I knew you'd be back, but once in a while I'd kick myself for being a darned fool and figure you wouldn't.'

'Anyhow, I'm here,' Blake drawled. 'Get out your handcuffs.'

'To Mexico with the handcuffs. Sit down. Both of you. Tell me about it. All I know about you since you left is that you went over to Deer Trail and 'most took the town apart one night.'

'Only thing about that is that I was leaving there in a hurry and bumped into three-four fellows who got in my way,' explained Forrest, helping himself to a chair.

'I had a talk with Craig Shannon yesterday. He told me how it was. You were lucky.'

'Not half as lucky as the Terrell gang,' Crabb amended. 'He might have rubbed out the whole mess of them.'

The disappearing little eyes of the sheriff twinkled. He liked the valiant doggedness with which Forrest's friends defended him.

'I meant he was lucky having a witness like Shannon present when the fireworks began,' Buzz explained. 'Hadn't been for that these miscreants could have got away with their story that he fired on them from cover and

190

started the rumpus.'

'Of course I was lucky,' Blake said. 'All the way through. In having a fine straight man like Shannon for a witness. In not getting loaded with lead while I was hightailing it over the fences or ducking around in the wagon yard. If I hadn't had every break in the world they would have fixed my clock.'

Bill stuck to his guns. 'They didn't get a break, did they? Four wounded, and nary a one planted in Boot Hill.'

'Did you round up those witnesses you went after?' asked Waggoner.

'I'm going to have to do a lot of talking,' Blake said. 'No use doing it several times. Bring in my lawyer Judge Vallery, that ranger Steve Porter, the district attorney, and my old sidekick Stone Heath, if he is still your guest, and we'll get it all over with in one pow-wow. Does that sound reasonable?'

'I would say so.' The sheriff grinned at him. 'I reckon, if you're telling the story of your wonderful adventures you'll forget where you got that file.'

'I have already forgotten. Before you start rounding up the audience, why not put us in the same cell as Stone Heath? We've got a few things to talk over.'

'Suits me.' He added, after a moment of hesitation: 'What the hell! You can all stay right here in the office if you like.'

Blake shook his head. 'No, sir. Wouldn't look good for you, Buzz. We've got to think of Ranger Steve Porter's feelings. When you get him here bring us all out of a cell. Kind of surprise him.'

'I'll surprise them all,' Waggoner beamed. He was pleased as Punch to have his prisoner with him again. It justified him against the criticism that had been going the rounds.

Stone Heath, very bored at reading the advertisements of a country newspaper for the third time, heard footsteps in the corridor and looked up to see who was coming. He let out a joyous 'Hi-yippi-yi!' at sight of his friends, but cut it short when it occurred to him that they had been arrested and brought in as prisoners.

Waggoner left them together. He was gone about an hour before he came back and unlocked the door.

'Everybody present,' he grinned, 'but I haven't told them whyfor they are here.'

He marshaled his prisoners into the office, bringing up the rear himself. 'Thought we'd have a little get-together meeting, boys,' he said.

Porter leaped to his feet excitedly. 'When did you capture Forrest?' he cried.

'I didn't capture him,' the sheriff answered.

'He just drapped in because he heard he was wanted. Gents, this is Blake's party. Seems he wants to make oration. If agreeable to everybody, we'll sit in and listen.'

The ranger moved his chair to the door and sat down there. Though he was puzzled and did not understand the situation, he had no intention of being caught napping again by some clever trick of the outlaw.

'I'll be very glad to listen to anything Mr. Forrest has to say,' the district attorney assented non-committally.

'It's a long story,' the accused man began. 'Perhaps I had better begin with the day I came into Sampson & Doan's store and first met Ranger Porter. Surprising as it may seem, I didn't know until I read the poster there that I was accused of robbing the Texas & Pacific train. The news did not greatly disturb me, because I knew I had four witnesses who could testify I was at a cow camp of the Circle Three B, seventy-five miles or so from Crawford's Crossing, at the very hour the train was being robbed.'

'Interesting if true,' commented Robinson, the district attorney.

'Interesting *and* true,' Blake said, smiling at him. 'Crabb and Heath were with me. We spent the night with two line riders of the Circle Three B. They are on their way to town now, and I am sure will be glad to answer questions.'

'Were they with you at the time the Valley Bank was robbed?' asked Porter acidly.

'We won't take up the Valley Bank matter today. I'm discussing the train holdup now. It is not possible I could have been at Crawford's Crossing then, because I have a copper-riveted alibi.'

'You were recognized by the express messenger,' Robinson reminded him.

'So I was,' Forrest agreed. 'That's important. I don't want you to forget that.'

Porter was not satisfied with the way things were going. 'If you didn't rob the T. & P. Express, who did?' the ranger said, flushing with resentment. 'You can't tell me you don't know anything about it.'

The answer of Forrest surprised greatly four of the men present.

'I know a lot about it,' he drawled coolly.

Vallery shot his cuffs nervously. He was afraid his client was about to make a serious mistake.

'What do you know about it, if you weren't implicated?' demanded Porter.

'I know who did do it.'

They stared at him in astonishment.

'Hadn't a thing to do with holding up the train, but you know the guilty parties,' jeered the ranger. 'That it?'

'That's it exactly.' Blake smiled pleasantly at young Porter. 'I thought somebody ought to be running down the miscreants, and since nobody else seemed to be concerned I broke jail and got busy myself.'

'But by Judas Priest,' broke in Vallery, 'do you mean to tell us that you actually have gathered evidence connecting other parties with this crime?'

'That is what I am trying to tell you,' Blake said placidly.

'And that you weren't in on it — had nothing to do with it?' Steve Porter insisted sceptically.

'No more than you had.'

'I don't believe a word of it,' the young ranger snapped.

'You will,' Stone Heath told him. 'And you'll thank Blake for putting you on the right track after you had bogged down.'

'Maybe it would be a good idea to listen to what Mr. Forrest has to tell us,' Vallery suggested. 'He seems to know more about this than we do.'

'A lot more,' Porter slipped in.

'After breaking jail I went to Deer Trail to find where my witnesses were,' Forrest explained. 'While I was talking with Craig Shannon I was attacked by Wes Terrell and his friends.'

'Not the way I read the story,' the ranger interrupted.

Buzz Waggoner offered confirmation of the prisoner's story. 'Blake is telling us the right of it,' he said. 'Craig Shannon told me yesterday, and whatever Craig says is so. Wes Terrell came up and recognized Forrest. He yelled for his friends to come and rub him out. They came running — Webb Lake and Pres Walsh and young Phil Decker. When they began pouring lead at Blake he lit out. They chased him to the wagon yard where they had the fight.'

'That the way of it, Forrest?' the district attorney asked.

'Yes, sir. I didn't answer their fire because I had to get out of there in a hurry. After they had me trapped in the wagon yard it was different. I knew I had to fight or be killed. *They did not want to arrest me.*'

Robinson slanted an inquiring look at the outlaw, in it curiosity blended with admiration. 'You must have had your hands full — four against one,' he said.

'I had luck,' Blake said simply. 'It was dark, and I was hidden among the wagons. They had to dig me out. I had a crack at Walsh first and slammed his head against a wagon wheel. Then Lake helped me out. He and Ter-

196

rell came on each other in the dark and didn't wait to find out they were friends. They blazed away, and Terrell went down. A moment later Lake saw me. He missed, but I hit his arm. That left only Decker. I played I was Walsh, got close, and pistol-whipped him. I lit out. My luck had certainly stood up.'

Stone Heath grinned at Forrest derisively. "You see, gentlemen, what it is to be lucky. That's all you need. A kid from school could have done it, with luck. All he had to do was to put out four bully-puss gunfighters yelping for his hide. Only four, not a dozen or two. I wish I was lucky like that.'

'Quit joshing, Stone,' his friend told him. 'If it had been light I would have turned my toes up to the daisies . . . Well, I rode over the hill and vamoosed. After I got to thinking it over, I sorted out two here and two there, and it seemed to add up to four. Why this sudden energy to wipe me out? They are enemies of mine, to be sure, but they have had several chances to start fogging during the past two years and haven't taken them. Why now?'

'A thousand dollars reward,' the ranger mentioned.

'So there is, and that might be the reason. But another one kept sticking in my mind. I was accused by Ray Terrell of leading the Texas & Pacific bandits. It would be good business to have me out of the way before I could prove myself innocent, if for private reasons of their own they did not want any more dust raised about the matter.'

'What private reasons?' asked Vallery, puzzled.

'Ray Terrell, express messenger on the train that was robbed, said he saw me with my mask off during the holdup. That wasn't true. He might just be trying to pay off the debt owing me because I shot down his brother Buck in self-defence. *Or maybe it was important for him and his friends to have suspicion directed elsewhere.* This looked to me like an inside job. How did the bandits know there was a big money shipment on board that day? They knew the payroll would be along soon. But on just what train? The express messenger would know. Maybe he wired them, after it was put on board, from some point up the line.'

'Wired them where?' Robinson asked.

'To some depot near Crawford's Crossing. My guess was Horse Creek, because I was going on the hunch that the Terrells did the job, and if they did they could stop there on the way from Deer Trail to the Crossing without going far out of their way. So I drifted in to the depot at Horse Creek and found out a telegram was sent from Santone on the twenty-third, the day of the robbery, to a Sam Jones, saying a baby was being sent on the Express that day, account of scarlet fever being in the neighborhood. Mr. Jones came in to get the telegram, but he didn't come back later after the baby, and there wasn't any baby on the train for him anyhow. The baby was the gold shipment.'

'By Judas Priest, I'll bet you are right,' Vallery cried.

The ranger stared at Forrest, doubt and admiration struggling in his face with chagrin. The idea of the telegram was reasonable. Why had he not thought of it himself? Yet there was no reason why he should. Lieutenant Bronson had been on this case and evidently had taken the word of the express messenger Terrell, since there had been no cause to suppose the man was not telling the truth. Forrest had just held up a bank. What more likely than that he and his gang would follow up by robbing a train? And maybe he had. Possibly his alibi was framed. It would not be hard to get some of his friends to swear to one. All four of his witnesses might be in the stickup as deeply as this man Forrest.

'Who was this man Sam Jones?' the ranger asked.

The prisoner directed his gaze at Porter. 'I don't know, but I can guess. He was described to me by four-five people at Horse Creek who saw him, and the description fits Webb Lake. He was riding a gray horse. So was Lake when he left Deer Trail the morning of the twenty-second.'

'You checked up on Lake?' Porter asked, suspicion still riding high in him.

Forrest turned to Crabb. 'Say your piece, Bill,' he drawled.

'Lake left Deer Trail at daybreak the morning of the twenty-second, along with Wes Terrell and Pres Walsh. They didn't show up again till Friday. I got that from Homer Burson, a kid who works at the corral where they keep their horses. Told him they were going hunting, but when they showed up they had no game with them and their horses had been ridden hard. Like Blake says, Lake was on a fly-bitten gray gelding. Wes rode a big bay with four white stockings. Pres Walsh had a round-bellied sorrel. The kid pointed the mounts out to me.' Crabb finished explosively: 'They're guilty as hell.'

'I think so,' Forrest agreed quietly. 'Inquire at the Horse Creek depot for a girl named Willie Fulwiler. She can tell you about Jones and the telegram. The man bought supplies at the store. He was seen by another man called Billy Boss. When Jones went into town to get the telegram he left three friends in the brush outside of town. This man Boss was looking for one of his hogs and bumped into them. They waved him round. His description of the horses fits the ones the Terrell gang were riding.'

Young Porter kept his eyes fixed on Forrest. He did not know whether these men were telling the truth or not. The prisoner had fooled him once. He did not forget that. The ranger wished he had had more experience in judging men. It would not do to let his admiration for this intrepid scamp get the better of his judgment. A man could have a winning smile and still be a villain. Robinson and Waggoner seemed to believe his story. But you could not put trust in a fellow notorious as a killer and known beyond question to have robbed a bank.

'It works out right neat, doesn't it?' he scoffed. 'These Terrells are your enemies. They claim you held up the train. When it's your turn you pass the buck back to them. I don't know any of these witnesses you have. Maybe you're all in it, each one alibi-ing the others.'

Blake showed no resentment. The white teeth flashed against the brown face in an amiable smile. 'Take it or leave it, Porter. Opportunity is like a bald-headed man with a beard, I've heard. You can catch him coming but not going. Maybe I'm offering you a chance to make a name for yourself. Maybe it is just a fairy tale. *Quien sabe?* If you are too busy to bother with it I reckon Buzz may want to take a crack at it. His political career won't be hurt any by digging up evidence to convict these train robbers.'

'Not none,' agreed the sheriff.

'I didn't say I wouldn't look into this,' the ranger said quickly, 'only I don't have to believe everything you say, not after the way you ran out on me once.'

The prosecuting attorney spoke. 'After we have talked with these Circle Three B riders we'll know whether Forrest's alibi stands up. Personally, I think it will. Why should he pull a windy on us when he knows it wouldn't stick? Morris of the Circle Three B will know if these line riders were off the job two or three days. Besides, I'm willing to believe the Terrells would do a job like this. If you don't report this to Lieutenant Bronson you may be making a serious mistake, Ranger Porter.'

Steve Porter flushed. He was boy enough to resent advice from an outsider. 'I'm going to report it,' he said huffily. 'But I'm going to insist Sheriff Waggoner keep Forrest here. In any case there is another charge against him.'

'So there is,' Blake said. 'Keep me well locked up, Buzz . . . Oh, one thing more, gentlemen. Too many of us know about the evidence against the Terrells. We'll have to be clams, to give Mr. Porter a fair chance to investigate without the suspected men getting notice of what is being done. If there is a leak among us it may be harder to get the necessary evidence.'

'As well as give them a chance to pull their freights for points north, south, east, or west,' Stone Heath added.

'If there is any talking done it won't be by the rangers,' Porter said.

The others too pledged themselves to silence.

CHAPTER 20

Curtis King Suggests

Janet followed her father into the little room he called his office. He sat down in the big armchair back of the table that served as a desk. Uncertainly, she looked down at him.

'Something on your mind, daughter?' he asked.

'I'd like to go down to Fair Play with you tomorrow, Father,' she said. 'I have some shopping to do, and we can pick up Helen and Bess there and bring them back with us.' She suggested the plan diffidently, her blue eyes doubtful how he would take it.

'Hmp! So you have some shopping to do.'

'Yes. You know Aunt Maud and Uncle Henry have been wanting me to pay them a visit. I promised long ago I would.'

'And if you were staying at the Vallerys you would hear all about how the trial was going, wouldn't you? I reckon you would attend some of the sessions.'

'I expect so. I'd like to go.'

He looked at her a long time without answering. It was characteristic of his forthright daughter, he thought, not to try to disguise her great interest in the outcome of the trial. Standing there, slender and straight, she was a lovely young thing. The small throat carried the fine erect head like the stem of a rose.

'Sit down, Janet,' he said. 'I want to talk with you.'

She drew up a chair and sat down.

The cattleman frowned at his daughter, not sure how to begin. If his wife had been still alive he would have turned this talk over to her, knowing that she would handle it with a mother's tact. Curtis King was a forceful individualist. He had made his way in a rough country by sheer force of character. But he knew very little of what was going on inside this girl's head.

'Texas has been a battlefield for fifty years, Janet,' he said. 'You know all about how we fought the Mexicans first and then the Comanches. After we had them both whipped came the Civil War. When we got that out of the way we found the state was a happy hunting ground for 'most all the desperadoes in the country. Seems like they all piled into Texas. The rangers helped and are still helping to mop them up, but decent citizens had to lend a hand too. Fact is, Janet, the cattle steals got so big we had to fight or go bust. It was neck meat or nothing with us. If we didn't win the thieves would. There wasn't any law to aid us. Well, we were hard and thorough — did things you couldn't justify in an old settled country.'

'I know, Father,' the girl said. 'I've heard about the horse and cattle thieves.' She wondered where this was leading.

'Remember, daughter, that though there was no law except the one we carried on our hips, there always was a clear line between those who were good citizens and those who were ruffians and scalawags. We wanted to build up West Texas and make it safe for women and children. They wanted it to stay a refuge for bandits. We wanted schoolhouses and churches and law and order. They stood for the six-shooter and rustlings and wild towns filled with human parasites contributing nothing to the welfare of the community.'

'Yes, Father,' she said meekly, and then spoiled it by grinning.

He pulled up to ask what she was laughing at.

'I didn't know you could be so eloquent,' she explained. 'Congressman Sanderson is nothing to you.'

'Too much oration,' he agreed. 'Well, I'll talk turkey.'

'And I'll listen,' Janet promised.

'About this Blake Forrest,' he went on,

leaning back in the big chair. 'I've never met him, but lately I've heard plenty. Quite a man, they say. One of those wild reckless devils that people like. A good cowhand — top rider — game as they come — makes friends and stands by them to the finish. But never forget that he has gone bad. He's a killer and he's a thief.'

'I wish you had talked to Stone Heath about him,' Janet said.

He shook his head. 'Wouldn't make any difference. You can't change facts. Heath is his friend. What Forrest does may seem right to him but not to us. Heath is wild himself. He makes excuses, but the man's record is there. Forrest has been a turbulent fellow. Where there is so much smoke there must be a lot of fire.'

'He never killed anybody except in self-defence, Stone Heath says.'

'I've heard another story. In any case, he robbed the Valley Bank. There's no doubt of that.'

Janet repeated the tale she had been told by Heath as to the reason for the robbery.

Again the cowman shook his head firmly. 'Excuses, Janet. I'll not deny I have some sympathy with Forrest, but laws are made to be obeyed.' There was a deep and searching inquiry in the steely eyes fastened on the girl.

'This fellow may be the kind that women like. I don't know. But I can't have my daughter interested in a scalawag like that.'

'Ought I just to turn my back on him, since he got into trouble on account of me?' she asked, standing to her guns, eyes unwavering.

'He didn't get into trouble on account of you. He got into trouble because he robbed a bank.'

'Anyway, he did me a service. I don't want him to think I'm ungrateful — that I haven't any interest at all in what becomes of him. I don't expect ever to speak with him again, but I need not act as if he were poison. It can't hurt me if he is wild — even if he has gone bad as you say.'

'No. Not if you keep your head and don't —'

He did not finish the sentence.

'Aren't you making too much of this, Father?' Janet said, a flag of pink flying beneath the brown of her cheeks. 'I'm not infatuated with the man, if that's what you mean. I wouldn't marry such a man if he was the last one in the world. I'm not crazy, you know.'

Curtis King was relieved, and at the same time a little ashamed.

'I have to be father and mother both now,' he told her, and his wistful smile was an apology. 'I reckon I'm too blunt, daughter. Your mother would have known how to handle this. All I was thinking is that I'd rather see you dead than married to a scoundrel who would ruin your life. But I ought to have known you better. You have as much good common sense as anyone I know. Fact is, I got to worrying, since I could see you had this scamp on your mind. Naturally you would have, seeing it was on account of you he got trapped in the first place . . . Yes, if you want to go down to Fair Play tomorrow I haven't any objections.'

Janet was a truthful girl, and she had some small qualms of conscience for what she had told her father. It had been the truth, but a little less than the whole truth. She would not consider marrying a man like Forrest, one who went his reckless way regardless of law. A sinner of his type, reckless and debonair and generous, might be a fascinating person to know, but he would be no safe husband for a woman who valued her happiness.

None the less her thoughts had a way of recurring to him whenever the pressure of immediate duties was lifted. There was something clean and big about him. She wondered as to his life — his background — the women he had known. Of course he was a man's man, but her own sex must have played a part in his life. She found herself jealous of those unknown women who marched past her in shadowy procession out of the dead years. No doubt he had been wild and taken his pleasures where he found them. All the carefree riders she had known crossed the railroad track to 'Hell's Half Acre' when they went to town. She had gathered this from snatches of their crisp crackling talk not intended for her ears.

Janet resented her weakness. She had been brought up in the narrow tradition that no nice girl ever gave a man a second thought until he had shown his preference for her, and that then she held him coyly in suspense until he had wooed her a suitable time. Now her mind was full of a man who not only did not want her but was in every way unsuitable. She must be a brazen creature, and such a fool about it that Stone Heath and her father had both guessed her secret.

The first man they met on the main street of Fair Play after they had stepped out of the surrey was Stone Heath.

'Thought you were staying at Buzz Waggoner's hotel,' Curtis King said.

'I was, but Buzz wouldn't have me for a boarder any longer.' The cowboy dragged his words, lazily. 'Seems I didn't hold up any train.'

'Do they know who did?'

Heath's face was a blank wall. 'I wouldn't know about that. I haven't heard of anybody being arrested. Except Blake Forrest.'

'He's still in jail of course.'

'Sure. His trial begins today — for the Valley Bank business.' Heath's gaze had picked up some men coming down the street toward them. All the amiable friendliness vanished from his eyes. They grew hard and cold.

Janet wondered. Her glance followed his to the four men straddling along the sidewalk. Three of them she did not know. The fourth was Phil Decker, a brother of her friend Helen. The Deckers had been close friends of their family for generations. The others were all older than he. They were hard-looking characters. One of them wore his arm in a sling.

Curtis King spoke to them. 'Good morning, boys,' he said. 'In town for the trial, I reckon. There will be quite a gathering.'

'We're here as witnesses,' Wes Terrell said, lifting his hat to the young woman. 'Aiming to help send that scoundrel Forrest to the pen.' He spoke to the owner of the Granite Gap ranch, but the gloating triumph was addressed to Heath.

'I don't wonder you don't like him,' Heath said with cool hardihood, 'after the way he has showed you-all up three or four times.'

'That'll be enough from you,' Pres Walsh cried angrily.

'Enough from all of you,' King ordered curtly. 'I'm surprised you don't know better with ladies present.'

Curtis King was a big man in West Texas, the owner of two large ranches with thirty thousand cattle and forceful as an individual. He had the habit of command and none of them cared to dispute it.

'We didn't mean to start anything,' Phil Decker said. 'Better move on, boys. See you later.'

He stopped to talk with the Kings. 'I'm expecting Helen and Bess in two-three days,' he explained. 'Helen's school closed Friday. She is right tired of teaching reading and arithmetic, and I expect she will enjoy being with you-all up at the Granite Gap for a while. Bess too. She hasn't been any too peart since the train wreck. It sure took the tuck out of her, though she's acting more like herself now.'

'We'll take care of her at the Granite Gap,' the ranchman promised. He was very fond of Bess Decker. She had lived with them for two years after the death of her mother ten years earlier. Her father was a boyhood chum.

'Soon as they get to town let us know,' Janet said. 'We'll be at the Vallerys'.'

The lawyer and his wife were very pleased to see their guest. They did not often have young people at the house and the good spirits of youth cheered them. Curtis stayed at the hotel.

After supper Janet made a chance to see the lawyer alone.

'Uncle Henry,' she began with no circumlocution, 'I want you to carry a note from me to Mr. Forrest.'

'Now look here, miss,' he retorted promptly, 'I quit playing Cupid a right long time ago. If you want any notes carried you get Curt to take them.'

Her grin was a mixture of cajolery and impudence. 'No, sir. You're going to take the note your own self. I've written it. Here it is. You can read it.'

'I don't want to read any of your love letters,' he said, waving it aside.

The girl's color deepened. 'Don't be silly, Uncle Henry. It's not a love letter. You know that very well. It's just a little message hoping that he will be acquitted. Read it. See if it isn't perfectly proper.'

'I don't care how proper it is,' he exploded, shooting the cuffs of both sleeves nervously. 'Point is, it isn't wise. Suppose this got out and folks talked. Don't forget that this man is a criminal and is going to the penitentiary for a long stretch of years.'

'How could it get out? Is Mr. Forrest the

sort of man who would . . . boast about it?'

'No. Still —'

She folded her hands and looked demure. 'I'm a young lady and I ought to think of appearances. For young ladies must be very very circumspect. Isn't that the word? He might misunderstand and think that I was very forward, a brazen young hussy.'

'That will do, young lady. I'll look at the note.'

While he was reading it, Janet made comment. 'We can't all be wrapped in cotton and laid away in moth balls until we are married, Uncle Henry. We're human, and when somebody does us a great kindness we have to show appreciation, even if the someone happens to be a young man.'

'I suppose if I don't take this note you'll get it to him some other way,' Vallery said, looking at her severely over his spectacles.

'Of course,' she said sweetly. 'But I know you are going to take it.'

He snorted. 'All right. I'll see he gets it, but I won't bring you back an answer.'

'There won't be any answer,' she said.

Having come to know Forrest pretty well, his lawyer reflected that she was probably right. The outlaw would not compromise her by so much as a sign of recognition.

Vallery had been a lawyer too many years

not to know that law and justice do not always walk hand in hand. Perhaps Blake Forrest ought to be shut up away from his fellow men. He had trod his own wild adventurous way, and it had led him into violence and lawlessness. Maybe he had 'gone bad,' to use the expressive phrase of the West, yet there was still a rather splendid loyalty and generosity in him. Did these belong behind the gray walls of a prison? If so, what about Jake Gildea? He was a mean, sly, ruthless scoundrel — and the leading citizen in his community. A queer twisted world, this.

CHAPTER 21

Forrest Says He Is Much Obliged

'Someone to see you, Blake,' Buzz said, and stood aside to let the visitor enter the cell. 'Meet Colonel King of the Granite Gap ranch.'

Forrest rose from the cot where he had been lying and shook hands with a strongly built, broad-shouldered Westerner who had cattleman written all over his face, bearing, and clothes. He was wearing a coat as a concession to the fact that he was in town, but it had fallen into wrinkled folds that might have been a contour map of a neighboring desert cut into draws and vegas by the erosion of wind and rain.

The prisoner offered his guest the only chair and sat down himself on the cot. His manner was courteous but reserved. The object of this call was not clear to him, and he waited for King to explain.

Of the two Curtis King was the embarrassed one. 'I've been talking to a good friend of yours, Mr. Forrest, a young fellow who is riding for me,' he said. 'You know who I mean, Stone Heath.'

'I know him very well. A top rider — good man in every way — entirely trustworthy.'

'He hasn't been with me long, but I have no complaint.' King threw away that opening and came bluntly to one nearer his heart. 'Fact is, sir, I'm greatly indebted to you for your kindness to my daughter when you found her lost.'

Blake had in his vest pocket a note from the young lady, but he did not mention that. It was a pleasant, harmless message, but he intended to destroy it before he was taken from his cell to the courtroom.

He waved the cattleman's thanks aside. 'I couldn't have done less, Colonel. You know that. She couldn't have met anybody who wouldn't have done as much.'

"That does not relieve me of my obligation, sir. If there is anything I can do for you — no matter what it is — I want you to call on me.'

The man on the cot shook his head. 'Can't think of a thing you can do, but I appreciate the offer.'

'Not short of funds, are you?' King blurted out. 'Trials cost money. Glad to make you a loan.'

'I'm obliged to you, sir,' Forrest answered, 'but I have drawn on my bank for a sum sufficient for my needs.' His smile was cynical. He might almost have said in so many words that Jake Gildea was paying the expenses.

The owner of the Granite Gap had a sense of frustration. He had come because he wanted to pay an installment on the debt he owed this man. If he could do this his daughter would feel less unhappy about it. But Forrest did not meet him halfway. There was a cool hardihood about his attitude toward his plight, a manner of indifference almost insolent, that would do him no good with the jury. None the less King persisted in finishing what he had come to say.

'I have another ranch in the Big Bend country.' he said. 'In case you are acquitted you might like to leave this section and make a fresh start. I can always use a top rider.'

'Sorry,' Forrest replied. 'Don't think I'll be able to accept that offer, sir. I expect to take a job to work for the state of Texas.'

'Haven't you any defence?'

'The best witness I have is old Jake Gildea. He won't say anything for me, but when the jury gets a good look at him they may vote not guilty on general principles.'

'You've given up, then. Are you going to plead guilty?'

'Why, no.' Forrest looked at him in mock surprise. 'There's no guilt in taking from that old skunk what belongs to me and doesn't belong to him.'

'The law —'

'Yes, I know about that,' the accused man interrupted. 'The cards are stacked for scoundrels like Gildea. When he robs widows it's a financial transaction. When I make him shell out his blood money it's bank robbery.'

'We can't make our own laws,' the older man said gravely. 'Not individually. We all have to abide by the group laws that our representatives make.'

'I've heard you made yours, Mr. King, in the days when the rustlers were pulling off the big steel in this country.'

'That was before law and order had come to the frontier.'

'I see.' Again Forrest's cynical smile flashed. 'But now they are here — and Gildea can pull off his crooked stuff with full protection.'

King understood that the prisoner realized he would be convicted and would stand up to his sentence without batting an eye. The ranchman was of the old fighting West himself, and he held to the view that it is what a man is and not what he has done that counts. He had seen a horse thief go into a burning house to save a child, with the chance of ever coming out alive nearly negligible, while a score of respectable citizens stood back daunted by the danger. Looking now into the hard reckless face of Forrest, he felt it was not an evil one. But he had not subdued himself to the discipline of the new era, and he would have to pay the price.

The cattleman rose. 'If there is anything I can do for you — now or later — I hope you'll feel free to call on me,' he said.

Forrest thanked him and said that he would.

The cattleman found Vallery in his office. The lawyer would be a very busy man for a few days during the court session. He had four or five cases coming up for trial.

'I've been to see that man Forrest, Henry,' the rancher told his friend. 'Looks to me like he hasn't a chance.'

'Not a chance, Curtis,' admitted Vallery, leaning back in his chair and stretching his arms in a characteristic nervous gesture. 'All I can do is get extenuating circumstances into the record, and I'm not even sure I can do that.'

'What does Robinson mean by bringing this riffraff from Deer Trail to testify against Forrest? I mean that Terrell crowd. The fight in the wagon yard had nothing to do with the bank robbery.'

With a mysterious smile Vallery explained. 'They think they are here as witnesses against

Forrest, but they are not. A little surprise for them.'

King did not know what he meant, but asked no questions.

CHAPTER 22

Bess Recognizes a Face

The case of the State of Texas *vs.* Blake Forrest opened next morning, but Janet and Mrs. Vallery did not attend the trial until the afternoon. The defendant's lawyer had told them the morning would be occupied in selecting a jury and in the opening statements of the lawyers. Since Janet did not want to seem too eager she punished herself by staying away from the first session. On the way to the courthouse they met Phil Decker and his sisters. Helen and Bess joined Mrs. Vallery's party.

Though the room was crowded, some men rose to give the ladies seats. Judge Jackman entered a moment later, and almost immediately afterward Buzz Waggoner brought in the prisoner.

The eyes of all present turned toward Blake Forrest and followed him down the aisle. At sight of the strong brown sardonic face, of the compact graceful body moving with such lithe and indolent ease, Janet felt hot emotion hammering through her veins. She thought he looked as little like a criminal as any man she had ever seen. He had not made the mistake of changing to store clothes, and as his cool gaze swept the room he seemed a very prince of vagabonds. Her mind flashed back to the hour when she had last seen him, when she had wished him luck and told him she was afraid he would need it. He needed it now, if ever a man did. But nothing in his bearing or his manner suggested this.

Helen Decker became aware that her sister was whispering to her, in a voice flooded with emotion.

'He's the man who saved me from drowning,' Bess was saying urgently.

The elder sister stared at the girl. 'Who is? Somebody here in the courtroom?'

'The man who just came in with Mr. Waggoner.' Bess added, swiftly: 'Can we ask somebody who he is?'

'I know who he is,' Helen answered. 'If you mean the man sitting down with Uncle Henry. But are you sure?'

'Of course I'm sure. How could I be mistaken? Who is he?'

'He's the prisoner — Blake Forrest.' Helen turned, all excitement, and whispered the news to Janet.

The heart of that young woman sang a wild tumultuous song of praise. He was, after all, a man among ten thousand, one of whom she could be proud.

'I knew he wasn't vile,' she told herself happily. 'How could he be and look like that? I knew he was good and brave and — splendid.'

'He can't be a bank robber, and I don't care if he is,' Bess murmured excitedly. 'I've got to thank him for saving me.'

Janet did not answer at once. She was thinking — swift, urgent, fugitive thoughts. They could not take him to prison — not now — the hero everybody in the county was praising — the man who had saved four lives from the flood and vanished unknown. She must see her father — and Uncle Henry. They would do something about it. They must.

She whispered to Mrs. Vallery. 'Something has come up — very important. I must see my father and Uncle Henry.'

Mrs. Vallery looked at the girl in surprise. What could have come up that was urgent? She had been sitting beside the girls. Nobody had even spoken to them.

'What do you mean, dear?' she asked.

'Let's get out of here a little while, please. We can't talk in this room.'

Mrs. Vallery led the way down the aisle to the door.

'Will you ask somebody to bring Father, Aunt Maud?' Janet said.

'Yes, but — what's it all about, my dear?'

Janet drew her to one side, but it was Bess who answered.

'Oh, Aunt Maud, the prisoner — the man sitting in there beside Uncle Henry — is the one who dragged me out of the river.'

Mrs. Vallery asked the same question Janet had. 'Are you sure?'

'Of course I'm sure. I'd know him among a million.'

A lounger near the door tiptoed into the courtroom and brought Curtis King to them. He heard incredulously what Bess had to say, but her certainty convinced him.

Five minutes later the bailiff of the court handed a note to Henry Vallery. Jake Gildea had just taken the witness stand, but the lawyer took time to read the message.

Bess says (so the scrawl ran) that Blake Forrest is the man who saved her from the flood after the train wreck. We'll have to get him out of this jam.

The note was signed by Curtis King.

Vallery forgot for a few moments the witness who was testifying, his mind busy with this new development. If this was true, why had Forrest not told him, so that he could somehow get it before the jury? The lawyer penciled a reply on the back of the paper and sent it by the bailiff to King. He wrote that after Gildea left the stand he would ask for a ten-minute recess.

The banker was a fat shapeless man who never took any exercise. His limbs were heavy, his body soft and flabby, the flesh of his red neck pendulous. The small eyes in the swollen face were crafty and suspicious. Because of his unwholesome personality, repulsive as a toad, he made a bad witness.

Robinson led him through his story as sketchily as possible. Though Gildea was the chief witness for the prosecution, he wanted to get him out of the way quickly. He wished the jury to fix its attention on the robbery and not on old Jake.

'Did the prisoner give any reason for demanding the money?' the prosecuting attorney asked.

'Some cock-and-bull story about a business deal I had with his mother once,' Gildea sneered. 'Nothing to it.'

'Were you in fear of your life when you turned over the money to him?'

'Yes, sir, I was. He is well known as a killer.'

Vallery at once raised an objection, which was sustained by the court.

'That is all,' Robinson said.

Gildea was rising to leave when Vallery stopped him. 'Just a moment, please,' he said affably.

Step by step he led the witness through the story of the holdup. Several times the banker snapped at him angrily, but he never lost his air of polite courtesy.

'Now about this transaction with the prisoner's mother. Will you tell the jury the facts in full?'

The prosecuting attorney objected as immaterial, incompetent, and irrelevant.

'If your Honor pleases,' Vallery explained, 'I want to lay the groundwork for proof that there was no robbery but merely the payment of a debt long due.'

After some argument the judge permitted the question.

The memory of the witness appeared to be very hazy as to details, but Vallery refreshed it with papers submitted to him for identification. It was the story of a sordid steal on the part of one managing property for a widow who trusted him. Apparently Gildea had skated on very thin ice, but he had escaped legal liability because Mrs. Forrest had signed papers whenever asked by him. By the time the attorney for the defence had finished questioning him beads of perspiration glistened on the red face of the banker.

Vallery shot his cuffs and moved to another point of attack. 'You say you turned this money over to the defendant because you were in fear of him,' the lawyer said in his gentle, almost apologetic, voice.

'Wouldn't you be afraid if a desperado — ?'

'Just answer the question, please,' Vallery interrupted quietly. 'Yes or no.'

'Yes, I was.'

'Did Mr. Forrest at any time draw a gun while he was in your private office?'

'He had a six-shooter strapped to his hip.'

'You have not answered my question.'

'His fingers were within a foot of the butt of his .45.'

'Answer the question, Mr. Gildea,' ordered the judge.

'No,' the witness snarled.

'Did you have a gun in the room, Mr. Gildea?'

'Yes.'

'Where was it?'

'In my desk.'

'About a foot from your fingers, maybe.'

Sharply the prosecuting attorney objected. The Court sustained the protest. Vallery smiled. He had got his point before the jury.

'It is known to you, is it not, Mr. Gildea, that this is still an Indian country and that many of our citizens who travel much still carry revolvers?'

Again Robinson objected. Vallery was satisfied to have the question ruled out. He made one last query, impressively, eyes fixed on the witness, words slow and deliberate.

'Is it not true, Mr. Gildea, that you turned this money over to the defendant voluntarily because of an uneasy conscience troubled by the fact that you had long owed it to him?'

'No,' the witness roared. 'Nothing of the kind.'

'That is all,' the lawyer said.

Gildea left the stand a much ruffled object of contempt, but Vallery did not flatter himself that he had shaken the fact of the robbery.

CHAPTER 23

'No Hero Tomfoolery'

Buzz Waggoner brought the prisoner into his office, where he found not only Mr. and Mrs. Vallery but the King family and the Decker girls waiting for him. Forrest did not know why his lawyer had asked for a short recess. The cool glance that swept the room now betrayed no curiosity.

'Something important has developed, Forrest,' explained Vallery. 'This young lady, Miss Bess Decker, says you are the man who saved her life after the train wreck.'

The prisoner looked more closely at the slim long-legged girl. He smiled at her. 'I told you that you'd sleep — and you did,' he said.

She grinned at him, shyly. 'Yes, doctor. How's the shoulder?'

'Fine, nurse. A little stiff yet, but otherwise good as new.'

Curtis King cut in. 'You saved the girl's life, sir.'

'I yanked her out of the creek, if that's what you mean,' Blake answered.

'We've been looking for you. So have the

230

Hunts, to thank you for saving little Myra.'

'Did I save her? I climbed a tree and brought her down, if she's the same kid I have in mind.'

'You swam the Funnel to get across to her, and you dragged out Finn Gunter and his little boy.'

'Sure. With a rope tied round my waist, so I had no chance of drowning. Glad I was there to give them a lift out, though. But what has this to do with the price of beans in Tennessee? We're keeping a heap of folks waiting in the courtroom.'

Vallery said, 'Perhaps you don't know that everybody in this part of the country has been anxious to find out who it is that saved four lives from the Funnel.'

His client was annoyed. 'What difference does it make? I was present, so I pulled out the folks I could reach. Mr. King has twenty men riding for him would have done the same. You're not going to make a fuss about it, are you? Because I won't like that. I'm not going to be made an idiot of with a lot of hero tomfoolery.'

Bess stood up to him, her eyes flashing. 'If you think you can save my life and not have me say "Thanks" you're mistaken. I was there. I saw what you did. Two or three times you went under and I thought you were gone. Every time you went into the river you risked being drowned — and you know that well as I do. So there.'

'I wouldn't argue with a lady,' Blake smiled, somewhat embarrassed. 'Now that's over with, I reckon. I'm thanked. Since you say I helped, I'll ask you to repay the favor. Let's keep this a secret among those now present. I wouldn't want to be joshed by the boys for the rest of my life, and I certainly will be if the paper gets this and prints a lot of hero stuff.'

'Wouldn't you rather be joked by the boys than go to the penitentiary?' Vallery asked.

'Don't see the connection,' Forrest replied.

'This story will sway public sentiment a lot, and if we can get it before the jury might affect their verdict.'

Curtis King took up the argument. 'We have to be reasonable, Forrest. You're up against a serious charge, and we have to fight it the best way we can. I understand your feeling. You don't want a hurrah made about what you did at the Funnel wreck. In your place I wouldn't either. But after all that's vanity. And think of us. You have done me two great services, for Bess is like my own child. I can't stand by and see you go to prison when it can be stopped perhaps. Can't you see that? I'm human. We feel — the girls are with me on that — we must get you freed if we can.'

'I'm perfectly reasonable,' Forrest said quietly. 'This Funnel Creek business hasn't a thing to do with the case.'

'But if it is brought out it might win you a verdict.'

'Look here,' protested the prisoner. 'Hundreds of cowboys in this county have gone into bank-full streams after stock. It's nothing to make a song about, and I'm not going to claim any credit for getting wet. That's out. It's not coming into this case. Understand?'

'I think you're wrong,' Vallery said.

'Maybe so, but I'm the fellow who has to go to jail, so nobody else can have any kick coming.' Forrest turned to the sheriff. 'All right, Buzz. Take me back to the courtroom.'

Janet did not say anything. Except to include her in his first sweeping gaze when he entered Forrest had not looked at her once. A heavy cold weight hung round her heart.

But Bess had something to say. She choked down sobs while she spoke. 'We couldn't make an idiot out of you because you're acting like one already. Why should you care what a lot of dumb cowboys say in fun when it may help you to get off by using what we know? And do you suppose Janet and I are going to feel happy to see you sent to prison for the rest of your stubborn life?'

'I reckon it's his say-so, Bess,' Curtis said

233

mildly. 'I feel the same as you do, but it's Mr. Forrest's right to do as he pleases about this.'

Forrest spoke to Bess, gently, smiling at her. 'You speak your piece right out, Miss Decker. That's all right with me. I appreciate your interest, but I just can't go around yelling that I'm a fair-haired hero. Every time I looked in the glass I would be ashamed of what I saw. Sorry, but it has to be that way.'

He and Waggoner walked out of the room.

'So he's going to prison,' Janet said, a bleak wind sweeping through her heart.

'Not if this story will keep him out,' Vallery said. 'I'm running this defence. I'll get the facts in whether Forrest likes it or not.' He glanced at his watch. 'Time I'm getting back to the courtroom.'

The others went with him.

After the bailiff had brought the court to order the prosecution called a plump pink-faced youngish man in jean trousers and a seersucker coat as its next witness. He gave his name as Homer Packard and said he was cashier of the Valley Bank. After Forrest had walked unannounced into the private office of the president, he testified, Gildea had rung for him and told him to bring the Holloway note from the safe. He had done this. Five minutes later the prisoner had left the bank hurriedly carrying one of the sacks used by the officers to carry money. Gildea had burst out of his office crying that the bank had been robbed.

Under cross-examination Packard admitted that when he had first answered Gildea's call to the office Forrest had been sitting across the desk from the president smoking a cigarette.

'Any weapon in his hand?'

'No, sir, but —'

'At any time did you see a gun in his hand?'

'Not in his hand, but on his hip —'

'Was anything said while you were there suggesting that this was a holdup?'

'Not exactly. Mr. Gildea told me to bring the Holloway note. I could see something was wrong.'

'Answer my questions please. Nothing more. You say that Mr. Forrest left hurriedly. What do you mean by that? Did he run?'

'No-o.'

'He walked?'

'Yes, but he acted kinda in a hurry.'

'Witness excused.'

After the prosecuting witnesses had given their evidence Vallery asked the court for a directed acquittal verdict on the ground that the prosecution had failed to show a robbery had taken place. The judge refused this request. Before the defence had called any witnesses he adjourned court for the night.

During the ensuing twelve hours Vallery was very busy. A messenger rode out to the Hunt ranch, another to the village where Finn Gunter lived. Ever since he had taken this case Vallery had differed with his client on one important point. He had held that Forrest ought to stay off the stand since he could offer no testimony that would help him and might be badgered into admissions that would prove fatal. Bluntly the accused man had vetoed this cautious policy. If he didn't get into the witness box everybody would know he was afraid, Forrest said. The jury was not fooled about this thing. They knew he had taken the money. He was going to get up there and face them.

Now Vallery withdrew his opposition. He had rearranged his defence and was going to make a try for acquittal on entirely different grounds. Knowing Texas and Texans, he thought there was a pretty good chance of succeeding.

CHAPTER 24

Bess Tells Her Story

Blake Forrest's testimony did not help him. He would not lie, and to tell the truth would have convicted him. When Robinson asked him if he had not robbed the Valley Bank his answer was an evasion, one almost insolent in its indifference.

'I talked the matter over with Gildea and he decided to pay me what he had owed my mother,' the accused man said with a cynical smile. 'I threw off the interest.'

'Answer my question,' Robinson snapped.

'Why, I've just told you,' Forrest drawled, surprised innocence in his face, 'that I had a nice little talk with Gildea and we agreed I had better take the money.'

'You threatened his life, didn't you?'

'I'm a peaceable man, Mr. Robinson.'

The judge admonished Forrest that he must stop quibbling. Robinson repeated the question.

'I don't recollect exactly what I said. Maybe I mentioned to him that he is some kind of a cross between a rat and a skunk.

He scares easy.'

'You're a notorious gunman, aren't you?'

Instantly Vallery objected. The court ruled that the inquiry had been put improperly, and the prosecutor reframed his attack to draw from Blake that he had killed three men in self-defence, two of them while serving as a ranger in pursuit of criminals.

'After you broke out of jail did you stop at some cache and dig up the money you took from Gildea?'

'You mean the money he gave me,' Forrest corrected. 'Maybe I did.'

'Is it true that before you had been out of jail twenty-four hours you engaged in a gunfight at Deer Trail?'

The cool gaze of Forrest swept the courtroom and came to rest on a group of three men standing by an open window near the back of the hall. The men were Wes Terrell, Pres Walsh, and Webb Lake. His thin smile was openly derisive.

'Hardly amounted to a fight,' he said carelessly. 'Some riffraff tried to murder me and gave up the job.'

There was a murmur of laughter among those present. Someone in the back of the room called out, 'You done said it, boy.' The judge wielded his gavel and looked severely at Stone Heath. 'The courtroom will be

cleared if there is any further interruption,'
he announced.

The prosecuting attorney waved a hand in
dismissal. He had got all he wanted out of
the prisoner. Forrest was leaving an impression of a hardy and dangerous man who moved
outside the law to gain his ends. No doubt
there was a certain sympathy with him in the
district, but it would not be enough to keep
him out of the penitentiary.

On redirect examination Vallery followed
the lead the prosecutor had given him.

'Where were you the second night after you
left Fair Play, Mr. Forrest?'

'In the brush,' Blake answered, a flash of
anger in his eyes.

'Did you not, in point of fact, spend the
night on the bank of the Funnel Creek?'

Nobody present could have failed to note
the resentment of the prisoner, though few
knew the reason for it. His hard gaze challenged Vallery, as did his curt reply. 'Nothing
whatever to say about that.'

'You refuse to say where you spent the
night?' Vallery continued blandly.

'I do. It has no bearing on this trial, and
you know it.'

The clash between the outlaw and his coun-
sel made a sensation, but it was nothing to
the amazement produced when the lawyer ex-

cused the witness and asked that Janet King be called to the stand. Her father was one of the most important men in the district. He and his family were looked up to by all who knew them. What could this girl have to say in favor of a man who had been on the dodge for weeks with a price on his head?

Janet moved down the aisle with light ease, apparently not conscious of the buzz of excitement running through the room. From every corner men craned their necks to look at the lovely girl. They watched the flow of the rhythmic body, the proud lift of the small head so beautifully poised above the slender throat.

She seated herself and waited. Vallery and his client were engaged in a whispered argument. Apparently Forrest was protesting bitterly at something and his lawyer was refusing to yield. The attorney had his way.

After a preliminary question or two Vallery came directly to the point he wanted to develop. 'Where and when did you first meet the prisoner, Miss King?'

'On the Mal Pais desert.' Janet added the date.

'What were you doing there?'

'I was lost, and had been for twenty-four hours. My horse had thrown me and I had been wandering around without food or water.

Mr. Forrest saw me. He fed me, looked after me, and brought me to Fair Play next day.'

Robinson jumped to his feet. 'I fail to see the bearing of this, your Honor. This desert meeting was long after the bank robbery.'

Suavely Vallery explained that he was bringing character witnesses to show that his client was not the kind of man to rob a bank. There was a verbal wrangle between the lawyers, after which the judge decided to admit the testimony. Evidently Miss King was taking the stand with the consent of her father. Judge Jackman was a politician, though an honest one. He saw no reason for antagonizing the owner of the biggest ranch in the county.

'How did Blake Forrest treat you, Miss King?' asked Vallery.

'With great consideration. As my father might have done.'

'When he brought you to Fair Play what occurred?'

'He took me to the hotel. Before he could leave town he was arrested.'

Vallery flashed a smile at the prosecuting attorney. He knew that even if Robinson objected to the last sentence of the girl it would still be in the minds of the jurors if not in the record. He had come to town knowing the risk he ran, in order to bring Miss King back to safety.

Janet was excused without cross-examination.

The bailiff called the name of Bess Decker. Again there was astonishment in the courtroom. It expressed itself in the shuffling of feet and the murmur of voices.

Bess was flushed and embarrassed. Vallery tried to put her at ease by using her first name and speaking in a gentle conversational tone. 'Have you ever met the prisoner?'

Bess looked at the man sitting beside her friend and nodded. When she spoke her voice was eager and excited.

'Yes. He saved my life when I was drowning in the Funnel after the train wreck.'

Instantly Robinson knew his case was lost. It did not matter that Forrest was guilty. The sudden startled shift of the eyes of the jurors to the face of the accused man, the swift approval of him that broke out almost in a shout from the astonished spectators, told the prosecuting attorney what the verdict would be. He adjusted his mind to accept this amiably.

'How did he save your life, Bess?' Vallery inquired.

The eyes of tue girl were starry. 'He swam into the river and dragged me out.'

'You are sure the man who rescued you is the prisoner?'

'Of course I'm sure. He was there all night.

242

After he had rescued me he jumped in and saved the little Gunter boy — then his father, Mr. Finn Gunter. I kept thinking he would be drowned. A big piece of driftwood hit him and smashed his shoulder. He was under the water a lot of times. Last of all he swam across the Funnel to get Myra Hunt out of a tree where the flood had washed her. It was terrible, Uncle Henry. I — I —'

She bit her upper lip, to keep back the sudden sob that swelled in her throat.

'It's all right, Bess,' the lawyer encouraged. 'Just one more question. Did Mr. Forrest tell you who he was?'

'No, he didn't.' She rushed on impulsively. 'I know he doesn't want me to say anything about it now. But when he came in yesterday and I recognized him, Uncle Henry, was I just to sit here like a bump on a log and say nothing?'

'You did exactly right, Bess. You may go now, unless Mr. Robinson has some questions to ask you.'

The prosecuting attorney shook his head.

The next witness was Gunter. He confirmed what Bess Decker had said. His small son followed him. Little Myra Hunt was too small to be called, but she too did her share. She sat with her father and mother near the front of the room and more than once waved an excited hand at the unresponsive Forrest. During a moment of silence she cried to her parents, in a voice audible to all, 'He called me Sugar when he tooked me from the tree.'

During all of which Blake Forrest looked dourly straight in front of him. They were making a fool of him, he felt. It was just as if he were sitting in front of a camera posing for the picture of a hero. He would never be able to live this down. Resentment toward Vallery was hot in him.

CHAPTER 25

Supper at Six

Buzz Waggoner took Forrest to his office while the jury considered its verdict. The sheriff overflowed into a chair and lit a cigar, after having offered a smoke to his prisoner.

'You sure did yore best to get into the penitentiary, Blake,' he wheezed, settling himself comfortably. 'By jumping Jupiter, you acted like Vallery and these witnesses who were talking you out of jail were yore worst enemies.'

'I'm not out of jail yet,' Forrest said.

He was beginning to get over his annoyance. That the testimony of the part he had played at Funnel Creek had helped him there could be no doubt. Yet he was glad people knew he had opposed its introduction.

Stone Heath and Bill Crabb burst into the room. They flung themselves on him joyfully.

'You doggoned sly old bronco-peeler,' Crabb shouted. 'Whyfor did you keep it under yore hat that you're the fair-haired lad who yanked half the population of this county out of Funnel when it went on a rampage? Looks like you ain't got good sense.'

'He's one of these here shy violets, Bill,' contributed Heath with a wide grin. 'If it hadn't been for the King young lady and little Miss Decker —'

'They came through wide and handsome,' the sheriff said.

'Y'betcha! Busted Robinson's case wide open. This prosecution has croaked, cashed in, handed in its checks.' Heath flung up his hat with a yell.

'The jury is still out,' mentioned Blake dryly.

'Couple of the boys can't write,' explained Crabb cheerfully. 'The others are learnin' them to print "Not guilty" on their votes.'

'I wouldn't offer two bits Mex against yore saddle for a conviction,' Waggoner said. 'In about five minutes they'll be sending for us to come back and listen to the good news.'

The sheriff was right. Inside of the specified time a messenger ran into the office, his face beaming, with the news that a verdict had been reached.

This was no settled community devoted first to law and order. On the Texas frontier men were judged by other standards than those which prevailed in New England. These jurors had fought Comanches to protect their wives and children. They had pounded through the brush after moss-horns with cactus and mesquite flogging their hands and faces. They had crossed deserts marked by the white glistening bones of cattle that had failed to rough through withering droughts. On the long trail drives they had ridden out blizzards, swum bank-full rivers, and dashed after stampeding herds while the lightning played on the horns of the stock. The two qualities that counted most in that wild land were courage and loyalty. No arguments were necessary to show that Blake Forrest did not belong behind the walls of a prison. He was their kind of man. He had the stuff in him that goes through to a finish.

When the verdict was read by the clerk the old Confederate war yell was lifted in a wild whoop. Judge Jackman did not attempt to curb the enthusiasm. He was among the first to congratulate the acquitted man. The prosecuting attorney beat him to it. Sensing the swift swing of public opinion, he wanted it understood there had been no animus behind the state's case. To see men struggling to reach Forrest one might have thought he was Fair Play's favorite son instead of one who had been posted all over West Texas as a bandit worth a thousand dollars to his captor.

Bess Decker laughed and cried and cheered. She waved her handkerchief and in her joy kissed Mrs. Vallery and her sister. Janet did not move or speak. She had been watching the dark impassive face of the prisoner when the words 'Not guilty' dropped from the lips of the clerk. Almost instantly the rush of the crowd had hidden him, but she knew he was still cool and reserved regardless of his private emotions. A hot wave of delight ran through her slender body. He was saved from prison, and she had helped to do it. He might never look at her again, but she had paid part of her debt to him. That was something he could not wipe out of his memory.

Mrs. Vallery worked toward the place where her husband and his client were standing. Craig Shannon shouldered a path for her.

'Open up for Mrs. Vallery, boys,' he called. 'Clear a way. You'll see plenty of Blake later. I reckon he'll be in circulation quite a while now.'

The lawyer's wife surprised her husband. After she had congratulated Forrest she invited him to come to supper that evening. 'I do so hope you will come,' she said, and looked so earnestly anxious that the refusal Blake was framing died on his lips.

'I'll be glad to come, Mrs. Vallery,' he said quietly, and added with a smile: 'I've been some annoyed with the judge for the way he handled my case, but it turned out he was right and I was wrong. It seems I was too thin-skinned about being afraid of the hurrah over the Funnel business.'

'If you insist on being a public character you can't keep people from talking about it,' she replied. 'That's the penalty you pay. After all, it isn't a crime to rescue people from a flood.'

'No, ma'am, and nothing to brag over either. What time shall I come?'

'At six o'clock.'

Forrest did not realize until he reached the lawyer's house that the Kings and the Deckers would be there for supper. Otherwise he would have excused himself. He did not want them to think that they owed him any more thanks. In point of fact it was the other way. Undoubtedly their testimony had kept him out of the penitentiary.

Bess met him on the porch, starry-eyed and shy. 'Are you still mad at me?' she asked.

'I haven't any time been mad at you,' he said, shaking hands. 'I just didn't want a fuss made about nothing.'

'Well, I'll be mad at you if you keep calling it nothing to save me from drowning,' she laughed, a little breathlessly.

'Mrs. Vallery didn't tell me you were going to be here,' he said.

'No. She was afraid you'd be scared away. It's a trap. You're not girl-shy, are you, except when they are lost in the desert or drowning?'

'Not of a nice friendly girl like you who nursed me when I was practically fatally wounded.'

'Janet is just as friendly as I am, but she isn't so pert. She behaves like a lady. I've always been a kind of tomboy, and it's time I stopped it.'

Mrs. Vallery came to the door to meet her guest. 'If Bess is quite through with you . . .' she said, smiling at the girl.

A wave of color swept the face of the very young woman. She was at the age of hero-worship, and just now her emotions were centered upon the man who had rescued her after the train wreck. In another month or two they would be seeking another object for outlet.

Her brother Phil appeared on the porch and diverted attention from Bess. Face red with embarrassment, he offered a hand to Forrest.

'I reckon you can forgive me easier for acting like a darned fool, since it was my head got broke and not yours,' he said. 'Maybe I'll learn more sense as I grow older.'

Blake shook hands with him and laughed. 'You'll have to forget and not me, since I sure took advantage of you when I pistol-whipped you, Phil. But at the time it looked like I had no choice.'

'You hadn't either, since I was training with a bad bunch.'

'I trained with them myself for a while. A man has to buy his own experience, I reckon.'

They all moved into the house.

Janet and Vallery were in the parlor. Miss King had very little to say, but Blake Forrest was very much aware of her. It was not only because of her lovely grace. She had an exciting personality, held very much in reserve. He caught a glimpse of it in the faint mocking humor of her eyes. There was a rich vitality in her beauty.

Curtis King breezed in from a business appointment. Before they sat down for supper he managed to get a word with Forrest alone.

'I've been hearing some talk. Nothing to it, maybe. I don't know. But the story is that Terrell and his crowd have been drinking and making threats against you. You don't want trouble with them, of course. I suggest you ride up with us to Granite Gap tomorrow. My proposition is still open about a job for you on my Big Bend ranch.'

'I can't let these fellows run me out of town, Mr. King. If hunting for me they will have to find me.' Blake looked quietly at the older man. He knew that from the viewpoint of the frontier he was on solid ground. A man under fire could not sneak away and still hold his head up.

'Now look here, boy,' Curtis answered impatiently. 'Circumstances alter cases. You have just got out of one jam. If you ram-stam into another right off you will practically be admitting you're one of these bully-puss gunmen who stomp around looking for trouble. Mind, I don't say you'll be one. I mean, that's how it will look to good citizens who will be watching you from now on. You have come to a fork in the trail, owing to the good break you got today. Be mighty sure you choose the right one.'

'That's all true, Mr. King. I'll say this. If Terrell and his friends don't die until I attack them they will live forever. I'll avoid a difficulty with them if I can, but I won't light out like a scared jackrabbit.'

'You don't have to do that. Just act as if you hadn't heard a word of their big talk and leave town with me. Anyhow, keep out of their way. I understand that Bronson of the rangers is about ready to arrest these scoundrels for the Texas & Pacific robbery. Soon as he does that they will be too busy to fool with you.'

Forrest smiled sceptically. 'Would you take your own advice if you were in my place, Mr. King? Let's say some enemies were threatening you. Would you run away and hole up?

Or would you face them down?'

'Not a parallel case,' the ranchman snapped. 'You ought to build up a reputation as a peaceful citizen. Everybody knows you're not afraid of these scalawags. You can afford to ignore them.'

'Just what I mean to do. I won't walk a step out of my way to meet them. But I can't go on the dodge because of them. It is not only because of what other people would say. Some day I would begin wondering myself if I hadn't sidestepped because they had the Indian sign on me.'

King gave up. 'All right — all right,' he said impatiently. 'Have it your own way. When you get older you'll learn that a man sometimes has to pay no attention to what folks say in a case like this.'

Mrs. Vallery called her guests to supper. It had been some time since Blake had sat down to a meal like this served with white linen and silver. The spring chicken and the flaky biscuits were delicious. He knew all present were trying to be friendly and to put him at his ease. Yet Blake was not comfortable. He did not belong in this group.

What disturbed him was not a sense of social difference. He had been well brought up by those who read good books and knew the contemporary niceties of behavior. His unease did not at all reach the surface. The reserve habitual to him except when with close friends bore no relation to shy gaucherie. In spite of his notoriety he moved in his world with distinction. But these people were good, definitely on the side of law, order, and morality, whereas his reckless feet had led him into wild and lawless paths. They were glad he had been acquitted, since he had done them a great service, but he knew they did not approve or condone the robbery of the Valley Bank. The life he had led, the things he had done, made a great gulf between him and them that was unbridgeable.

CHAPTER 26

A Bluff Is Called

Blake and Janet wandered to the porch after supper. Bess was helping their hostess clear away the dishes, and Curtis King had retired with Vallery to the library to talk over a cattle contract. The soft velvet night lapped the ugly little town and magically softened its rawness to a thing of beauty. The moon and stars were out, enough to give a light that might be dangerous. Forrest remembered what the cattleman had told him and was careful to stand behind the thick bougainvillea vines.

Their small talk died away. Except in his moments of gay recklessness Blake was inclined to listen rather than to speech when he had nothing to say. With his friends he could sit brooding for half an hour and let his thoughts flow on instead of words. Now his mind was full of this girl in summer blue and white, whose beauty was tempered like a fine blade, who was so sweet and gracious and withal mysterious. He could only guess at what the woman behind this enchanting flow of life was like.

The excitement in Janet grew keen. To be with this man sent pulses of emotion beating through her blood. She told herself not to be a fool. After tonight she would probably never see him again. What she must do now was to make talk — about anything — it did not matter what. She snatched at the first subject to hand.

'I suppose you will be leaving this part of the country now,' she said, and felt a wave of color beating into her face. Why had she mentioned that? Perhaps he would think she was begging him to stay, or that she meant he was disgraced and ought to go.

He gave her question back to her. 'Why?'

'I don't know — I thought maybe —'

'That I had better try a new start where people don't know I am a bank robber who got off by a fluke.'

She did not evade his challenge, though a breathless tremor passed through her bosom. For the first time he had opened a door into his life.

'*Are* you a bank robber?' she asked, her voice so low it just reached him.

'You heard the evidence,' he said.

'I think you took the money.'

'So I'm a criminal.'

'No,' she protested.

A sardonic smile rested on his hard lean face.

'Perfectly justified? Just taking what was my own from a scoundrel who had stolen it?'

She shook her head. 'No. You can't right one wrong by doing another.'

'Then I'm guilty.'

'Yes, but that does not make you a criminal — if you don't keep the money.'

His gaze searched her face. 'I see. A conscience fund, sent back by a repentant sinner who finds he can't sleep nights on account of his evil deed.'

She looked at him steadily, her body stiffening at his sneer. 'It would be an unpardonable weakness, wouldn't it, for a man who makes his own laws?'

'What's the object of laws?' he asked curtly. 'If it's to bring about justice, I would call them a failure. A lot of politicians go to Austin and fix things up to favor slick scoundrels against decent honest people. Take the case of Jake Gildea. He would have robbed Mother Holloway of her home if I hadn't butted in, and she's as fine a little woman as ever lived in Texas. He took all my mother had and without doubt shortened her life by reason of worry and too much hard work. But the law says he is a good citizen because he didn't hold a gun to their heads and only betrayed their confidence to steal what they had nice and legal. If I had shot him down when I was a boy public opinion would have said he got what was coming to him, but because I only helped myself and Mother Holloway to what he had euchred out of two widows I'm a bandit.'

'I didn't say you are a bandit,' Janet corrected gently. 'And I'm not trying to tell you what you ought to do. Nobody but you can decide that. Maybe I said more than I should.' She felt the color storming into her cheeks again. 'I'm only a girl, and of course it's none of my business. But you asked me, and I told you what I think. Likely I'm wrong.'

Forrest did not answer. Two men were moving up the dusty road. He watched them.

'You had better go into the house,' he said quietly.

'What do you mean?' she asked, startled at the change in him. Her eyes followed his, and fear rose to her throat. 'Those men — you think —'

The call of a coyote sounded.

'It's all right,' her companion said. 'They're friends.'

He moved to the gate to meet them. Janet walked into the house.

Stone Heath and Bill Crabb joined their friend. He knew they had come to bring him information, but ignored this. With an elbow on the top of the gate, he grinned derisively at them. 'We've just finished a top-notch supper — fried chicken, biscuits that melt in your mouth, mashed potatoes with gravy, string beans, real coffee, and strawberries and cream to top off with. If you've come for a hand-out, I'll find out if Mrs. Vallery has any wood she wants chopped.'

Abruptly, Stone Heath said, 'Got your gun with you, fellow?'

'No. I left it at the hotel. One of you want to hock it?'

'Better take mine,' Crabb said, and drew a .45 from the scabbard under his left arm.

'What's the urge?' Forrest asked. 'I'm a guest of the Vallerys. They don't either one look dangerous to me.'

'It's the Terrell bunch,' Crabb explained. 'They are up at Peake's Place getting roostered. If a jury hasn't sand enough in its craw to convict you, why they aim to take a hand. That's the talk they are making.'

'Did they mention what kind of hand?'

'Not necessary. You know what they mean.' This from Heath.

'I reckon you boys were not present during the pow-wow while they were making oration.'

'No. Buzz Waggoner brought us the word. Said to tell you to look out.'

Forrest drummed with his forefingers on the

gate. 'Second time this evening this has been mentioned to me. Maybe there's something to it. I don't want a mixup with these birds if I can help it. Not an hour ago I told Curtis King there would be no trouble if they would leave me alone. But I don't aim to let them run me out of town.'

'What's Lieutenant Bronson doing?' Crabb wanted to know impatiently. 'Why doesn't he put them under arrest and try them for the Texas & Pacific robbery?'

'He will, soon as he thinks he has evidence enough,' Blake said. 'The rangers move slow, but they get there. . . . Do you reckon these scoundrels know where I am now?'

'Sure they know. Everybody in town has heard that Mrs. Vallery gave you an invite to supper.'

'Then what's to prevent them from coming down here and lying in wait behind those cottonwoods to blast me when I come out from the house?'

'Not a thing in the world,' Heath answered promptly.

'I wouldn't like that,' Blake said placidly. 'Mustn't be any trouble here. I wouldn't want the other guests frightened. Reckon I'll step in and say good night to my hostess. 'Back in a couple of minutes. Stick around.'

Forrest walked back into the house. 'I find

I'll have to be leaving,' he told Mrs. Vallery. 'Some business has come up unexpectedly. I have enjoyed your hospitality very much. It was good of you to ask me.' To her husband he said: 'See you at your office in the morning, Judge.'

The cattleman watched him, eyes slightly narrowed. 'Do you expect to see me too?' he asked.

'Yes, sir. I'm still thinking about that Big Bend offer.'

'Janet says your friends are outside. That's good — to have friends who stick by you when you need them.'

Forrest nodded, understanding the warning. He was being advised not to appear without them as long as he was in town.

'They're tough *hombres* and hard to shake,' he said carelessly.

From the moment he had re-entered the room Janet's eyes had not left Forrest. She knew that this business which had come up was serious. A cold wave drenched her heart. Was he heading into more trouble, after all that he had been through? She did not know why her father had told him covertly not to stir out without his friends, but she was sure there was a reason.

When he shook hands with her, she said in a low voice, 'You'll be careful, won't you?'

His surprised gaze fastened a moment to hers. He answered, smiling at her, 'From now on I'm going to be the kind of a guy that takes an umbrella out for fear it will rain.'

Heath and Crabb were waiting for him outside. They walked down the dusty road toward town. Again Bill offered him his gun.

'You might need it — sudden.'

'Not I,' Blake said gaily. 'I'm a reformed character.' He put it in the words of a Negro spiritual.

' "I wrastled with Satan and I wrastled with sin
Stepped over hell, and come back agin." '

'Are Wes Terrell and Pres Walsh and Webb Lake reformed characters?' Heath asked dryly.

'No information on that point, Stone,' Forrest said cheerfully, and continued to sing:

' "Isaiah mounted on de wheel o' time,
Spoke to God-A-Mighty 'way down de line." '

'Just out of plumb idle curiosity I'd like to know what you're figuring on doing when you get back from the camp-meeting,' Heath suggested.

'Me? Why, I'm going up to my room at the hotel to play seven-up with you boys. After that I'm going to bed.'

'Not going to pay any attention to the brags of these scoundrels?'

'Not a bit. If it's just talk it will die down. If they mean business I'll duck it if I can.'

'And if you can't?' Bill wanted to know.

'Why, that will be a bridge to cross then, and not now.'

'We heard Wes says for you to light out of Texas if you know what's good for you.'

'Did he sent me railroad fare?'

'You want to go heeled, Blake,' remonstrated Crabb. 'If they knew you weren't toting a gun —'

'They would shoot you into rag dolls,' Heath finished for him.

When they turned into the hotel it was by the side door leading through the barroom. A rowdy group of half a dozen were drinking. The three friends had walked into the very crowd they were trying to avoid.

Into Heath's ear Forrest dropped a word of instruction. Rapidly Blake led the way toward the door opening into the lobby. He did not reach it. Terrell caught sight of him and gave a yelp of surprise.

'Here's the damned buzzard-head,' he called to the others.

With three swift strides he had cut off his enemy from the lobby.

Forrest moved to the end of the bar and rested his left forearm on it, so that he faced the row of men lined up in front of it. He stood there negligently, at apparent ease, watching with a cynical smile the consternation his arrival had produced. But his eyes, half hooded by sleepy drooping lids, had the glittering pounce of a hawk.

Three of those in the place were casual bar flies lapping up free drinks. A new round had just been ordered and the glasses were full. The spongers did not wait to empty them. Swiftly, without actually running, they got out of the line of fire. One vanished through the door. A second took refuge behind a table overturned by him in his flight. The third lay down back of the bar.

'So you came here looking for trouble,' Lake said in a flat hard voice. His right arm was in a sling, and the belt he wore had been shifted so that the weapon in it could be drawn by the left hand.

'No, sir,' answered Forrest, dragging the words. 'Trying to duck it. Heading for my room where I could hide under the bed.'

"I'll bet you're plumb scared, Blake,' Heath

said, following instructions.

'Quivering like an aspen,' his friend admitted, with a cool laugh. 'Why wouldn't I be with these bully-puss wolves howling for my blood? Looks like the end of the trail might be in sight — for somebody.'

'You don't reckon it would do any good for you to beg off,' Heath proposed, his grin insolent in its mockery. 'Mebbe if you'd get down on yore marrow bones and beg pretty these Bill Hickok gents would let you go this time.'

The sudden appearance of his enemy flanked by two devoted friends had taken Terrell at disadvantage. He had no doubt they had walked in prepared for a battle. No question but they had heard of his threats and were here for the showdown. The gaze of the big man slid to his companions, to Pres Walsh and Webb Lake, and found no comfort there. They would fight if necessary, but they had no relish for a fracas of this sort. Meanwhile they waited for their leader to make the decision.

Wes Terrell shirked making it. His shifting eyes picked up Bill Crabb, who was standing near the back of the room, feet apart, body leaning forward, fingers hovering near the butt of a .45. A split second would bring the man into action. The bully's gaze slid to Stone

Heath, notorious for his recklessness in a county where few men were overcareful of their lives. He too was ready to send crashing death across the room at an instant's warning. And most dangerous of all Forrest himself, as swift and accurate a shot as any man in Texas, jeering at him with the devilish assurance that always shook the nerve of his foes. With Lake reduced to left-hand shooting this was a long way from being good enough. It would not be an even break, and Terrell wanted a sure thing when he started guns blazing against Blake Forrest.

'Don't start anything in here, gentlemen,' the bartender begged.

'That's right,' Terrell said. 'There are ladies upstairs. We don't want to alarm them. If you fellows came here looking for us —'

'He's going to insist we go outside and settle this, Heath,' the unarmed man at the end of the bar said. 'A sure enough bad man from Bitter Creek. Just crowding us into a fight, wouldn't you say? Yes, boys, I'm shaking in my boots. Pimples running up and down my back.'

A wild surge leaped up in Terrell to fling away caution and finish this now. He had hated this man bitterly for years. The fellow had killed his brother, humiliated his pride, defeated him at every turn. Some day there had to be a settlement. Why not now? Why not take him at his word, walk out into the street, and let the roaring guns end the feud?

The impulse died. Terrell could not buck up his will to go through with such a battle. It would mean death for four or five men, and very likely he would be one of them.

Terrell ate the threats he had been making all evening.

'Whoever told you we were looking for you lied,' he said flatly. 'If this town wants to make you its fair-haired hero that's all right with us. We've got our own opinion of you and we're not afraid to tell it anywhere, by thunder.'

'Except when Mr. Blake Forrest happens to be present,' Heath added.

'Then or any time,' Terrell boasted, saving face. 'Come on, boys. Let's get out of here where the air don't smell of skunks.'

He swaggered out, Lake and Walsh at his heels.

Heath gave a whoop triumphant. 'You dog-goned old buckaroo, they don't want any of your game,' he cried.

Crabb pounded Forrest on the back with a hamlike fist. 'I never did see such a bad man-tamer. You take the cake, boy, with all the frosting on it. And you unarmed all the time.'

'It was you boys who bluffed them out. Terrell sized you up and threw in his hand.'

'Come out of yore forts,' Heath called to those in hiding. 'Fourth of July all over and no fireworks. Your drinks are still waiting on the bar for you.'

The innocent bystanders reappeared, still a little shaken from fright. 'Did you say that Mr. Forrest isn't armed?' one of them asked, after he had emptied his glass at a gulp.

'Not this time,' Heath explained. 'But next time he meets those birds he will be. Bet yore boots on that.'

Forrest led the way upstairs to his room. He knew that inside of an hour all Fair Play would be listening to the story of how he had called the bluff of the Terrell gang and made them back down from their threats. At what had taken place he did not feel pleased. Not an hour ago he had thought he could avoid trouble by walking around his enemies and keeping his distance. Now he knew they would not let him do that. Again he had trodden on their corns, by no wish of his. He knew how dangerous it was to trample down their inflated vanity. Nothing less than his death would satisfy them now.

'I'm a fine guy at ducking trouble,' he said sourly. 'Unless Bronson puts them all away in the pen, guns are going to start smoking right soon. A fellow with a rep like mine hasn't a chance to live peaceable.'

While they played seven-up Blake's mind was gloomily busy with the perverseness of fate.

CHAPTER 27

Lieutenant Bronson Makes a Roundup

Buzz Waggoner seated the guests he had invited to his office.

'Glad to see you, boys,' he said heartily. 'Like I told you, Mr. Robinson wants to talk over with you your evidence in the Texas & Pacific train robbery.'

'About time he got busy,' Wes Terrell said, his ugly mouth set in a sneer. 'I'd got to thinking this killer Forrest had the Indian sign on Robinson. Why wasn't the scalawag arrested the minute the jury acquitted him of the bank holdup?'

The prosecuting attorney showed no resentment. 'We weren't quite ready then,' he answered. 'The evidence wasn't all in order.' He turned to Ray Terrell. 'You're still prepared to swear, as you did in the affidavit you signed, that you absolutely recognized Forrest when his mask slipped?'

'Bet your boots,' the express messenger replied promptly. 'I'd know that bird among a thousand.'

'He seems to have an alibi,' Robinson mentioned. 'His friends Heath and Crabb claim to have been with him sixty or seventy miles away from the Crossing when the train was stuck up.'

'Sure they claim it,' Walsh snarled, putting his boots on the table and spitting tobacco juice at a crack in the floor. 'Why wouldn't they, when they were in it up to their necks their own selves?'

'They're a bad bunch, the whole mess of them,' Wes Terrell urged angrily. 'Don't let them fool you, Robinson. Why, only last night the three of them were all set to rub us out, and they would have done it too if they hadn't seen we were waiting at the gate for them.'

'I heard about that,' Waggoner said mildly, his tongue in his cheek. 'You kind of showed 'em up, eh?'

The door opened. Lieutenant Bronson walked into the room, followed by Steve Porter and another ranger. Waggoner waved a fat hand blandly.

'We're turning the meeting over to Lieutenant Bronson,' he said.

Wes Terrell leaped to his feet, uncertain what this might mean. Webb Lake did not move. His cold slaty eyes fastened on the officer of rangers. Nothing to be alarmed about, he told himself. It would be the job of Bronson to arrest Forrest and bring him to jail. It was his business also to run down the evidence. Probably he had come to talk it over with them again. Yet there was a sinister quality in that moment of chill silence while the lieutenant looked them over that disturbed Lake and all his companions. Moreover, the point stuck out like a sore thumb that if Bronson had come merely for information he did not need to bring two of his troopers with him.

The lieutenant sat on the edge of the table, one foot dangling.

'Like to gather the loose threads together a little closer, boys,' he said. 'Where were you standing when you recognized Forrest, Ray?'

'In the express car. He wasn't ten feet from me.'

'How many men did he have with him?'

'Three.'

'Did you know any of the others?'

'Not for sure, but one of them looked to me like that fellow Stone Heath. About the same build, and he walked with the same you-be-damned cocksure way.'

'Weren't you surprised that Forrest didn't bump you off after you had seen him without his mask?'

'He didn't know I'd seen him. I turned away quick.'

Swiftly the ranger officer swung round on Wes Terrell. 'You left Deer Trail very early the morning of Tuesday, April 22, in the company of Walsh and Lake. Where were you between then and Friday afternoon?'

A chill wind swept through Wesley Terrell. He had a queer feeling of collapse at the pit of his stomach.

'We went hunting,' he said. 'Why?'

'Where did you hunt? Who did you meet while you were away?'

'We were in the brush country back of Dry Valley. Didn't meet anybody after we left the road. What's the idea, Bronson?'

'Bring back any game with you?'

'No. All we got was a wild boar and a white-tail too gaunted to take home.'

'Anybody with you except your two friends here?'

Terrell hesitated a barely perceptible instant. 'Yes. We picked up Luke Schrader at his place seven miles outa town and he went along.'

'What the hell is all this questioning?' demanded Walsh with a blunt manner of resentment three-fourths bluff.

Bronson was a slender broad-shouldered young man with a hawk nose and steely eyes that had a tremendous thrust. 'Any objections to explaining your movements?' he asked Walsh quietly.

'I dunno whether I have or not,' answered Walsh sulkily. 'I don't have to answer all the fool questions a dumb ranger flings at me.'

'Not if you don't want to, Pres,' the lieutenant said. 'Suit yourself.'

'I have no objection to giving you an account of my whereabouts,' Lake spoke up. 'That is, if you're interested in where I was too.'

'Fine.' Without the slightest warning Bronson exploded a question under him that was like a bomb. 'Were you in the village of Horse Creek on Wednesday, April 23, about noon or a little later?'

The wooden face with which Lake looked at him did not betray how wildly the man's heart was racing.

'No, sir, I was not,' he snapped.

'Didn't meet a girl named Willie Fulwiler, who was spelling her father at the depot while he went home to get his dinner?'

'Never heard of her.'

'Then of course you couldn't have got a telegram from her that arrived while you were there, one addressed to Sam Jones and signed Mamie, mentioning that a baby was arriving on the evening express . . . No, keep your hands right where they are, Pres. We have every last one of you covered.'

'You can't do this to us,' roared Wes Terrell, attempting bluster. 'We won't stand for it a minute.'

'Throw up your hands, all four of you,' ordered Bronson, crisp command ringing in his voice. 'And don't make a mistake.'

Eight hands went into the air, reluctantly.

'Disarm, them, Steve,' the lieutenant continued.

When this had been done Bronson continued his interrogation.

'When you sent the telegram I have mentioned, Ray, from Santone, how came you to be so careless as to file it personally instead of by a kid you could have got to do it for a thin dime?'

'I didn't file any telegram,' Ray Terrell made sullen response.

'We're prepared to prove you did. A witness has already identified you without your being aware of it. Four people picked you out in the courthouse during the Valley Bank trial, Lake, as being the man who called himself Sam Jones at Horse Creek. Your gray gelding has been identified too. A little undercover work, you understand. Wes Terrell, Pres Walsh, and Luke Schrader were seen with you riding away from Crawford's Crossing not an hour after the holdup. And finally, Wes, a woman — a friend of yours — has been crowded into doing some talking.'

'That's a lie,' blurted Terrell, perspiration beading on his face. 'The whole thing is a frameup.'

'You'll find it's not,' Bronson told him. 'You're in a jackpot for big stakes holding a busted flush . . . Sheriff, have to borrow some handcuffs from you.'

'You aiming to arrest us?' Ray Terrell said, his face white.

'I have already arrested you . . . Put on the cuffs, Steve. I reckon Buzz will help you.'

'With a heap of pleasure,' Waggoner agreed. He added, drawling the words, 'Maybe it will be a comfort for you to know that Blake Forrest tipped us off you and yore pals had done this. He worked it all out, fitting the pieces in like a puzzle. You tried to hang it on him, and he figured the best defence was to find out who did it. So, putting this and that together, he dug up enough to hand you boys a nice long jolt in the pen. What loaded him with suspicions first was yore anxiety to rub him out before he could prove his alibi.'

'He's trying to shift this from himself to us,' Wes Terrell snarled, his face ugly with rage and fear.

'You'll have a chance to prove that at the trial,' Bronson told him. 'All right, Buzz. I reckon your prisoners are anxious to see their new quarters.'

The sheriff led the way down the corridor.

'You'll pay for this plenty, Buzz,' threat-

276

ened Walsh. 'You can't get away with a dirty trick like this. Think we're fools and don't see that you and the rangers both are playing in with Forrest? I hear you and that scoundrel usta be in a cattle-rustling gang together, and everybody knows the rangers are for him because he was once one himself. We'll get a crack at you yet, and at Bronson too for that matter. Don't think anything different for a minute.'

'I wouldn't get in a sweat if I was you, Pres,' the sheriff advised, without heat. 'If you can show a jury you didn't rob the train I won't make any holler about it. All is, I'm sheriff of this county.'

After the prisoners had been locked up Waggoner returned to his office with Bronson to rejoin the prosecuting attorney.

Over his cigar, a broad-rimmed cowboy hat tilted back on his head, the fat sheriff made a prediction. 'If you haven't enough evidence, Robinson, after a couple of days there will be more waiting for you back there in one of those cells.'

'You think one of the prisoners will break down and turn state's witness?' Robinson asked.

'That's why I put them in separate cells. Yes, sir. Two of those tough customers are false alarms. Maybe three. The only one I'd back to go through to a finish is Webb Lake.'

'We have evidence enough,' Lieutenant Bronson said. 'By the way, you'd better get a cell ready for Luke Schrader. My boys are bringing him in today.'

CHAPTER 28

Forrest Takes a Job

At the Granite Gap ranch, as with others of the big cattle demesnes of the open range, the lavishness of the hospitality was almost feudal. Never a day passed without at least half a dozen guests sitting down to dinner either with the men or at the family table. Any stranger crossing the country was welcome to stay for the night.

The main house was a big low rambling log building with a long wide porch along the whole front of it. A wide hall cut the house into two parts and permitted a passage of air to temper the summer heat. Two ramblers and a bougainvillea vine shaded the porch from a sun at times too torrid. A careless garden, not too well kept, sloped down toward the men's quarters a hundred yards away. In it bloomed roses and sweet williams and a dozen other old-fashioned flowers, some of them more or less choked with grass.

Curtis King had built the house soon after the Civil War, and had since added wings as his family grew and his circumstances became easier. In the older part of the house the floors were of whipsawed lumber and the space between the logs of the wall still mud-daubed. This was the part where the boys and their father lived. The gallery outside of their domain was strewn with saddles, bridles, spurs, lariats, and chaps. They lived an untidy and casual existence, and Janet had long since given up trying to make them orderly.

In the newer wings the young woman dominated. There were samplers on the walls instead of bearskins. Here the old furniture of the family — four-poster walnut beds, valuable French mirrors, heavy wardrobes, and comfortable rockers on thick-napped carpets — suggested an entirely different outlook on life. There was a good piano. In the bookcase were sets of Scott and Smollett, leather-padded volumes of Tennyson and Byron, and some wordy and unrealistic fiction by writers whose names are no longer remembered. Janet could play old-fashioned tinkling melodies and could sing in untrained voice the sentimental songs of the day.

It was a well-favored land of plenty. A large irrigated garden, taken care of by an old Mexican, produced an abundance of fresh vegetables. From an orchard planted at the wide entrance of a canyon came peaches, plums, cherries, and berries. In season watermelons were as plentiful as blackberries. The ranch supplied most of the needs of those who subsisted on it, with the exception of clothing and such essentials as tobacco, coffee, tea, and sugar.

But the Granite Gap was no idler's paradise. There was always enough of work for all. Young though she was, the management of the house was in the hands of Janet. She made out the lists for food that went to town and superintended the cooking in a general way. With the bunkhouse she had nothing to do. The ranch employed so many riders that a separate cook took care of the employees.

Between the life of the cowboys and the young woman at 'the big house,' as the large rambling southern home of the Kings was called by those on the payroll, a sharp division line existed. In the careless atmosphere of the place, democratic though it was in one sense, no brush-popper ever overstepped by a hair the proper respect due Janet. The sons of Curtis were hazed like any other youngsters, but the name of his daughter was never mentioned at the bunkhouse or around a campfire.

When Blake Forrest arrived with Stone Heath he turned his horse into the big pasture and walked with his friend to the bunkhouse. A message came by young Curtis King that his father wanted to see Forrest at the big house. After he had washed up and shaved, Blake strolled up and was met by Curtis King on the porch.

'Come in,' the ranchman said, and led the way to his office. 'This is how it shapes, Forrest. My foreman at the Big Bend ranch, Will Ellison, has picked up quite a bunch of stock for himself and wants to start on his own. I've talked with stockmen who know you, and they all tell the same story. You know cows. You understand every angle of the business.' He stopped, looking at his guest with shrewd appraising eyes.

Blake guessed what was in his mind. 'That's not all they said,' he suggested with a smile.

'You're right,' King answered promptly. 'They said you would make the best foreman in Texas — if you'd quit helling around.'

'I've quit,' the young man told him.

'Fine,' the owner of the Granite Gap answered, no certainty in his voice. 'When did you quit? After you walked up from Vallery's house the other night and almost had a battle with that Terrell outfit, hardly an hour after you had promised me you would walk round them if you could?'

'Here's my story about that,' Forrest said quietly. 'My friends came to tell me the Terrells meant trouble. I didn't want them to waylay me outside the Vallery house, so I decided to go to my room at the hotel. We took the short cut through the bar to the lobby and walked into the enemy. Wes Terrell headed me off. I wasn't armed. Nothing left to do but make a bluff. I walked to the end of the bar and began deviling Terrell to start smoking. He thought we had come in there to fight the thing out. Like I figured, he hadn't sand enough in his craw to go through. His friends waited for him to say what it would be, and he said "Nothing doing." That's all there was to it.'

'Glad to know that. Now these scoundrels are locked up, there won't be so much pressure on you. Well, as I said, Ellison wants to quit. Not right away, but in three-four months. My idea is for you to go down to the Big Bend ranch and learn the ropes so as to take his place. We can fix up a deal by which you get a small cut in on the profits as a bonus.'

'Let's get this clear, Mr. King,' the younger man said bluntly. 'Are you making me this offer because you think I'm the best man you can find for the place, or because you feel indebted to me for bringing your daughter back to town?'

The ranch owner leaned back in the armchair, his steel-hard eyes fixed on the other man. 'I don't mix sentiment with business,

Forrest. If I didn't think you the man for this job I wouldn't offer it to you. There's danger in it, and mighty few I know could handle it satisfactorily to me. Nothing can alter the fact that I'm eternally grateful to you for saving my daughter, but that is a debt I can't offer to pay.'

'Then I'll say that you have hired a hand, Mr. King. There's a little matter I want to clean up before I go. It will take me two or three days. Will next week be soon enough to start?'

'That will be fine. I think we'll both be satisfied.' King looked up at his daughter, who had just appeared in the doorway. 'You might shake hands, Janet, with the new foreman of the Big Bend ranch.'

Janet offered her father's employee a small firm sun-browned hand. Strong white teeth gleamed between the red lips in a smile of obvious pleasure.

'I'm so glad,' she said.

Looking into her eyes, he noticed the mobile quality of them. The color was blue, but of variable shades. They darkened with excitement. He had seen them still and deep, quiet pools of mystery. Now they were wide-open, eager. He thought, and gave no hint of his feeling, that the flame in them could burn into a man's veins and set his pulses hammering.

'I hope you won't be sorry,' he replied, 'since you are responsible for it.'

'I — responsible? Am I?'

'Only that you were an instrument of fate. If I hadn't met you on the Malpais I wouldn't have gone back to Fair Play — and if I hadn't done that nothing else following would have happened the way it did. Probably the rangers would still be combing the hills for me.'

'I hope they will never do that again,' she said, and as she looked up at him her bosom grew warm with emotion.

'He's a respectable citizen now — no more helling around,' King explained.

'The repentant sinner we were talking about the other day, Miss Janet,' added Blake with a sardonic smile.

The ranchman looked at his strong brown face, all the weakness of youth ironed out of it — took in the lean and well-knit body, lithe and graceful as that of a panther. He guessed that this cool customer would waste precious little time repenting.

'Better ask him for supper, Janet. I have a lot to talk over yet with this young man.'

'You will stay, won't you, Mr. Forrest?' invited the girl. 'We would all be glad to have you.'

He hesitated. 'I sort of promised the boys at the cook shack —'

'We have fatted calf, prepared especially for prodigal sons,' she broke in. 'And anyhow Bess would never forgive us if we didn't keep you here. So that's settled.'

She turned swiftly and went her light-footed way through the door.

'Sit down again, Forrest,' his employer said. 'Want to talk over with you the Big Bend layout. There's an enormous lot of thieving going on down in that country. Mexicans running wet stock across the river. Raids across the border and counter-raids. Outlaws on the dodge in the brush and helping themselves right and left. I read in the Galveston *News* the other day that there are now seven hundred fifty warrants out in Texas for horse thieves, and that counts only the known ones. Up here we are comparatively honest, but down along the border it's grab what you can. This is a man-size job I'm offering you. Outside of Captain Nelly's rangers, who have to cover half of West Texas, Judge Colt is all the law there is. You will need nerve and diplomacy. Bandits will ride into yore cowcamps for grub, and you will have to put up with them as if they were honest men, unless you have evidence against them. Not one man in a thousand could do what I'm asking you to do, and that is to make money for me and stay alive yoreself.'

'Maybe I would be safer locked up in the penitentiary,' Forrest said, with a grin.

'I've a notion it's the other guys won't be safe,' King told him. 'You walk through trouble as if it wasn't there, and usually you find it isn't. . . . Want to wash up for supper?'

Blake grinned, amused at the thought that had occurred to him. He was getting to be quite a society man. If he did not look out some girl would cast an eye on him, after which he would be a brand snatched from the burning.

CHAPTER 29

A Bank Deposit

Craig Shannon and Blake Forrest dismounted at the hitch rack in front of the Valley Bank. The younger man untied the saddlebags and flung them over his left arm. Together they walked into the bank.

Two men were in sight. Homer Packard, behind the cage, was cashing a check for the owner of the largest saloon in town. At sight of Forrest the cashier forgot what he was doing and stared at him from a face gone suddenly white.

'You — again!' he gasped.

Blake smiled, pleasantly. 'Like to have a little talk with Mr. Gildea,' he said. 'Is he in his office?'

'Yes, but —'

'Then we'll just walk in and surprise him. He'll be glad to see us.'

Packard looked at Shannon, started to ask a question, and thought better of it. 'Maybe I'd better tell Mr. Gildea that — that you're here,' he got out.

'We'll tell him ourselves,' Blake said. 'No

need troubling you when you're busy.'

He started for the door of the inner office, but stopped at an abrupt hoarse summons from the cashier.

'Put up your hands — quick! Or I'll shoot the daylights out of you.'

Through the bars of the cage the barrel of an unsteady revolver protruded. Blake grinned. 'My goodness, Craig,' he drawled. 'This is a holdup. The young man aims to rob us.'

Shannon did not throw up his hands either. He snapped, sharply, 'Don't be a fool, Packard,' and added, 'we're here on legitimate business.'

The saloonkeeper dryly gave the cashier advice. 'I reckon you better put yore popgun up, Homer. Mr. Shannon hasn't took to sticking up banks for a living.'

The bank clerk withdrew the gun, uncertainly. 'I wasn't talking to Mr. Shannon,' he explained, the color slowly beating back into his face.

Blake looked around, as if to see who else was present. 'Must have been me he meant. You hadn't ought to be so abrupt with the customers of the bank, Homer. I've come to make a deposit.'

He opened the door of the office and walked into the room. Shannon followed him and closed the door.

The small piggy eyes of Gildea lifted from the document he was reading and instantly registered alarm. 'What you doing here?' he demanded, his voice shrill, beads of perspiration on his swollen face. 'Get outa here, you fool. You can't do it twice and get away with it.'

Forrest put the saddlebags on the desk. He unstrapped the fastenings and lifted some canvas sacks from them.

'No need getting excited, Mr. Gildea,' he suggested. 'I've come to make a little deposit in the bank. Like to have you count it. I make the total six thousand four hundred and twenty-two dollars.'

Suspiciously Gildea watched him empty the money from the sacks to the top of the desk. His heavy inert body did not move. Only the little eyes were quick with life. He did not understand what this was about, but he knew there was not to be a second robbery. The presence of Shannon ought to have told him so from the first, he admitted to himself. But this did not make any sense. Forrest had brought back, so he said, exactly the amount he had stolen, not counting the Holloway note. Why had he done this? The jury had decided that this money belonged to the man who had taken it from the bank. He was under no obligation to return it. Had he come back to deposit it in the Valley Bank as a deliberate gesture of triumphant defiance?

'Are you in this, Shannon?' the banker snarled.

'Merely as a witness, Jake. Blake wanted a friend along so that there wouldn't be any mistake as to what had taken place. I was glad to come.'

'Well, what the hell *is* taking place?' demanded Gildea. 'If he thinks he can deposit this money in my bank, he's wrong. I won't take it from the scoundrel.'

'Maybe it would be a good idea not to decide that until you have heard Blake's proposition,' the cattleman said.

'I'm not interested in any of his propositions. He robbed me of this money and got away with it before a fat-headed jury. I won't have any more dealings with him. None whatever. That's flat.' Gildea slammed a fat fist on the desk to stress his point.

'Now suppose we count the money,' Blake said quietly. 'I'm not expecting you to deposit this money in my name, Gildea. I'm bringing it back to you for private reasons of my own. You wouldn't understand them. Not necessary you should. The point is, you get the mazuma, and that's all you care about.'

'You mean you're giving me this money?'

the banker shrilled.

'You've got the idea. You're a heartless thief and always will be. I haven't any more respect for you than for a sidewinder. But I'm bringing back to you the same dough that I took. Now get busy counting it. I don't like to breathe the same air as you longer than is necessary.'

Gildea counted the gold and the notes. 'You want a receipt for this?' he asked.

'Yes. Send for Packard and turn this over to him. Both of you will sign the receipt.'

Five minutes later Forrest and his friend walked out of the bank and remounted their horses.

'I'm not sure yet I wasn't a fool for taking the money back,' the younger man said with a wry grin. 'He owed it to me, with compound interest added.'

'He owed it to you, but that wasn't the right way to collect.' Shannon slanted a puzzled inquiring look at him. 'What made you take it back, Blake?'

Forrest knew why, but he did not tell him. That was strictly his own rather shamefaced concern. When a man has followed his own sweet will for years, realization that the opinion of another is extremely important comes to him with a shock. The only answer the cattleman received was a jingle sung by rail-road builders.

'Hollered at the mule and the mule
    wouldn't gee,
So I whopt him in the head with the
    singletree,
And it's "Go on, mule, you better stop
    saddlin'." '[1]

'You're a fine rooster,' jeered Shannon, intent on stirring up a reply. 'Damn my buttons if you make sense. To get that money you take a chance of working for the state of Texas ten or fifteen years, then when you're sitting pretty you turn it back to that old vinegaroon instead of living at the top of the pot with it.'

'No trouble to make a case out against me as a prize lunkhead,' Blake admitted cheerfully. 'I certainly got myself in a jackpot where I was sweatin' like a nigger at election.'

'Then by gilt-edged luck you work out of the tight and find you can't use six thousand dollars anyhow. That the way of it?'

'I reckon. Fact is, Craig, sometimes a man does a crazy thing and finds out later he doesn't want to stick by it. I've been a wild

[1] Stepping high to avoid putting its weight into the load.

coot, but I'm not the right stuff to make a thief of, by General Jackson. My folks didn't start me right for it.'

'Now you're shouting, Blake. Keep that in mind. For years you've had the reputation of being a bad man when you didn't deserve it. Now you'll have to walk a chalk line till folks see you've quit snorting around. Why don't you get married?'

Forrest looked at his friend, a droll gleam in his eye. 'Picked the lady for me yet, Craig?'

Shannon smiled. 'Wouldn't surprise me if you had picked her.'

For reply the young man gave him another stanza about the mule which had better stop saddling.

CHAPTER 30

'All Women Marry on a Chance'

Janet walked into her father's office with a newspaper in her hand.

'Have you read this piece about Blake Forrest?' she asked. 'The one that tells of his taking the money back to the bank?'

Curtis King reached for the paper. 'No, I haven't. Let's see it.'

A strange last chapter [he read] has been written in the Valley Bank case of alleged robbery. Today Blake Forrest, who was recently acquitted at Fair Play of holding up the bank, walked into the office of Jacob Gildea and turned over to him six thousand four hundred and twenty-two dollars, the exact sum he was charged with taking.

It appears that the whole trouble arose from a misunderstanding as to whether Mr. Gildea wanted Forrest to have this sum in payment of an old debt said to have been due. Finding that this was not the case, the accused man returned to the bank the amount in dispute. The affair is now closed to the satisfaction of all concerned.

The cattleman gave a whoop of jubilation. 'Bully for Forrest. That starts him right again. I'm sure pleased to read this.'

'So am I.' A faint glow of crimson streamed into her cheeks below the tan. 'I have to tell you something, Father. When we spoke about it before I told you I didn't love him and that I wouldn't marry him if he was the last man in the world. That's not true, though I didn't know it then. I'll marry Blake Forrest — or I'll never marry.'

He frowned at her, his keen eyes searching her face. 'Has he asked you?'

Her eyes were as steady as his. 'No. He has never said a word to lead me to believe that he cares anything for me. I'm just shameless — hoping he'll ask me and afraid he won't.'

Curtis King showed in his tanned rugged countenance no sign of softness, but his heart went out mightily to this forthright girl who was confessing to him the folly that had swept her from the prudent moorings of her traditional and conventional upbringing. He loved in her the gallant and defiant courage that faced the truth. His impatience was the index of the disturbance that moved him. Because he could find no other answer he fell back on the time-honored formula accepted by his and her world.

'That's foolish talk. A nice girl doesn't fling herself at the head of a man who doesn't woo her. She waits, until she is sure he cares for her, and after a suitable time —'

'Yes, I know all about that, but I'm not a nice girl. I'm a crazy little fool who has fallen in love.' She added, with a touch of bitter contempt for herself, 'Maybe you could whip it out of me.'

He brushed that aside with a gesture. 'All girls are romantic. Just now Bess is all steamed up about this man. I don't blame her, since he saved her life at the risk of his own. There's something about the fellow to take a woman's eye — or a man's, for the matter of that. He stands out from the herd, perhaps because he bulls his way through and doesn't give a cuss what people think. Point I'm making is that there's a lot of romantic nonsense that isn't love.'

'Yes,' she agreed. 'Bess is romantic about him. Maybe I am too. But it's more than that with me. When I'm not with him I'm just passing dreary time until I can see him again, and even then I'm not happy since I'm just another girl to him. Nothing else matters any more — not my work, or fun, or music, or anything I used to be so interested in before I knew him. I'm not telling you this for sympathy. I know I have to buck up and work out of it myself.'

Nobody looking at the immobile face of the cattleman could have guessed how proud he was of this daughter's spirit. He knew that back of the radiant animal vigor there was an inner beauty fine and rare.

'I'm sorry about this, Janet,' he said quietly. 'It's bad enough to fall in love with a man who doesn't care for you, let alone one who has spent his whole life proving he wouldn't be a good husband.'

'Why wouldn't he be a good husband? You've just said that returning the money starts him right. I don't know all he has done that is wrong, but it doesn't matter now. If he has made his own laws he hasn't broken them. There's nothing weak about him — and nothing to despise. He is a strong man, unafraid. Since he isn't evil, a woman would be proud to have him for a mate.' She ended on a little note of laughter. 'I seem to be making a speech.'

'It isn't that I don't like him,' King said gently. 'I don't know any young man I admire more. But I wouldn't choose him as the man for you to marry. There's something tempestuous about him. Every time he walks into a saloon, men eye him. The woods are filled with his enemies.'

'And with his friends,' she cut in. 'Not colorless fair-weather friends, but men devoted to him through thick and thin.'

'Yes. He draws men to him. I'll say that. He has plenty of character — of a kind. But he is a marked man. Someday he will have to kill again or be killed. There would be little happiness for his wife.'

'You don't know that. All women marry on a chance. I'd like to take mine beside a man who strides along so fearlessly and so splendidly.' Again she pulled up with a murmur of rueful laughter. 'But why go into that, since he has never thought of asking me to marry him?'

King paced the floor, greatly disturbed. 'I'm afraid you're laying up grief for yourself, daughter. Unless you are overstressing your feeling for him. Sometimes girls imagine they are in love when it's only a temporary fascination.'

'No.' Janet shook her head decisively. 'It hit me when I first met him, though I tried to argue myself out of it. This is for keeps. But don't worry about me. I'll get through it somehow. I told you because — well, if the miracle happens and he does ask me, you won't be so shocked.'

'I wouldn't stand in your way — if you are sure you love him,' he said, and put an arm around her shoulder.

'That's fine,' she grinned bravely. 'Now all I have to do is to get his consent.'

'I've never known a man good enough for you,' he said gruffly. 'You're like your mother.'

Janet looked out of the window and her eyes grew wider. 'Well — well, talk of angels and you hear the clip-clop of their horses' hoofs. Mr. Forrest is just returning to our midst.'

Forrest unsaddled, put his horse in the pasture, and reported at the big house. His employer met him a little stiffly, with a feeling of puzzled resentment, even of hostility, the cattleman knew to be unfair. The new foreman was not to blame because Janet had fallen in love with him. Apparently he had not made a move to win her affection, but the father of the girl was affronted that he could ignore, even unconsciously, a gift so precious. Though he would not have chosen such a marriage, he felt unreasonably that Forrest ought to wish it.

'Are you ready to take off for the Big Bend ranch?' King asked curtly.

'Yes, sir. Tomorrow morning.'

'Good enough. Come up after supper and

I'll talk things over with you. I've been thinking about getting some imported bulls. White-
face, I reckon.'

'I'll be up, sir. Like to get off early and
make it in a day if I can.' Blake offered a
suggestion. 'If you can spare me Stone Heath
I would like to have him on the Big Bend
ranch. He's a man I know and can trust. It
would be nice to feel I had him back of me
on this job.'

'That will be all right. I'll send him down
in a week or two with some supplies.'

King rose from his chair. Blake felt that he
had been dismissed. He was conscious of a
change of atmosphere, of a lack of cordiality.
It was nothing he could definitely place, but
it was there nevertheless. He wondered what
could be the reason for it.

CHAPTER 31

Janet Forgets to Mail a Letter

Since Forrest was leaving early in the morning and her case was desperate Janet waited shamelessly in the shadow of the porch to meet him accidentally after he left her father. She heard the droning of their voices a long time before there came to her the sound of a chair being pushed back. Presently the broad shoulders of the new Big Bend ranch foreman bulked in the doorway.

Janet moved forward a step or two and he caught sight of her. Before she could begin the approach she had selected he took speech out of her mouth.

'I've been hoping to meet you,' he said. 'Is there somewhere we can talk — alone?'

'I want to get a letter off tonight. One of the boys would take it to Midway, but if you wouldn't mind riding with me —'

She stopped, breathlessly, to watch the effect of this. It was a daring suggestion, for that time and place. No unchaperoned young woman could ride out into the desert at night with a young man except at the risk of starting talk.

Without an instant's hesitation Blake said, 'I'll catch and saddle, Miss King.'

'Black Hawk is in the pasture. You'll find my side-saddle on the south side of the barn, fourth from the end. I'll meet you there in fifteen minutes.'

Janet went into the little room where her father was still sitting. She thought he looked older than usual. His big body was slumped in the chair dejectedly. With the point of a pencil he stabbed at a sheet of paper. When he looked up he could tell at once by her starry eyes that a pulse of excitement was beating strong in her.

'I'm going down to Midway to mail a letter, Father,' she said. 'With Blake Forrest.'

Surprised, and doubtful, he asked, 'Do you think that wise?'

'We spent a night together alone on the desert,' she reminded him.

'I don't mean that. Of course it's all right. I'm thinking of — gossip.'

'It may be the last chance I'll ever have to be alone with him, Father. I don't want to be a coward and not take it.'

'Who proposed this trip?'

'He said he wanted to talk with me. I suggested we ride.'

Curtis King threw up his hands. 'All right.

All right. Don't be out too late. He'll come to the house here for you, I reckon.'

'I said I would meet him at the stable.'

'No. Start from here. I'll be on the porch and see you off myself. We'll have nothing furtive about this.'

'That would be better,' she nodded. 'Thanks, Father, awf'ly, for understanding.'

She hurried from the room to change her dress. Helen Decker knocked on the door as she was getting into her riding costume. The school-teacher showed surprise.

'Are you getting ready for the midnight ride of Miss Pauline Revere?' she asked.

'Something like that. I'm carrying an important letter to the post office at Midway to get it off on the morning mail.'

'It must be very important,' Helen said dryly, adding with a cowboy drawl: 'I 'low all yore riders are plumb wore out and couldn't make out to tote it for you.'

Janet laughed softly, a wave of color flushing her brown beauty. 'This is a very particular letter. It takes two of us to make sure it gets on its way safely.'

'I see. And the other half of the two is the reformed bank robber.'

'How did you guess it?'

'By not being entirely blind, deaf, and dumb,' Helen answered. 'I could even guess the letter wouldn't be so awfully important, if it wasn't for giving you a chance to share a lovely moon with the bandit who is also a hero.'

'It's to Sampson & Doan ordering a keg of ten-penny nails and a horse collar . . . Father says we may ride to the post office. You don't think it's too brazen of me, do you? I asked him to go with me.'

'Your father?' Miss Decker inquired innocently.

'We're not talking about father.'

'Oh, your Robin Hood! Did you have to rope and hogtie him before he would agree to go?'

'He was very nice about it.' Janet pulled a boot over a very well modeled leg. 'You haven't answered my question.'

'You'll go with him just the same if I think it's . . . brazen, won't you?'

'Yes. I may never see him again.'

'I think he's not good enough for you, dear, but if you're in love with him I hope to goodness he has sense enough to know his luck.'

They clung to each other, in a swift embrace, as girls do.

'Some day you'll understand better,' Janet said with a tremulous laugh. 'We're all alike. We want our mate, the one man in the world. It's the way we're made. There's no use

305

preaching Madame Grundy to us.'

Curtis King helped his daughter to the saddle. His hard eyes met those of Forrest. 'I'll expect you back by ten-thirty,' he said.

'We'll be on time,' the younger man replied.

It was a night of countless stars. The moon suffused the desert, softening its harsh and dessicated details to a vague and magical loveliness. They rode knee to knee, in silence, their supple bodies synchronizing with the motions of the horses.

Janet caught herself wondering at her emotion. She was in a world reborn, one filled with beauty that flooded her being, and just now she was as much alone in it as Eve had been with Adam.

'I've been to Rosedale since I saw you last,' he said. 'I called on Jake Gildea and took him back his money.'

'I saw it in the Rosedale *Herald*,' she answered. 'I'm glad.'

'You told me two wrongs do not make a right. I didn't want to see it that way. I fought against it, but — I had to give in.'

'Are you — sorry?'

'No. It was something to be wiped out before I could make a new start.'

She brushed back an escaping tendril of soft hair, to get rid of the sudden telltale moisture that filmed her eyes. 'You've turned that new leaf.' Her voice was almost a murmur.

'Yes. All the wild irresponsible crazy days are dead.' The old sardonic smile touched his lips. 'I'm for law and order, and peace — and I'm going down into a country where I'll have to pack a gun every minute, and use it sometimes.'

'I wish you weren't going,' she said.

'Why?' He flung the question at her almost harshly.

She picked words out of her agitated thoughts, to tell something of what was in her mind and to conceal more.

'It isn't fair to send you down there — into that lawless country — now of all times — when you're just starting to —'

Blake tossed her argument aside. 'Nothing to that. A man has to do his job. Robbers and rustlers must be checked or all honest people will have to leave the country. I'm glad to go. It's a great chance for me.'

'You'll be careful?'

He did not hear what she had said. His mind was on something else, the gulf that separated them, the lawless years that had made him what he was and the quiet gentle ones that had fixed her character. Yet, desperately conscious of them, he deliberately broke down the dam his will had built.

'I have thought of you ever since I left, day

and night,' he cried, his voice low and rough with feeling. 'I can't get you out of my mind. When I try you keep crowding back. Before I go I have to tell you that . . . I've had no better sense than to fall in love with you.'

The tumult of a joyous song flooded her being. Love irradiated and warmed her like a fine and potent wine. 'I have thought of you too,' she said, almost in a whisper. 'Day and night.'

'How have you thought of me?' he demanded. 'As a brand snatched from the burning, a reclaimed sinner to whom you've done your Christian duty?'

Her eyes turned to his strong face, so intensely masculine, the look in them that a woman has for only one man. She felt the wild beating of her heart against her ribs.

'You never were a sinner to me.'

He swung from the saddle and lifted her to the ground. His hungry gaze searched the young face raised to his, found in it the gift of shy and eager surrender. He drew her into his arms.

Slowly they rode back to the ranch house, neither of them remembering that they had not mailed the letter which had been the excuse for their ride.

Curtis King was waiting for them. He heard the news with an imperturbable face, but it was none the less a relief to him. One look at the radiant countenance of Janet told him that for the hour at least she was supremely happy. The future would have to take care of itself.

'We want to be married at once,' Blake explained. 'I know that is hurrying things, but our idea is for Janet to go down to the ranch with me now.'

'Have it your own way,' King said. 'You're not the man I would have picked for her, Forrest. Too much you-be-damned dynamite in you. But maybe she knows what she wants better than I do. I'll say this. If you don't know you're getting a girl out of ten thousand you're a plumb fool.'

Forrest agreed. 'If I didn't know that I wouldn't want to marry her.'

CHAPTER 32

The Forrests Go Pioneering

So they were married. They drove down to the Spur (⊢⊏) ranch, stopping a couple of days at the Southern Hotel in San Antonio to rest and do some shopping. From here they headed the buckboard south to their new domain.

At the Granite Gap the conditions of life had been comfortable and pleasant. The ranch was within reach of a railroad, and even luxuries could be obtained if desired. But as they pushed through the brush in the direction of the border Janet realized that they were moving into a pioneer world and that every mile was carrying them farther from civilization. She was not disturbed by this. Indeed, it was a delight to her to feel that she was setting out with her man to help conquer a land so entirely primitive.

When they camped out on the journey, the buzz of mosquitoes in her ears, she made light of the discomforts. If at the end of the long trek she was discouraged at the sight of her new temporary home, a small house made of split logs set upright in the ground, she gave no sign of it.

Janet was too happy to let material hardships affect her spirits. She sewed curtains for the small diamond-shaped portholes which served for windows, and she cooked in a Dutch oven as if she had been used to nothing else all her life. As she worked snatches of song bubbled from her lips. She and Blake found it easy to laugh often together, for they were living in a rose-colored world of youth and love.

'It won't be for long,' he promised. 'Ellison is leaving at the end of next week. Then I'll be the Big Boss and we'll move up to his house. It's very comfortable, not exactly what you've been used to but a lot better than this.'

As the weeks and the months rolled along Janet discovered that her volcanic man was always gentle and considerate in their relations. From the gossip she picked up she learned that he was becoming very popular with the vaqueros of the Spur. Nonetheless she could see that his word was law. No loudmouthed bully, his quiet suggestions were more potent than the hectoring commands of a bully-puss majordomo.

Blake carried his difficulties on his own broad shoulders and did not bring them home to Janet. He ruled by the right of the strong. From the Mexican cook she heard the details of an encounter that fixed his supremacy once for all. A huge vile-tempered scoundrel called Buck Spelvin had ruled the roost at the bunkhouse of the Spur. Even Ellison had walked cannily round him, knowing that the fellow had a local reputation as a bad man. When Forrest took the reins Spelvin had watched him from slitted eyes filled with a malignant and jeering defiance. The new foreman was aware the man was a disaffectant and a creator of trouble, but he waited patiently, overlooking more than one contemptuous affront, to choose an occasion of quarrel that suited him.

It came about a week after Ellison left. At a night campfire Spelvin drew a gun on a harmless young Mexican rider who accidentally tripped over his foot and spilled some coffee on him. A stream of threats, decorated with obscenity, poured from the hairy throat of the bully.

'Put up that gun, Buck,' Forrest ordered, his voice low but clear as a bell.

'Maybe you can make me,' the ruffian sneered, jumping to his feet.

'Maybe I can,' the foreman answered, still quietly.

Every man around that campfire knew a challenge had been given and accepted.

Forrest rose in one swift lithe movement, his gaze fixed on the enemy. He made no motion toward the revolver in the scabbard at his hip.

'Better put it up, Buck,' he suggested again, evenly, but with cold steely authority ringing through the words.

The unshaven heavily jowled face was thrust forward furiously. Urgent impulse was twitching at the fellow to fling bullets at the foreman, to rub him out before he could lift a hand in self-defence. What daunted him was fear, not of Forrest but of these hard-bitten riders whom he had bullied. One of them, Stone Heath, a new man just arrived, was known to be a close friend of the boss. Spelvin knew he could kill the foreman, but his horse was in the brush, unsaddled, and he would probably be surrounded before he could get away. In that case he would likely be wiped out before he could rope, saddle, and escape.

'Not on yore tintype, Mr. Foreman,' the ruffian growled. 'My gun's waiting right here ready for business. If you want any of my game, come a-smokin'.'

Blake recalled the advice of the lieutenant of rangers under whom he had first served. He was a grizzled old officer who had fought Indians, Mexicans, and outlaws. 'When you start for a bad man, son, keep going. You've got an edge on him because you're inside the law and he is out. Nine times out of ten he'll throw in his hand and quit.'

All of which might be true, but it was small comfort to think this might be the tenth. As Forrest moved forward, evenly, not too fast, with the light strong stride that characterized him, he realized that the crook of a finger would send him to eternity.

'No occasion to go crazy with the heat, Buck,' he drawled. 'Can't have my boys shooting each other up, and by the jumping Moses, I won't. Put that cutter back in its holster before you make a mistake.' In his voice there was complete assurance, in his bearing an almost indifferent certainty. His eyes bore into the blustering bad man. Not by an instant of ragged haste did he hurry his pace.

'Keep back, fellow,' shrieked the rider. 'Keep back, or by God, I'll pump lead into you.'

'No, you won't,' the foreman corrected. 'You'll turn that .44 over to me like a lamb.'

Blake held out his right hand as he approached. The other man drew back, excitement and uncertainty in him struggling for mastery.

'Don't you come a foot nearer,' he yelled. 'Not a foot.'

'That's no way to talk,' Forrest remonstrated quietly. 'When I say, "Give me the gun, I mean —" '

He stopped. The time for words was passed. Out went Blake's left, all the drive of his plunging body back of it.

In his uncertain English the Mexican cook had told Janet the swift denouement.

'The big boss he jump — queek, oh, very queek. His feest land smack, like the keeck of a mule, on Buck's jaw. And Buck, he roll over and lie steel. The big boss say, "Get his gun, Stone," and walk back to the fire. That is all, *señora*. Except that Buck he saddle his bronco and beat it *muy pronto*.' Pedro laughed, savoring in memory his pleasure at the cool efficiency of the new foreman. 'Then the big boss he sing, like he do sometimes, and the vaqueros they theenk, "Here is the man for us at last." '

Janet liked the enthusiasm of the cook. She shared it herself.

'What did he sing?' she asked, smiling at the pockmarked little Mexican.

'He sing, *señora,* about dry bones in a valley.'

Later in the day Pedro heard his mistress singing the same song, in her lilting untrained contralto.

'Dry bones in the valley,
  I really do believe.

315

Dry bones in the valley;
Oh, some of them bones are mine.

Some come a-cripple,
Some come a-lame,
Some of them bones are mine.
Some come a-walking with a hickory
cane,
Some of them bones are mine.'

Even though she found life in the primitive brush country a never-ending joy, Janet devoured eagerly all the letters that came from the family she had left at the Granite Gap ranch. Newspapers came to them seldom, since they had to travel fifty miles to get the very irregular mail. It was in a letter from Bill Crabb that they read a piece of news which interested them both.

I take my pen in hand, oldtimer [wrote Crabb], to let you know the latest news about them dere friends of yours, the dadgummed Terrell outfit. Well sir, Robinson got a conviksun against all five of the skunks and Judge Jackman he got real generous with their time and handed them a fifteen-year jolt. No kick coming from anyone. You will not be plesed to hear that on the way back to jail Wes

Terrell shot Buzz Waggoner and the whole caboodle eskaped. Somebody had sliped Wes a gun. The doc says Buzz will make the grade. Nobody knows where the Terrells have lit out to. Some say Arizona. Well, Arizona is welcome to them, I say.

When do you aim to send for me, you blamed old vinegaroon. Since you and Stone have gone this country has got awful tame. Don't seem like the men have any guts or the women any jingle. I'll be down there riding the chuck line if you don't give a job to that old top-rider,

yore friend,
BILL CRABB

'Why don't you send for him, Blake?' his wife suggested. 'You need men you can trust.'

'I just hadn't got around to it,' Blake said. 'I'll write him tomorrow.'

Bill arrived three weeks later with a wagonload of supplies and a sack full of letters, newspapers, and books.

CHAPTER 33

In the Brush Country

The cow business in that lower country was a precarious and uncertain one. All over the West during the day of the cattleman, rustlers hung on the outskirts of big outfits and carried on their nefarious business. But near the border the natural hazards of the stockmen were greatly increased. When the northern market broke, for one reason or another, many thousand longhorns were shipped to Indianola, Galveston, and other points for consumption by the packeries, which sold the beef as 'salt junk' or killed for the hides and tallow alone.

During the days of reconstruction after the war both land and cattle were almost without value. Only the hides would bring cash. Cattle drifted south during the winter. Thousands of them bogged down and died in the bayous and creeks. According to the custom of the country anybody could help himself to what was called a fallen hide, regardless of the brand on it. Unscrupulous hide-hunters did not wait for the cow to die a natural death. The skinners became as busy as the old buffalo-hunters had been.

When Blake Forrest came to the Big Bend those conditions were a memory, but the men who had been active in the big steals still nested in small clearings all over the great thickets of this lower land. Another source of peril was the raiders from Mexico. In the dark of the moon it was an easy enterprise to cross the Rio Grande, round up a bunch of fat stock, and swim them over the river for sale to new owners. Men not yet in middle life could tell stories of how Juan Cortina, most famous of the *bandidos,* plundered and murdered in South Texas. Some of them had heard him make his boast that the gringos were raising cattle for him.

Against these foes and the natural ones of flood, drought, and blizzards, Forrest and his men waged incessant warfare. There was at first little law in the land, though the rangers and the cattlemen enforced occasional rough justice. Cowboys rode the line and failed to return to the home ranch. Comrades found their bodies where they had made their last stand. Swift reprisals followed. Outlaws were run down and shot or hanged without benefit of judge or jury.

When Blake Forrest returned after one of these primitive expeditions — sometimes un-

dertaken by the Spur outfit alone and sometimes with the help of rangers or other stockmen — he never talked to Janet of what had
taken place. She noticed that for days he was
grimmer, that her happy little jokes died down
too easily. She watched the tight lines round
his mouth, and knew he was living over again
the unpleasant memories of how he had punished white-faced killers now lying in shallow
graves somewhere in the mesquite. At such
times she was very tender and patient with
him, using all her wiles to woo him out of
the black mood hanging heavy over him.

His duties took him away from the home
ranch a great deal, sometimes for weeks at
a time. During the roundup of cattle for the
trail drive she would not see him for long
stretches; then unexpectedly he would ride in,
dusty, gaunt, unshaven, and red-eyed, to stay
for an hour or two and then push off on a
fresh mount. She was expecting a baby soon,
and though she never complained she missed
him tremendously. But it was the lot of pioneer mothers to be much alone, she knew,
and she kept her chin up and met him when
he came with gay and cheerful stories of what
had taken place in his absence.

Coming home on one of these flying visits,
he told her a piece of news that had reached
him. A stranger had drifted into the cow camp

320

and had dropped the casual information that he had spent the night recently with the Terrell gang.

'He met four of them — the two Terrells, Lake, and Walsh, I'd guess from his description of them. His opinion is that they are operating in stolen horses.'

Janet's heart seemed to stand still a moment. 'You don't think they will — start anything?' she asked.

'No. They're holed up here on the dodge like plenty of other outlaws. Scoundrels of their stripe aren't hunting trouble. They are ducking it. Anyhow, they wouldn't dare hurt you.'

'I'm not thinking about myself,' Janet said.

'If you're worried about me, Sugar, you can forget it,' he said cheerfully, his strong arm round her shoulders. 'I reckon I'm about the last man in this part of the country they want to meet. They don't aim to stir up a hornet's nest that will set McNelly's rangers on their tails.'

'They might waylay you.'

He shook his head decisively. 'No chance. I'm with a big crew most of the time. They will steer clear of us. When I'm riding the brush alone they won't have any way of knowing where I'll be.'

Her smile was a little wan. 'You always say

you are so safe, but I worry about you just the same.'

'Don't do that. No need of it, sweetheart. I have a fine bunch of vaqueros ready to fight for me at the drop of the hat. No gang of bandits would want to tackle the Spur outfit. We're too strong. And you want to remember that this lawlessness in the brush and along the border is being mopped up by the rangers mighty fast. They are doing a thorough job in getting rid of these Gone-to-Texas gents. . . . There's something else I want to talk about with you. I can't get off just now myself, but I want to send you back with Stone Heath to the Granite Gap until after the baby is born. I know you don't want to go, but —'

'I don't want to go, and there's no need of it. All the time I was away I would be unhappy. We can get Doctor Broderick at any time inside of two hours. I'll do far better here than I would at the Granite Gap. As I told you, I've had a letter from Helen Decker. I think she would be glad to come down and stay for a long visit. She is good company, and it would be nice to have her.'

'If you can get her to come I won't insist on your going north,' Blake compromised. 'Better write her tomorrow.'

He did not like to leave Janet at the almost deserted ranch, with so many long hours to be lived through alone, but there was nothing else for him to do. They were in a pioneer country, and this was one of the penalties they paid. He felt she was in no danger. The border raiders had been quiet for a good many months, and the outlaws in the brush would do her no harm even if they visited the ranch to get food. None the less he would be greatly relieved to have Helen Decker with Janet. Helen would not only relieve his wife's loneliness. She was a competent and energetic young woman who would take charge of the household and not let her friend overdo.

Janet watched her husband ride away. He stopped at the rise beyond which the road dipped out of sight. She lifted a handkerchief into the breeze and he waved a hand in farewell. A moment later he disappeared over the brow.

Slowly she walked back into the house. Old Pedro's kind heart was moved at her distress.

'*Señora,* I cook fine supper,' he promised. 'All the theengs you like. You weel say, *"Bien servido, gracias a Dios."* '

Janet smiled gratefully, then hurried into her room where she could quietly weep a little.

CHAPTER 34

Some Gone-to Texas Gents

Blake King Forrest lay in his crib and waved in the air fat pink bowed legs. He chortled happily at Helen Decker, who was making funny faces for his amusement. Janet smiled at the performance. Privately she was of the opinion that this three-months-old baby was the most remarkable child in the state of Texas. He was a source of perpetual interest to her.

Her husband had left that morning to join his men at the roundup and would not be back for two or three days. But Janet had ceased to worry about him. Of late the brush outlaws had been less bold, daunted by the vigilance of the cattlemen and the energy of the rangers. Moreover, she had learned that Blake Forrest was a man the banditti on the dodge preferred to leave alone. They detoured for him as widely as they did for the rangers.

'Some riders coming up the road,' Helen mentioned. 'Quite a delegation. Four — five — six of them.'

324

Janet watched the approaching horsemen. They were white men, not Mexicans. She was surprised to see so many, for just at this time all available males were busy with the beef roundup. A vague alarm filtered through her. It quickened to active fear when she recognized some of the visitors.

They dismounted at the bunkhouse and Stone Heath came out to speak with them. Outside of Pedro he was the only man who had been left at the home ranch.

Helen frowned. 'Two of them are Wes and Ray Terrell,' she said. 'I didn't know they were in this part of the country. Haven't heard anything about them since they wounded Mr. Waggoner and escaped.'

'Yes, and another one is a man who rode for us. His name is Buck Spelvin. He is a hard case. Blake had to get rid of him. . . . They're coming to the house now.'

Heath walked beside the leading horses. He called to Janet, as soon as he was close enough, in order to allay her fears, 'These men are out of grub, Mrs. Forrest, and would like to get some from us.'

Spelvin swung from his saddle and straddled forward to the porch. His upper lip lifted in a sneer. 'I'm right sorry yore husband is not at home, Mrs. Forrest,' he said. 'I sure would admire to meet him.'

'You met him when you were here before,' Janet said quietly. Her heart was beating wildly like that of a captured bird held in the hand, but she did not intend to let this formidable combination of enemies know she was afraid, even though her fear was for her baby and her husband.

Heath smothered a laugh, not too carefully. The bully swung round on the big blond cowpuncher.

'You got anything to say, fellow?' he demanded angrily.

'Not a thing,' Heath drawled. 'Blake said it all.'

'When I wasn't expecting it and he had about a dozen of his gang with him he jumped me,' Spelvin flung out furiously. 'If you want to take it up for him —'

But Stone Heath had received explicit instructions covering a case like this. They were for peace and not war.

'No, sir, I reckon Blake will have to fight his own battles, frail and crippled though he is,' the Spur rider said mildly. If there was a faint chuckle of sarcasm in the voice, the outlaws could not prove it.

'I didn't know you were down here in the border country,' Helen said to her cousin Ray, with no trace of friendliness.

'You got nothing on us, Cousin Helen,' he

replied. 'We didn't know you were here either.'

'Please don't call me cousin,' she told him tartly. 'I haven't any kin who rob trains and have to hole up in the brush.'

'She and that skim-milk brother of hers throw down on folks when their luck is out and play in with the family enemies,' Wes Terrell snarled.

The tawny eyes of the red-haired girl flashed battle signs. 'If anyone threw down on you it was yourselves. I never knew what — what scum you are until I saw you trying to ruin Phil. Thank God he saw in time what poor trash you are.'

'Don't you talk thataway to me, girl,' Wes cried. 'I'll not stand for it a minute.'

'That's the way I'm talking,' Helen retorted, a heat of anger in her voice. 'I never was afraid of your bluster and I'm not now.'

Terrell glared at his cousin, who was facing him with level eyes, her color high, her small fists clenched.

'You always were a vixen, a little redheaded devil who needed whopping,' he said, restraining himself with difficulty. 'For two bits Mex I'd take my quirt to you now.'

'Have you got down to fighting young ladies, Wes?' asked Heath contemptuously. 'If you've got to have war maybe you'd better pick on me.'

'Please — please! Let's not have trouble,' Janet begged.

'We won't, Mrs. Forrest. Heath is right. We're not making trouble for ladies.'

Webb Lake swept off his hat as he spoke. Even though he had ridden far through the dusty chaparral he contrived to look immaculately clean. He was of a type known to all old-timers on the frontier. In his youth he had drifted to the West because of a certain wildness in the blood that had set him in revolt against the tame conventions of a small settled community. Of a good family, well educated, with plenty of ability, he might have made for himself an honored place in his new environment if he had possessed sufficient stamina. But there was a weak streak in him. He became a periodic drunkard and fell in with evil companions. For many months at a time he did not touch liquor, then went on a long spree that would bring him to the verge of collapse. Yet in spite of the failure he had made of his life Lake still retained the sediments of decency. Nobody had ever seen him show lack of respect to a good woman.

'Unless they devil us into it,' Wes Terrell added harshly.

'No if about it,' Lake said firmly. 'You and your family are quite safe, Mrs. Forrest. We are here, madam, to ask the favor of buying some provisions from you. Don't be alarmed, please. Under no circumstances would we do you the least harm. The bark of the boys is a lot worse than their bite.'

Janet took instant comfort. Her instinct told her that this quiet little man with the cold slaty eyes was to be trusted. He might be a scoundrel, but he was a clean one. Women would be as safe with him as with her own husband.

'Speak for yoreself, fellow,' Spelvin flung out angrily. 'I'll play my hand any way I damn please.'

Lake looked at him, quietly, steadily, from opaque eyes cold and hard as ice. 'I'll speak for all of us, Buck,' he said.

'Sure, sure. We got no trouble with these ladies. They don't need to be scared of us.' This from Luke Schrader, a heavy-set man with a Teutonic cast of countenance. 'All we want is grub, boys.'

'You can have what you want,' Janet said. She turned to Heath. 'Stone, you know where the key to the storehouse is. Will you serve Mr. Lake and his friends?'

Webb Lake looked down with interest at the infant in the cradle and snapped his fingers at him. The baby wriggled joyfully and chortled at the man. Janet picked up her son, preparatory to walking into the house. Moved by some wise instinct, she handed the child to the outlaw.

'He's very fond of men,' she said. 'See how he takes to you at once.'

The man was embarrassed but pleased. 'The little codger sure has taken a strangle hold on my finger,' he said. 'He's a mighty husky boy for his age, ma'am. Looks a lot like you.'

Pres Walsh's ugly lip curled. 'Maybe you could get a job in the nursery, Webb,' he suggested.

Janet retrieved her baby. 'See Mr. Lake gets what he needs, Stone,' she said to Heath, and walked into the house by way of the open gallery.

At the store Heath waited on the customers. It was not usual for the Spur ranch to sell supplies to outsiders, but in a country so sparsely settled it was only neighborly to let strangers purchase necessities occasionally. The present visitors bought flour, bacon, beans, meal, coffee, sugar, salt, and other staples, but when it came to paying for them, their ideas and Heath's differed.

Wes Terrell's thin slit of a mouth stretched to a grin. 'Put it on the hook, Stone,' he said. 'We're all good friends of yore boss. He'll be glad to know he has accommodated us.'

330

'This is supposed to be a cash on the barrel-head deal, Wes,' Heath mentioned.

'Not for such close pals as we are,' Walsh replied derisively.

Mildly the Spur rider stuck to his point. 'Blake won't like it, boys. This ranch doesn't run a general store. My advice would be for you to settle now.'

'Who cares about yore advice?' Wes Terrell wanted to know.

'Fact is, Heath, we're a little short of funds right now,' Lake explained. 'Dollars don't grow on huisache or mesquite bushes.'

The six riders presently departed, their saddlebags laden with parcels and sacks of provisions tied on behind. At the corral they stopped a few minutes while Walsh roped a buckskin gelding that took his fancy. The last Heath saw of them was when they dipped over the rise in the road, the Spur horse following at the heels of its new owner.

Stone reported to Janet, with bitter self-criticism. 'I'm a fine guy to leave in charge,' he said. 'To let a bunch of scalawags ride off with a first-class cowpony and about seventy-five dollars' worth of grub. Blake will like that fine.'

'You did exactly right,' Janet told him. 'We got rid of them pretty cheaply, it seems to me. The last thing Blake would want would be for you to have any trouble with them here.'

Helen Decker's tawny eyes smouldered with anger. 'To think that two of them are my cousins — just common thieves.'

Stone Heath looked at this red-headed girl, so vivid and so violent, and there was nothing impersonal in that gaze. He knew — he had known for some time — that she was a woman who could make his life exciting and give it value. Without her, existence would be a pretty tame affair, he felt.

'We're not responsible for scalawags who happen to have the same folks we do,' he said.

'No, but they can make us blush just the same,' she cried bitterly. 'What makes men run to seed, Stone? They had the same grandfather I did, Colonel Philip Decker, a splendid man of honor and integrity, who commanded one of J. E. B. Stuart's regiments in the war. And look what riffraff they are now.'

Heath shook his head. 'I wouldn't know, but once Blake and I were both headed in that direction. So was yore brother Phil. We pulled up in time. If we hadn't —'

'But you did,' she protested. 'That's the difference. There was something in all of you that wouldn't let you go any farther. You didn't have it in you to be bad men. When you-all came plunk up against a choice, you went right. They didn't. What's the matter with them?'

'A weak strain, I reckon. Their grandpaw Judd Terrell wasn't any such man as Colonel Decker. He stayed at home and ducked the war — branded stock that wasn't his, I've heard say. He just wasn't the right stuff. It is coming out in his grandsons. . . . Well, you'll likely never see them or any of their crowd again.'

As a prophet it turned out that Heath was partly right and partly wrong.

CHAPTER 35

Helen Changes Her Mind

'Somebody coming up the road hell-for-leather,' Buck Spelvin said, and drew up his mount.

His companions stopped, watching horse and rider.

'He's sure whipped out — him and his fuzzy both,' Ray Terrell commented. 'Something wrong with him, the way he's hanging to the horn.'

That the man was desperately sick all of them could see. He pulled his spent pony to a halt and clung with both hands to the pommel, body swaying. The gray face of the rider was ghastly. The outlaws could not miss the reason for it. On the man's shirt, not far below the heart, was a wet red stain.

'Raiders,' he gasped. 'Juan Cuero's band — headin' for the Spur.'

Walsh and Lake swung from their saddles in time to catch him as he slid down. They put him on the ground, his head pillowed on Lake's arm.

'He's gone. Heart quit beating.' Walsh looked up at the others, who were grouped around them.

The eyes of the wounded man fluttered open. 'They got me — at Sibley's ford.'

His body collapsed into a heap. He was dead.

'Anybody know him?' Wes Terrell asked. None of them did.

'He must of knew the Spur riders were at the roundup and was trying to warn Mrs. Forrest,' Schrader guessed.

'Looks like,' agreed Wes Terrell. His anxious eyes slid down the road. Beads of perspiration had broken out on his forehead. 'Cuero never rides with less than twenty-thirty men. We better be lighting out, boys. If they're making for the Spur they'll be along right soon.' He turned and walked swiftly to his horse.

'Damned soon,' agreed Spelvin. 'I aim to ooze into the brush *pronto*.'

Lake rose to his feet. 'Just a minute, boys. There are women and a baby at the Spur. Do you aim to leave them at the mercy of Cuero's devils?'

'You can ride and warn them if you feel thataway, Webb,' answered Wes Terrell harshly. He could not keep his gaze from the curve of the road three hundred yards away.

Fear had wiped the strength out of his flabby face.

The cold eyes in Webb's pallid face blazed. 'Warning them is not enough, you yellow wolf. Likely they won't have time to saddle. We've got to fight for them.'

'For Blake Forrest's ranch and family. Not on yore life. Anyhow, it's every man for himself now. I'm lookin' out for Wes Terrell.'

'Our cousin is there with Janet,' Ray said to his brother. His face was drained of color. There had always been a suspicion that he was not a game man. Ray himself had lived with the knowledge that he was timid.

'She done told you half an hour ago she is no kin of ours,' Wes flung back, almost in a shout. He was on the edge of panic. The story ran that Cuero and his men were no better than Apaches. 'She made the choice, not us.'

'I know, but — that doesn't matter now.' Ray had always been a pale shadow of his brothers. Their big blustering strength had eclipsed him. 'We've got to save her, Wes.'

'Don't be a fool,' Wes cried. 'Webb claims he is going to ride back and warn them. They'll saddle and get into the brush all right.'

'There may not be time,' Ray urged.

Lake cut into the argument. 'No time for talk. Someone has to get word to Forrest.

Luke, you do that. Ride like a prairie fire was after you. Me, I'm burning the wind for the Spur. Those of you who are men will take my dust. The rest can go to hell.'

Already Schrader had started on his errand. Lake mounted, swung his horse, and jumped it to a canter.

Buck Spelvin ripped out an ugly oath. 'I'm just blamed fool enough to back Lake's play,' he said, jeering at himself.

Walsh and Wes Terrell turned into the brush. 'Come on, Ray,' the latter called over his shoulder.

As Ray pulled himself to the saddle he made his choice and in doing so turned his back on shame forever. His horse galloped down the road at the heels of Spelvin's bay. Terror pursued him. He looked back fearfully to see if Cuero's raiders were in sight. The sting of a quirt quickened the pace of his flying cowpony. An urgent desire was in him to get ahead of Spelvin.

At the end of a long stretch rising to the brow of a small hill he turned his head again. The panic in him filled his throat. Far back on the yellow ribbon strip of road rose a cloud of dust. He knew that horses in motion had stirred up that powdery screen.

The ranch house was just ahead of him. He saw Lake leap to the ground and drag a rifle from its boot beside the saddle. Already he had shouted a warning to Stone Heath, and that young man was running into the house.

Stone stopped to snap an order at Pedro, who had just emerged from the kitchen. 'Cuero's raiders headed this way. Get yore gun. Fill a box with grub and take it to the fort house.'

'We'll need water, Buck, plenty of it — for a siege.' Lake's voice rang crisp and sharp. 'I saw their dust as I came over the hill. What weapons are at the ranch I'll gather.'

'Can't we all get away?' Ray Terrell asked. 'Riding double?'

'Too late. Turn your horse loose. You won't need him. Help Buck with the food and water.'

Lake plunged into the house. Already Janet was snatching the baby from the crib. Helen Decker was at the other side of the room. She had just lifted a rifle from its rack on the wall.

'How close are they?' Janet asked. Her lips were colorless, but there was no quaver in the voice.

'We have just time to fort up,' Lake answered quietly. 'Don't be frightened. We'll stand 'em off.'

Stone Heath came into the room carrying a rifle and a revolver. A belt of ammunition hung over his arm.

'Everybody to the fort house,' he cried. 'Get a jump on you.'

The fort house was the original ranch dwelling. Here Forrest and his bride had lived until Ellison vacated the larger house for them. It had been built to withstand Indian attacks. The walls of upright split logs, the small diamond-shaped windows, the sod roof, had all been designed to make the place as nearly invulnerable as possible. The door was of heavy oak supported by great iron bolts stretching from below each hinge to the opposite jamb. In front and in back of the two-room cabin there was no brush or cover of any kind for a hundred yards except that afforded by an old smokehouse and by a cave for potatoes, turnips, and other roots.

Toward this the men and women now hurried. Janet carried her baby and his bedding. The others were laden with weapons, food, buckets of water, and blankets.

'Any wood?' Lake asked.

'I packed some in yesterday,' Heath replied. 'It's where I sleep.'

'They're coming,' Helen cried.

All of them knew it. None of them had been moving too fast for frequent swift glances at the brow of the hill where the raiders must first appear. They came over it at a gallop, a long stream of them that seemed to have no end. When they saw the house they lifted their guns and waved them in the air, shouting defiance and threats at the gringos.

'We're holed up just in time,' Heath said. 'All in, boys. Careful about splashing that water, Ray. We may need it all.'

One of the raiders caught sight of them and raised a shout. Bullets sprayed the walls and the ground in front of them.

'Hurry, Stone,' Helen cried.

Heath came in, slammed the door, and bolted it.

'First thing I learned about Mexicans from my dad was that they can't shoot straight,' he said contemptuously.

'We won't bank on that too heavily,' Lake said. 'Where is the safest place for the ladies?'

Already Pedro was working at the puncheon floor. He edged up a loose corner, got his fingers underneath, and lifted a square section which served as a trap door. Below this were steps which led down into a cellar.

He went down these, to make sure no snakes had found a den there.

'We'd better each take a porthole so as to cover all four sides of the house,' Heath suggested. 'Pedro can load our guns for us when we get busy.'

'I can help do that,' Helen said. 'Behind

these walls I'd be perfectly safe, and I'm not going to sit down there in a cellar all the time.'

She was looking at Heath, a little defiantly. He smiled at her.

'That's the spirit, Miss Helen,' he told her. 'We'll sure call on you when you're needed. Till then I reckon we menfolks would feel easier if you'd get down where a stray shot couldn't reach you.'

Her eyelashes fell before his steady gaze. 'All right. I'll do as I'm told. But they are not firing just now. I want to speak to Cousin Ray.'

Helen walked across to Terrell. He was standing on a stool at one of the lozenge-shaped openings, a rifle in hand.

'Where is Wes?' she asked.

Ray felt a queer flush of shame running through him. 'He — didn't come.'

'But you came, Cousin Ray.'

'I felt I had to come, Cousin Helen.'

She nodded, her steady gaze on this man who had always been the least consequential of the Terrell clan. 'I want to tell you how ashamed I am of what I said. Maybe — maybe we won't get out of here. Will you forgive me and shake hands?'

'Nothing to forgive. All you said was true. We've turned out a pretty poor lot.' He stepped down from the stool. 'Sure I'll shake

341

hands. Glad to do it. I always thought a heap of you.'

He offered his hand. She took it, then suddenly leaned forward and kissed him.

CHAPTER 36

Cuero's Raiders North of the River

Into the cow hunt camp at Buck Creek a man pounded heavily on a weary mount. Seated on a box, the cook looked up from the potatoes he was peeling to watch this crazy rider's approach. The man must be a fool. His horse would never amount to anything again. Some dumb tenderfoot probably. In the days of the Comanches, not more than four or five years ago, a fellow had to kill a horse sometimes. But the red raiders were on reservations now. They did not have to sweep the frontier for food, since Uncle Sam bought Texas bullocks and had them driven to the door of the agency.

'Where's Blake Forrest?' the man in the saddle croaked from a dust-filled throat.

'At the cow hunt — over on Dutch Flat.' The cook looked at the sweat-stained heaving horse and said severely, 'Yore bronc won't ever be worth a damn, if it lives.'

'Cuero's raiders are headin' for the Spur ranch,' the messenger said. 'Get horses — quick.'

'Goddlemighty! Whyn't you say so?' The

343

cook woke to instant activity. He snatched up a rope and loped across the flat toward three or four hobbled horses.

Luke Schrader slid to the ground, unfastened his own rope, and followed the cook.

'Take the blue,' the Spur man shouted. 'He's faster than the sorrel.'

Within five minutes they were galloping across a rolling prairie as fast as their mounts could travel. It was half an hour later that the cook lifted his hand in a sweeping gesture.

'There they are — right below us.'

A man was chousing a wild-eyed steer out of the thicket. The cook rode forward and intercepted him. 'Where's the boss, Lem?' he called.

' 'Lo, Sam! What you doing here? He's right over the hill with the gather.'

'Cuero is raidin' the ranch. Get the boys together. Come on, you.' The last words were shot at Schrader over the cook's shoulder. Sam was already taking the hill.

Forrest heard the news in a grim tight-lipped anguish, but he wasted no time in indecision.

'Rope my claybank, Mac — fast as you can,' he told the nearest rider. To Crabb, orders crackled out sharply. 'Round up the boys already in from the brush. Leave somebody here to pick up the others later. Don't wait for them. Cut across to the camp and pick up what rifles are there. Then get to the ranch fast as you can.'

He turned, striding toward the remuda. No use wasting energy in running, since it would take Mac a minute or two to rope and saddle his mount. Schrader walked beside him, carrying on with the story.

'Heath won't be alone. Webb Lake and couple of the boys pulled out for the ranch soon as we heard the greasers had crossed the river and were makin' for the Spur.'

'Sure of that? How did you hear it?'

'Met a man wounded by Cuero's devils. He was alive and no more, hanging to the horn. They got him at Sibley's ford. 'Most as soon as we got him to the ground he died.'

'Did he say how many men Cuero had with him?'

'No. Hadn't time. Went West too soon. But I looked back from a hill and saw the raiders pouring down the road. A big bunch of them.'

'Who went with Lake?'

'Buck Spelvin for one. I dunno for sure who the other was. Not Wes Terrell. He said he was saving his own hide, damned yellow coyote. Say, pick me a fast horse and I'll side you.'

'See Mac about it. I can't wait.' Forrest slammed a restive fist into the palm of his hand. He was in hell, ridden by a terror he could not shake. His wife and baby were in danger. Why had he made so sure that the day of the raiders was over? Why had he left them at the mercy of a murderous ruffian such as Juan Cuero?

For forty years there had been war along the Rio Grande between the Mexicans south of the river and the gringos north of it. There had been years of patched-up peace, but the resentment between the races had never died down since the days of the Alamo and San Jacinto. The feeling of many of the Texas cowboys was so bitter that they had no scruples about stealing stock from Mexicans across the line. Long before the Civil War the raids and counterraids had resulted in the deaths of hundreds of Texans and Mexicans.

The most notorious border bandit of the frontier days was Juan Cortina. He was powerful, daring, brutal, cruel, and able. His followers could be counted by hundreds. In 1859 he captured Brownsville and killed several citizens, and for many years subsequently his murderous raids were a scourge to the Lone Star State. Between the Rio Grande and the Nueces River vast numbers of cattle roamed. Of these Cortina took heavy toll. He stocked half a dozen ranches of his own in northern Mexico, and he sold thousands to dealers who shipped to Cuba and other markets. In time he became respectable, a politician of power, a general in the Mexican army.

But other raiders took his place, and one of the worst of those was Cuero. Close pressed by rangers and *rurales,* he had given pledges of reformation. For a year, prior to this time, there had been no *bandidos* scouring South Texas. The ruthless activities of the rangers had deterred them. The common talk ran that the old wild days were forever past. Blake Forrest, like others, had been lulled to a false sense of security. Now he bitterly repented his credulity.

Mac was cinching the saddle on the claybank when the foreman reached him.

'Give me your six-shooter, Mac,' Blake told the man. 'You can get another at the camp on your way to the ranch.'

Forrest vaulted to the saddle and jumped his horse to a gallop. He went out of sight as if he had been fired from a gun.

A tenderfoot devoured by anxiety as was Blake might have decided that his problem was to get his horse in a straight line between two points at the greatest possible speed. The foreman of the Spur knew better than that. By carelessness he could easily founder the claybank. He had to get the maximum speed consistent with saving enough stamina to cover the necessary miles. This required a nice judgment. He had to restrain the urgent impulse to hold his mount to a gallop.

Moreover, another question had to be decided. About halfway between him and home lay the Buchanan ranch. Would he gain time by detouring for a mile to pick up a fresh horse? Or had he better keep on to the Spur on his jaded claybank? The settlement of that debatable point he pushed back for determination to the moment when he would have to make a choice. It would depend upon the condition of his mount.

He rode across prairies and plunged through thickets of huisache and mesquite. Brush whipped his face and catclaw tore at his legs as he pounded forward. At times he slowed down to a road gait for a few minutes, but only to give the horse a rest sufficient for it to carry on again at a run.

The sun began to slide down toward the western horizon. In a couple of hours now it would set, Blake figured. The long reaching stride of the claybank had eaten up many miles, but he knew he had been asking too much of the horse. It was very weary. Better turn off to the Quarter-circle M B and pick up a mount from Buchanan.

Before he had traveled the cutoff to the ranch more than a few hundred yards he met a cowboy in a homespun linsey-woolsey shirt and black and white checkerboard trousers thrust into the tops of old dusty boots.

'By gum, if it ain't Mr. Forrest,' the tow-headed youth was beginning when Blake cut him short abruptly.

'Give me that horse. And ride back to Buchanan. Tell him Cuero's raiders are at the Spur and for him to gather what men he can quick as God will let him. My boys are on the way from the cow hunt.' The words that issued from the dust-caked throat were almost a croak.

Blake swung to the saddle the line rider had vacated and gave the horse a touch of the spur. It jumped to a canter.

'Hey, you ain't going on alone,' the cowboy shouted after him. The Spur foreman did not answer. Already he was disappearing round a bend in the road.

'He's surely in a hell of a hurry to go to sleep in smoke, which he will certainly do if Cuero's *bandidos* are still at the Spur,' the Quarter-circle M B rider mentioned aloud to himself. 'He ain't thinkin' of himself, I reckon, but of that wife and kid at home. I never did see such a turrible look on a man's face before.'

The youngster turned the drooping clay-bank toward the Quarter-circle M B ranch house. He knew that inside of twenty minutes he would be headed for the Spur with all the men Buchanan could hastily pick up.

CHAPTER 37

Besieged

Cuero made no immediate attempt to capture the fort house at the Spur ranch. He had not crossed the river to fight but to loot, to destroy, and to drive back with him as many horses and cattle as he could collect. Experience had taught him he must strike swiftly and be gone. By sunup next morning he must be back across the Rio Grande. This meant that he had to round up his herd before darkness. Already he had gathered a bunch of longhorns and was holding them a few miles down the road. The rest he expected to get at the Spur.

Meanwhile he had turned loose his men to enjoy themselves. Some of them had broken open the store and were helping themselves to ammunition, knives, tobacco, clothes, and food. Others were tearing through the house smashing furniture, ripping up bedding, breaking windows, and defiling the place. One slim lad came capering into the yard wearing the best silk dress of Helen Decker.

A few random shots tore into the walls of

the fort house. Some drunken raiders rode up even to the door and beat upon it defiantly. Those inside had an easy chance to mow down these careless aggressors, but did not take advantage of it.

'No sense in us rarin' up and making them mad before we have to,' Heath advised. 'The more time they fool away at the store and the big house the better for us. Before they go they'll give us plenty of trouble, but if they wait too long we may have help from the boys at the cow hunt.'

Lake nodded, grimly. 'Hope they decide to have a bonfire and burn the big house. Anything to keep them too busy to tackle us in earnest.'

Stone Heath turned his post over to Pedro temporarily and went down the ladder to the cellar. A lighted candle had been stuck into the dirt on a kind of shelf in the wall.

'How's every little thing doing down here?' he asked cheerfully. 'Doesn't seem to be much going on upstairs with us. The greasers are busy looting the storehouse and ripping things up at the house. I hate to mention, Miss Helen, that one of them is prancing around in that blue silk dress of yours.'

'You think maybe they'll leave without really attacking us here?' Janet asked.

'No can tell. I figure they'll try to rush us

before they go, but when we stand them off and make it cost them plenty, Cuero is likely to give it up as not worth while.'

He spoke with a good deal more confidence than he felt.

'There are only five of you, and there must be a hundred of them,' Janet said.

'But we're forted up, with plenty of ammunition, and they're in the open. All we got to do is to hold the fort till Blake comes busting in with the boys. . . . How is young Blake King Forrest making out?'

Stone strolled across to Janet, took the baby from her arms, and danced him gently up and down until he wriggled with delight. The cowboy's laugh was easy and carefree. 'Young fellow, when you hear the firecrackers poppin' don't you get scared. Remember we're having a kinda special Fourth of July, kindness of Señor Juan Cuero.'

Both Helen and Janet knew he had come down to cheer them. His nonchalance was a fraud. Nothing would please these raiders more than to wipe out a few helpless gringos, and if they made a determined attack the odds would be too great for the defenders.

As he was leaving Helen said quietly, 'I'll be up there if you need me.'

He smiled, looking at her very steadily. 'I don't reckon I'll need you upstairs, but I'll certainly need you a lot later.'

Her eyes did not waver. 'When you need me I'll come, Stone.'

The young man looked over her shoulder at Janet. 'Shut yore eyes, Mrs. Forrest,' he drawled. 'Miss Helen started something with Cousin Ray, and it's catching.'

Their long kiss was not exactly cousinly.

Stone went up the steps three at a time.

'I'm so glad,' Janet said, and clung to her friend in a warm embrace.

For the moment they forgot the desperate plight in which all of them stood.

'Cuero is calling his men together,' Buck Spelvin told Heath as the latter reappeared. 'Getting ready for to rush us, looks like.'

From a cowhorn a bugler sounded the recall. The men straggled back from house and store carrying their loot. Cuero talked to them, with excited gestures, waving a hand toward the fort house repeatedly as he exhorted. Shouts from his followers interrupted the heavy, strongly built leader.

'Viva Cuero! Maten los gringos!'[1]

Apparently the attack was to be made on foot. A number of men were assigned to hold the horses. The outlaw chief did not take the trouble to scatter his forces in order to give

[1] Long live Cuero! Death to the Americans!

the defenders less chance of hitting the charging Mexicans. Evidently he expected to storm the house at the first rush.

'Don't get goosey, boys,' warned Lake. 'Be sure you get a bead on your man before you fire. They'll do a lot of wild shooting, but we can't afford to do any. Some of them will reach the house and start banging on the door. Doesn't make any difference. They can't bust in. Won't have time, since we'll be pouring lead into them while they're hammering at it.'

Heath confirmed this prophecy. 'That's whatever. It will look scary to see them running at us, but if we keep our heads, all they'll get will be lead pills and plenty of them. . . . Here they come.'

They raced across the open like ants, shouting and whooping as they came. Without waiting to aim, they fired as they ran. The answer from the blockhouse was withering. A bandit dropped — another — and another. In the packed jam of men even flurried shooting would have had deadly effect, and the defenders were cool frontiersmen used to danger. Even Terrell had lost his shakiness, now that the emergency was upon them. He dropped two bandits during the rush for the house.

Most of the Mexicans faltered — and broke. A group of them reached the door and began hammering at it with the butts of their rifles or with their shoulders. One of them doubled up and went down, shot through the head. The rest turned and scattered, flying back for cover. In the retreat a huge giant in a wide gold-trimmed sombrero flung up his hands and slid forward on his face. His sprawling body lay motionless in the dust.

The firing died down. Stone's gaze swept the room, to take in the casualties. All of the party were still on their feet, but Ray Terrell was looking down with a surprised expression at his bleeding forearm. A bullet had passed through the flesh halfway between the wrist and the elbow.

'Ten of 'em down,' Buck Spelvin shouted jubilantly. 'Leastways, four are down for keeps and the rest are crawling or limping off.' He let out the old rebel yell he had heard so often when he had been a seventeen-year-old youngster with Mosby. 'And nary a one of us even touched.'

The women were standing on the stairs, their eyes searching the room.

'You're hurt, Ray,' his cousin called, and ran to his side.

'A slug hit me in the arm,' he explained.

'We'd better get him downstairs and dress the wound,' the Spur cowboy said.

Helen supported the wounded man. He

laughed, a little embarrassed by so much attention.

'It's only a flesh scratch, I can make out to walk alone, Cousin Helen,' he mentioned.

Assisted by the women, Lake dressed the arm. Before coming to the frontier he had studied to be a doctor, though he had never qualified for practice. The job he did for Terrell was a creditable one.

The Mexicans were busy holding an animated discussion. It broke up, to await the result of an offered flag of truce. A bowlegged vaquero approached the fort house cautiously, stopping several times to wave the white rag. When he was about fifty yards away he stopped and poured out a spate of Spanish. The purport of it was that General Cuero would let them go in peace if they would surrender and give up their arms.

'We'd be murdered like Crabbe's men were,'[1] Spelvin cried bitterly. 'Tell 'em to come and get us if they want us.'

'Better play for time,' Stone Heath suggested.

---

[1] In April, 1857, Henry A. Crabbe of California led a troop of filibusters into Sonora, under a secret pact to assist Ignacio Pesqueira to become governor of that state. Prior to the arrival of Crabbe's forces, Pesqueira had defeated his enemies and achieved his ambition. To retain his popularity he repudiated the Americans and attacked them. After several skirmishes the filibusters were penned up in Cavorca. Crabbe's forces were besieged for a week. They ran out of food, water, and ammunition. Under promise of their lives they at last surrendered. Fifty-seven gaunt survivors were led out to the plaza, and stood against a wall, and died by the fusillade.

'That's right,' assented Lake. 'We'll ask for a quarter of an hour to talk it over.'

The bowlegged Mexican told them that Cuero would give them five minutes, no more. At the end of that time he would storm the house and wipe the defenders out, *muy pronto*.

During the armistice the defenders reloaded their weapons and discussed the outlook. They decided to offer a counter-proposition in order to gain a few minutes more. If Cuero would send all of his men away but half a dozen, to show good faith, they would accept the proposed terms.

To this the Mexican leader consented. Seven or eight of the bandits stayed with him. The rest rode over the hill, taking their loot with them.

Lake said, grimly, 'He'll have them back here in no time when he finds we're not coming out to be massacred.'

The bandylegged vaquero came forward again with his white flag to tell the besieged they might now come out safely.

CHAPTER 38

Blake Says Thanks

While he was still a long way from the ranch Blake heard the far faint popping of many guns. He gave his horse the spur and drew from underneath the belt of his leathers the .45 revolver he had borrowed from Mac. From the tracks on the dusty road he could tell that many riders had traveled it recently toward the ranch. Cuero usually rode with a large band. If he appeared on the scene alone they would probably rub him out instantly. The sensible course would be to wait for Buchanan and his own boys, but this was something he could not do. His wife and baby were at the focal point of that heavy firing he heard.

The gun explosions died down. Had the *bandidos* captured and exterminated the defenders, or had they been driven back? He was consumed with a feverish anxiety.

Blake dragged his mount to a halt and swung into the brush. For over the hilltop just this side of the ranch a disorderly mob of riders were appearing. From the loot they carried he could tell they had plundered the house and store. A cold wave of fear splashed through him. If they had captured the house —

He tore through the brush, keeping out of sight of the road. As he came out of the clearing he saw half a dozen Mexicans on horseback in a group. They were facing toward the old fort house, their eyes fixed on a vaquero with a white flag who was approaching it.

The heart of the foreman lifted with joy. The Americans had taken refuge in the old log ranch house and were still holding their own. That there had been a battle was clear. Four dead bodies lay stretched in the open and several wounded men could be seen under the cottonwoods.

Swiftly Blake sized up the situation. Cuero had sent his men away temporarily to trap the defenders into surrender. If the gringos gave up their arms the bandit leader would call back his men and start the massacre. That was his plan.

Blake's eyes blazed. For once Cuero had lost the game. He had moved too slow. Inside of fifteen minutes Buchanan's cowboys and the riders from the cow hunt would be on the scene.

The Spur foreman rode into the open. He put his horse at a canter and let out the 'Hi-yippi-yi!' of the Texas cowman, to warn those in the house that he was not an enemy. The marksmanship of the Mexicans did not worry him much. Everybody knew they could not hit a barn door.

The leader of the bandits turned and caught sight of Forrest. The heavy-set Mexican had a dark pockmarked face, sensual and cruel. He gave a shout and moved his horse in the direction of the Texan, at the same time dragging out from a scabbard a revolver.

The two men rode toward the apex of an acute angle formed by the directions they took. Cuero shouted a malediction and fired. The hat of the foreman was half lifted from his head by a bullet tearing through the crown. Blake's .45 crashed an answer a fraction of a second later.

Cuero caught at his stomach. His face contorted with pain. The weapon dropped from his hand and he began to sag.

Leaning low in the saddle, Blake dashed across the open. He shouted his name aloud, over and over, since he did not want to stop lead sent by his friends. The man with the white flag turned a frightened face in his direction and scuttled away for safety. As the foreman reached the house, he flung himself from the saddle. Two or three bullets tore into the log walls of the house as he shouted for admission.

The door opened. He ran into the house and Stone Heath with a whoop of joy slammed the door shut and bolted it.

'My wife?' asked Blake hoarsely.

'Fine as the wheat. The baby too. And Miss Decker. None of us hurt except Ray Terrell. He got a pill in his arm.' Stone pointed down the ladder to the cellar. 'Hot zicketty, I'm glad you got here, fellow.'

A moment later Janet and the baby were in Blake's arms. He had to choke down the hot emotion that filled his throat.

'I — thought I'd never get here,' he said roughly.

'It's been — terrible,' Janet murmured, clinging to him. 'With little Blake here and — all these terrible men. How did you get through them?'

From the top of the ladder Stone called down. 'Looks like they're fixing to go. They're carrying away the fellow you dropped. Must have been someone important.'

'Cuero, I think,' Blake told him. 'He was all tricked up with fine clothes. Buchanan's men will be here soon, and there will be a bunch from our cow camp dropping in. The *bandidos* are beginning to figure they have run into a hornet's nest, don't you reckon?'

Forrest joined the other men upstairs. It was

clear the raiders were wavering. The sound of the firing had brought them back over the hill and they were gathered in groups of excited gesticulating men. Several of the band had been killed and more wounded. Though Cuero was not yet dead, it was plain he had ridden on his last raid. They had come to the Spur to raid a defenceless ranch, not to fight a desperate battle with grim Texans who had their backs to the wall. There was still desultory firing, but no longer any heart in the attack. Without a leader, the *bandidos* did not know whether to finish the job or call it a day and ride for the river.

At this critical moment Buchanan's men appeared over the brow of the hill. The Mexicans had had enough. They fled, in a shower of bullets, leaving their wounded behind them.

To the men who had saved his wife and child Blake made brief thanks. 'Nothing I can say, boys, but thanks. Some of you counted me an enemy, but you acted like good Texans and rode hell-for-leather to save women and a baby, knowing you'd likely never come out alive.'

Buck Spelvin growled an embarrassed and ungracious explanation. 'Hell, I just came to get a crack at Cuero's raiders. I never did like greasers.'

'Now you're here, Buck, you'd better stay,'

Forrest suggested. 'There will always be a place at the Spur for you.'

'No, I reckon I'll drift to Arizona with Lake and Terrell,' he said. 'This ain't no healthy spot for us. Too damned many rangers.'

Forrest knew that Lake and Terrell would have to leave the state or be captured eventually. The sooner they left the better for them.

'If you are heading for Arizona pick the best horses you can find on the Spur,' he said. 'In case you're ever up against it drop me a line. I'll never forget what you've done for me today.'

'I reckon you would have done it for us,' Ray Terrell said, flushing with confusion in which pleasure had a share.

He was a man of inherently good instincts who had been led astray by others gone bad. It had been a long time since he had felt as satisfied with his conduct as he did now. He meant to take another name in a new country, send back the money he had taken as his share of the express robbery, and cut loose from lawlessness. Forrest was an example of how reformation was possible for a man who had transgressed the law.

'I'd ask you and Lake to stay here, but it wouldn't be safe,' Forrest said. 'Arizona is a good bet. It's coming on the map as a cattle country. You boys ought to do well out there.'

Hard on the heels of Buchanan's men came the riders from the cow hunt. They reported a brush with the departing bandits.

Before the defenders of the fort house had evacuated it, Juan Cuero had passed away. The wounded outlaws begged for mercy without expecting it. They were surprised when Forrest treated them like prisoners of war until the rangers arrived to take charge of them.

The raid of Cuero was the last invasion of Texas for a generation, in fact until the rise of another notorious bandit named Pancho Villa. Law came to West Texas. The bad men gave up their evil ways or were wiped out. The rangers and the cattlemen together cleared the brush of its nefarious inhabitants.

Under new and better conditions the Spur ranch prospered. Within five years the Forrests were its owners. Stone Heath was the foreman. He had a share of the increase and was on his way to become a man of substance. He was a respectable married man and father, and his two children had red hair like their attractive mother. By this time Blake King Forrest had two small sisters. The five youngsters played together as one family.

Sometimes Blake and Stone talked over the old wild days when they had walked so carelessly on the edge of lawlessness. They agreed that these were better ones. They were doing their part to build up a Texas where women and children would be safe, and in this they were only carrying on the work started by Austin and Houston, the ideal for which Travis and Bowie and Crockett had died at the Alamo.